ᴿ
ᵉᶻ

"You d̶ ... y fair, do you ... mmm."

Sliding her arms around his neck, she kissed him back, letting him do with his hand whatever he wanted.

And what he apparently wanted was to get her naked.

In seconds her blouse was open, her bra unclasped, and Taylor's mouth was on her. Claire felt her head spin as hard need took hold of her.

"Tell me what you like," he whispered as he bit the lobe of her ear. "Tell me what you want."

"Listen to me," she panted. "Please. I have to tell you . . ."

"What?"

"I had fun with you today," she said, her voice low and husky. "I enjoy your company—"

"Same here."

"But . . ." DROLD PUBLIC LIBRA

He eyed her. "But we're not going to have sex," he finished for her. "Are we?"

RECEIVED JUN 1 3 2006

Avon Contemporary Romances by
Marianne Stillings

SIGHS MATTER
MIDNIGHT IN THE GARDEN OF GOOD AND EVIE
THE DAMSEL IN THIS DRESS

ATTENTION: ORGANIZATIONS AND CORPORATIONS
Most Avon Books paperbacks are available at special quantity discounts for bulk purchases for sales promotions, premiums, or fund-raising. For information, please call or write:

Special Markets Department, HarperCollins Publishers, Inc., 10 East 53rd Street, New York, N.Y. 10022–5299. Telephone: (212) 207–7528.   Fax: (212) 207–7222.

MARIANNE STILLINGS

SIGHS MATTER

AVON BOOKS
An Imprint of HarperCollinsPublishers

This is a work of fiction. Names, characters, places, and incidents are products of the author's imagination or are used fictitiously and are not to be construed as real. Any resemblance to actual events, locales, organizations, or persons, living or dead, is entirely coincidental.

AVON BOOKS
An Imprint of HarperCollins*Publishers*
10 East 53rd Street
New York, New York 10022-5299

Copyright © 2006 by Marianne Stillings
ISBN-13: 978-0-06-073483-1
ISBN-10: 0-06-073483-3
www.avonromance.com

All rights reserved. No part of this book may be used or reproduced in any manner whatsoever without written permission, except in the case of brief quotations embodied in critical articles and reviews. For information address Avon Books, an Imprint of HarperCollins Publishers.

First Avon Books paperback printing: April 2006

Avon Trademark Reg. U.S. Pat. Off. and in Other Countries, Marca Registrada, Hecho en U.S.A.
HarperCollins® is a registered trademark of HarperCollins Publishers Inc.

Printed in the U.S.A.

10 9 8 7 6 5 4 3 2 1

If you purchased this book without a cover, you should be aware that this book is stolen property. It was reported as "unsold and destroyed" to the publisher, and neither the author nor the publisher has received any payment for this "stripped book."

For Sharon

*You knocked on my door and invited me
to your birthday party, remember?
You said you wanted to get to know me better,
because I seemed so . . . normal.
Thank you for sticking around all these years,
even after learning the truth.*

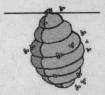

<u>Surveillance</u>
Sir Lancelot's secret lookout.

Chapter 1

August
Port Henry, Washington

Blue sky . . . treetops . . . straw hat . . . breasts.

With a touch of his index finger, he caressed the knob as though it were the soft curve of her shoulder. After a brief mental tussle between his half angel, half devil conscience, both sides concluded it wouldn't harm the taxpayers any if he allowed himself a moment or two of reverent reflection on the wonders of . . . nature.

Detective Taylor McKennitt popped his gum, then fine-tuned the focus on his binoculars. Under his breath, he murmured, "Claire Hunter, you are still one very fine-looking woman." He grinned and blew out a short breath.

Thank God he'd gotten over her. A lesser man would have been captivated at the sight of her in those blue jeans and white knit top. But Taylor had moved on. She was no longer his almost girlfriend but simply an assignment, and he was free to appreciate her attributes from afar without getting his knickers in a twist.

Good thing, too, since he hadn't anticipated seeing her here. Originally, his intent had been simply to check out the farm, see if all the ducks were in order, so to speak. He'd expected to catch a glimpse of Sadie Lancaster, Claire's aunt, but not Claire herself; not today, anyway.

He sharpened the image, and his grin widened. Damn, he loved this job.

Shifting position, Taylor jammed his hand under his jacket, into his shirt pocket, and withdrew his cell phone, punching the autodial with his thumb. As he waited for the call to ring through to his brother, Claire turned, bent, and lifted a cardboard box.

Taylor's gaze followed her every move as his mind drifted to the night they'd spent together eight months ago. He felt his chest warm remembering what had happened between the two of them, and the sultry, sensuous things she'd whispered to him in the dark . . .

". . . hit by a bus, or just plain stupid?" His brother's impatient voice jolted Taylor out of the land of ancient history.

"Sorry," he growled in response. "I'm working. Got a little . . . distracted."

"So, what's the haps? Where are you?"

"Doing a little recon." Since the *recon* had morphed into ogling his brother's wife's best friend, Taylor felt it best to keep the details and the locale to himself. "Where are you?"

"On the road," Soldier said. "Spent the day at the precinct in Seattle gathering all the data I could on our new case. Heading north on 101 now. ETA in Port Henry's about fifteen-thirty."

Taylor checked his watch. "That's in an hour. You stopping by the PHPD, or going straight home?"

"Straight home into the arms of my beautiful wife."

"Gag me."

"If only," Soldier said dryly. "Mostly I need to mow the lawn before it gets dark. Hey, you staying with us tonight? We can start going over these files. Betsy's getting your usual room ready."

"Can't do it until tomorrow night," he said, his eyes locked on Claire. "Today, uh, threw me a few curves. I'm hip-deep in forms and figures, and looking a little behind." He adjusted the focus as she turned around.

"Sounds like you're looking at a righteous bust," Soldier quipped.

Taylor snapped his gum and smiled. *Yeah, I'd like to stay on top of this one,* he thought but did not say. Banter and innuendo with his brother were one thing, but this was Claire . . .

"Listen, Jackson," he said instead. "I've got to hand my cases off to Atherton and Stewart and meet with the lieutenant, so I won't see you until around noon tomorrow."

Detective J. Soldier McKennitt—Jackson, to his brother—gave a grunt of acknowledgment.

Taylor popped his gum and peered through the binoculars as Claire carried a cardboard box to the faded green Ford pickup parked in the barnyard. She set the box inside the bed of the old rattletrap, leaning in to adjust its position.

"Speaking of good-looking women," Soldier said. "How you doing in the girlfriend department? Been seeing anyone special?"

As he watched, Claire continued loading boxes into the truck, unaware that Taylor's eyes followed her every move.

"I'm seeing someone special right now," he muttered under his breath, his gaze held in thrall by the woman whose fawn brown eyes had mesmerized him the day they'd met, and whose fire had turned to ice the morning they'd parted.

"What was that?"

"Nothing."

With a hard blink, Taylor filed away his memories of that night with Claire in the mental folder marked "Finished Business"—in front of the time he'd paid back Ronnie Sherwood in the second grade for a black eye, and just behind the day he'd discovered Paula had been unfaithful . . . the first time.

With renewed enthusiasm, Taylor said, "You picked up all the case files?"

"Yeah."

"Tell me a little about Mortimer. What exactly are we dealing with here? Any Feds looming on the event horizon?"

As Soldier began addressing the details of the case, Taylor listened while he carefully scanned the scene below.

The Lancaster farm was set in a deep and lush little valley that cupped Claire in its rustic hand. The centerpiece of the tableau was the century-old two-story farmhouse. Faded blue with peeling white trim, it matched the barn standing back against a cluster of towering firs. In the yard between the two buildings, a trio of brown chickens bobbed and pecked at the hardpan, while an enormous goose waddled about, beak in the air, honking orders to the indifferent clouds.

That was the extent of her protection? Three chicken dinners and a goose-down pillow on the wing? No other houses or farms close by. Not a good thing for two women alone.

". . . but no FBI," Soldier was saying. "After you and I go over the case files, we can talk to Mrs. Lancaster, see if she knows anything."

"What do you think? Is the Lancaster woman in any kind of danger? Is Claire?" His heart skittered a little at the thought.

There was a moment of silence, then, "I hope not, but from what I've read so far, I just don't know."

Down in the barnyard, Claire finished loading boxes, then twisted, raising her arms in a lazy stretch. As she did, the screen door at the back of the house eased open, and for a moment, Taylor expected to see a man emerge, a boyfriend maybe. His fingers froze on the binoculars.

But it wasn't a man who appeared, just a mostly white calico cat. Taylor resumed chewing his gum and relaxed his grip on the binoculars.

He'd forgotten about her snooty cat. The feline in question slinked down the steps, blinking as though the sunlight were a personal affront.

What in the hell was that damn thing's name? Princess? Fluffy? Happy? Dopey? No, wait. Those were dwarfs. It was Ag-something. Agatha? That was it.

". . . going to be okay with this," Soldier was saying, "since it's Claire, and you two have a sort of a history?"

"Not a problem."

"You're *sure*." Soldier's voice carried a note of caution in it. "Because Betsy and I, well, we thought maybe you and Claire—"

"Been there, done that, bought the T-shirt, bad fit, donated it to Goodwill. The end."

"Well, as long as you're sure," Soldier drawled.

"I am. Tonight, e-mail me what you can on Mortimer."

"Copy." There was a hint of defeat in Soldier's voice. Then, "Okay, apparently this whole thing got started from a tip. A woman. She called from a pay phone in Port Henry, wouldn't give her name."

"Mrs. Lancaster?"

"Possibly, but there's no evidence to support it. However, if this woman's accusations are valid, Mortimer's involved in conspiracy, fraud, maybe even homicide."

"They're playing our song."

"Yeah," Soldier said. "Let's see if we can catch this guy with his hands in the cookie jar before somebody gets hurt. Uh, Tayo?"

"Yeah?"

"If you ever *do* want to talk about it . . ."

"I won't."

As Taylor jammed the cell phone back in his pocket, Claire shoved the last box farther into the bed of the truck and brought the tailgate up, slamming it so hard, the screech-and-bang echoed through the clearing to where he lay hidden in the high grass on the hill behind the farm. Turning, she went back into the farmhouse.

In the time he'd been flat on his belly watching the place, the sun had rolled down from the top of the sky and into the August mist drifting above the horizon like a windblown veil. It was a nice summer afternoon, just the kind of day a man liked to spend lying naked on cool sheets— with a woman.

Speaking of whom, the kitchen door swung open, and Claire stepped out, walking down the steps to the truck. She tossed her leather handbag through the open window and onto the passenger side, then removed her hat and set it in the huge wheelbarrow resting under an apple tree near the driveway. When she turned in his direction to fluff her hair, he finally saw her face full on.

He shook his head and snapped his gum.

Yeah, it was a damn good thing he was over her, all right. As a professional, there was no way in hell he'd let his personal feelings interfere with a case, especially when it could turn deadly.

Claire and her aunt deserved his vigilance and instincts because the women were probably unaware of Mortimer's proclivities, and with so much at stake, it put them in a world of danger.

Claire set the last cardboard box next to the first three she'd plopped onto her best friend's Oriental carpet, then eased back and let her body settle into the velvet cushions of the camel-back sofa.

"There you go, my dear," she said to Betsy. "These old books and magazines should keep you company on those long nights when your husband leaves you to go traipsing all over the Northwest looking for bad guys."

Claire watched as Betsy McKennitt, radiant in her eighth month of pregnancy, surveyed the four boxes next to the coffee table. Moving her swollen body toward the adjacent wing chair, she attempted to sit, but given her advanced state of pregnancy, performed what appeared to be some kind of reverse-thrust docking maneuver.

Resting her hands on her tummy, she huffed out an exhausted breath and panted, "No lung . . . capacity. I'll be glad when the baby drops . . . so I can breathe . . . again."

She moved her right hand around to her lower back as she stretched the left toward a pink Depression glass candy dish sitting on the coffee table. Stirring the peanut M&M's noisily with a straight index finger, she finally found the one she wanted, plucked it out, and tossed it into her mouth. Munching happily, she glanced at Claire. "Cute earrings. Are they new?"

Claire's fingertips went to her earlobe as she tried to recall which pair she'd put on that morning. Ah, the beaded dangles. "Thanks. They're my new faves."

Betsy tossed another candy into her mouth. "What do you have now, like ten bazillion pairs? You are such an earring slut."

"Pity me." Claire sighed. "I'm an addict. Some women collect shoes, some collect handbags, some collect men. Me, I'd sell my body for a cute pair of earrings."

"You staying at your aunt's farm tonight, or going back to Seattle?" The candy dish rattled again.

"Going back." Claire glanced at the clock on the mantel. "It's almost six," she said, thinking of the three-hour drive that lay ahead of her. "I'm not on rotation at the hospital until Tuesday, so I'm taking advantage of the weekend off and painting the master bathroom. Once the roofers come next week, the Seattle house will finally be ready to put on the market."

Since she didn't live there—and hadn't for twenty years—and since Zach certainly never would, what was the point in hanging on to the old place? She'd only kept it this long because she couldn't bear to relinquish the part of her childhood the house represented. The part when she'd been young and innocent, had a whole family, and had known no fear.

But she was older now, maybe old enough to let her parents, and her memories, finally be at rest.

Betsy crunched another candy. "New topic. How's your love life?" Betsy's hazel eyes narrowed on her.

"What love life?"

"Guess that answers that." She searched the bowl of M&M's, snared a red one. "It's Friday night, Dr. Hunter. You're young and beautiful, and very, very single." She sent Claire a look of exasperation. "Any men in your life at all, even in your wildest dreams?"

"If there were, you'd be the first to know."

Her friend's lips quirked into a wry grin. "Maybe you should try one of those online things. Don't they have one for doctors? Hot-docs-dot-com or something?"

Claire snorted a laugh. "I'm not a hot doc, and I think those sites are, well, not for me is probably the most diplomatic thing I can say."

"But aren't you looking for one? A hot doc, I mean?"

"I'd have more luck with a hot dog," she said dryly, "if you get my drift."

Betsy snorted. "Oh, come on. You're just not trying hard enough. Men fall all over you. I've seen it happen."

"Been too busy."

Betsy looked like she wanted to expand on the topic, but wisely kept chewing. Swallowing, she eyed the candy dish again and plucked another victim from the bowl. "Okay. Different subject. How's Aunt Sadie?"

Claire leaned back against the cushy softness of the couch. "I haven't seen much of her since she got engaged to old Mortie."

Betsy blinked. "Aunt Sadie's getting married? At her age? What is she now, a hundred?"

"Very funny. I swear, though, she acts like a teenager sometimes." Claire shook her head. "I hope I have that kind of . . . *enthusiasm* for the opposite sex when I'm sixty-five."

Claire thought for a moment about her aunt, a woman who had shelved a fabulous career to be both mom and dad to her and her twin brother, Zach, when their parents had died within a year of each other.

"So who's her boyfriend?" Betsy asked. "Did he used to be in showbiz, too?" She put the bowl down. "I need water. All this chocolate's making me thirsty."

"I'll get you some. Stay put."

When Claire returned from the kitchen, glass of water in hand, she said, "Mortie isn't an actor. He runs a thriving business." Handing the glass to Betsy, she said slowly, "Maybe *thriving* isn't the right word."

"Aunt Sadie's engaged to a ne'er-do-well?" Betsy said. "How long—"

"No," Claire interrupted. "No, he's enormously successful. What I meant was, he's uh, well, he's a . . . now, don't laugh. He's a funeral director. Mortimer's Mortuary. You know, down on Taft."

Betsy's blond brows shot up to her hairline. Then, quirking her lips, she said, "*That* Mortimer? Aunt Sadie's engaged to a *mortician*?" She snorted a laugh, then covered her mouth. Solemnly, she mumbled, "I hear that's a serious undertaking."

"I should *never* had told you."

"Mortimer's is very popular. People are just dying to get in."

Claire flattened her mouth. "You can stop now."

"Marrying into the family, he'll get free medical care, right? So he can come to you if he starts . . . coffin."

"Not another word, I swear—"

"Competition's pretty stiff, I bet." She grinned broadly. "Speaking of sex."

Claire laughed. "We were not speaking of sex!"

HAROLD PUBLIC LIBRARY

"Well if we weren't, we should have been. So." She slid a calculated look at Claire. "Heard anything from Taylor?"

Claire stopped laughing and clamped her mouth shut.

Undeterred, Betsy said dryly, "You remember my husband's brother, don't you? Tall guy, athletic, dark hair, blue eyes, hunky, sexy, available, and interested in *you*?"

"Vaguely," Claire murmured.

"Claire . . ."

"Betsy . . ." Claire scowled. "I knew it was only a matter of time before you got around to Taylor. Yes, he is attractive, and as hunky as they come."

"Any sentence that contains the words *hunky* and *come* has my approval."

"For a woman in such an advanced state of pregnancy, you sure have a one-track mind."

"Honey, have you seen my husband?" She fanned her face with one hand. "*Hello*. If you had a husband like Soldier, you'd have a one-track mind, too." Slapping her own cheek, she widened her eyes as though something had just occurred to her.

"Oh, wait. You could have a husband like mine if you got involved with his brother." She slapped her cheek again. "Oh, wait. You did get involved with his brother, but you chickened out."

"You can stop slapping yourself now. Your

eyes are starting to cross." Resting her head against the back of the sofa, she groused, "I'm not blind, for God's sake. Taylor is handsome, not to mention—"

"—Smart, funny, compassionate, responsible, sweet," Betsy finished for her. "Yeah. I can see why you can't stand him. When was the last time you had sex?"

"Like I said, I've been very busy."

"There is no *too busy for sex*, my dear," Betsy corrected. "What you haven't done is make time for finding a *partner*. I know for a fact that men come on to you constantly. You've *got* to be horny as hell." Taking a breath, she said softly, "What's wrong?"

When Claire didn't respond, Betsy shook her head and sent her a look of sympathy. "You know, both Soldier and I thought you and Taylor really had something good going. You two are perfect for each other. Listen, I care about you. I want you to be happy. You really think it's over between you and Taylor?" She looked thoughtful for a moment. "Avoiding him is not the same thing as being over him, Claire. I think you still have feelings for him. I can see it in your eyes when you talk about him. I think he still has the hots for you, too, and—"

"Great," Claire laughed. "He can look me up on hot-docs-dot-com."

Betsy arched a brow. "You know, I'll bet they have one for detectives . . ."

Claire grinned. "Hot-dicks-dot-com?"

"Sounds like a porn site."

"I'm leaving now." Claire laughed. Grabbing her purse, she pulled out her car keys. "Look, I'm ready to get married, and as soon as some nice guy comes along, I'll walk down the aisle, and then make a baby or two. But it won't be with Taylor."

"And nothing could ever happen to change your mind."

Claire flattened her mouth. "Nothing."

Behind the wheel of Aunt Sadie's ancient pickup—the windows down to let in a cooling breeze—Claire tried to relax, but her conversation with Betsy had stirred up all kinds of memories, emotions, and worst of all, desires—for Taylor.

Letting a sigh past her lips, she thought of what Betsy had said, how certain Betsy was that Taylor was a match for her in every way. But sometimes people who seemed meant-to-be had insurmountable barriers between them others simply couldn't comprehend.

The truth was, Detective Taylor Sean McKennitt might not be right for her, but he was impossible to forget.

She glanced at her watch. A little after ten. Stopping for dinner and gas had put her a bit behind schedule, but there really was no rush. This late on a Friday evening, Seattle traffic should be doable. With any luck, she'd be home by eleven.

As she turned another corner, she bit her bottom lip, remembering, and cursing Taylor's rotten hide for being so damn unforgettable.

Another bend in the road. She downshifted to ease the truck around it, and realized what she'd done.

Damn his hide again. She'd been so preoccupied with her thoughts, she'd missed the on ramp to I–5. Now she was stuck on a service road until it met up with the highway.

A big truck or SUV or something had come up behind her, and she reached to adjust the rearview mirror. Shifting gears, she slowed to make another of the many hairpin turns along the narrow country road.

On the straightaway, she noticed the guy had moved closer. What was he trying to do, pressure her to increase her speed? These hills were too winding for her to risk going any faster. A missed turn could send her into a gully, or right off a cliff.

She kept her speed even, but the guy behind her inched up.

"Back off, will you," she growled under her

breath, trying to get a look at the driver in her mirror, but it was impossible to see anything beyond the glare of his headlights.

She blew out a breath. Probably some teenager in a mad rush to get somewhere. Downshifting, she gripped the wheel and concentrated.

Another glance told her he'd crept closer still. His high beams filled the cab, too bright, hurting her eyes.

"What a total *jerk*."

Her jaw snapped shut as he lurched forward, tapping her bumper.

What in the hell was he *doing*?

She looked for a place to pull off and let him go by, but the road had been virtually chiseled out of the mountainside and turnouts were few.

He tapped her bumper again. Her heart pounding, she lowered her head and kept her eyes on the road. She would not let this creep make her speed, but maybe a little space between them would be a really good idea. She pressed on the accelerator.

But he rammed her once more, shoving her ahead of him as he laid on the horn. The blare was shocking, invasive, filling her head with noise until she found it hard to think. She wanted to cover her ears, roll up the windows, but she didn't dare let go of the wheel for fear of what he might do next.

Shifting into second, she tried to slow down, but he was right on her bumper, pushing her around the next bend too fast—way too fast.

Hysteria thickened her mind, but she fought it, fought for control, fought to comprehend what was happening.

He slammed into her harder. He was deliberately trying to run her off the road, and if she didn't do something . . .

She threw it into first and stomped on the brake. Tires squealed as the smell of burning rubber filled her nose. The rear end of the old pickup skittered to the side, but did not slow. The momentum and force of the vehicle behind her continued propelling her down the hill.

The blast of his horn made her head ache. Her knuckles hurt from gripping the wheel. The core of her body was one tight coil.

Her headlights reached out as if to showcase the disaster that lay ahead. And there it was— the turn too sharp to make.

Claire felt the tires lose their hold on the road as the truck rocketed across the oncoming lane. She clung to the wheel and cranked it as hard as she could to keep from plunging over the edge of the road into the black ravine below.

Reaching down, she yanked the handle of the emergency brake. Her tires screamed. Gravel and dirt sputtered and spewed as the truck skidded in a wild semicircle. Her body bending over the wheel, she held on, leaning into the skid, holding her breath.

Her ears rang and her hands shook as the truck jolted to a stop so violently, her head banged hard against the door frame. For a moment, tiny stars burst behind her lids as darkness threatened to envelop her.

The blast of his horn continued, scrambling her brain, making her skin crawl. Then he slammed her again, and she screamed.

The front of the truck slid forward, dipped toward the ravine below, and stopped. Her body strained against the seat belt as she was thrown forward.

The vague sound of tires squealing told her he was backing away. She shifted her body, trying to get a glimpse of him, but he'd doused his lights. All she could see was a square shadow moving slowly away, into the night like an alien creature returning to the void of deepest space. Then the flash of bloodred taillights as he hit the brake before disappearing around the corner.

For a moment, she simply sat there panting, the sound of her own breath like a raspy saw. She sobbed without shedding a tear, and tried to slow her breathing, her thundering heart, her terror.

A wave of dizziness spun her brain in circles

and she thought she might be sick. Then she remembered hitting her head. The pain was starting; the dizziness increased.

Keep it together. Don't pass out. Don't . . . Don't . . .

Grasping the steering wheel with trembling fingers, Claire let her damp forehead rest against the backs of her hands as her eyes closed.

In the shadow place of her mind, far, far away, a car door slammed.

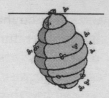

<u>Burglary</u>
Fast-food eating establishment.

Chapter 2

As Claire roused herself to consciousness, she heard heavy footsteps crunch over gravel, grow louder, come nearer. She pushed away from the steering wheel and turned her head into a beam of light shining directly into her eyes.

Raising her palm, she squinted past it, trying to see.

"Ma'am?" came a deep voice from behind the brilliant aura. "You all right in there?"

He ran the light around the interior of her truck, giving her a respite from the glare. She lowered her hand, and blinked. Impressions filtered into her brain. Tall man. Young. Uniform. Handsome. . . .

"Z-Zach?" Joy lightened her heart for a moment. Then just as quickly, turned to sorrow. It couldn't be Zach. The realization made her want to cry.

"No, ma'am. Was Zach with you?"

"No." Her voice was a mere whisper. "S-sorry, Officer. Zach is my brother. You remind me of him."

The light flicked into the bed of the truck.

"You doing okay? Had anything to drink tonight, ma'am?"

God, her head hurt. It was hard to think, to remember.

"I was run off the road," she explained. "Somebody in a huge SUV or something purposely shoved me off the road."

"You get a license number?"

"No."

"Make or model? Color?"

She shook her head, which hurt like hell to do.

"After he hit me," she said, "I think he turned off his lights. All I could see were his taillights as he drove away. I'm pretty sure it was an SUV, though. One of the gigantic ones. The taillights were big and square."

"You sure you're all right? You look a little woozy."

"I hit my head. Passed out for . . . What time is it?"

He checked his wristwatch. "Ten forty-five."

Forcing herself to remember what time it had been when she'd lowered her head to the steering wheel, she had a vague recollection of the clock on the dashboard. There had been a ten, but whether it was followed by a twenty-something or a thirty-something, she couldn't say.

"Maybe I should call an aid unit," the officer said.

Her head wasn't bleeding, the nausea had mostly dissipated, her vision was clear and not blurry, and she could recall most of the events leading up to the accident. If she had a concussion, it was probably not severe.

"I'll be fine," she said. "I'm a doctor. Just bumped my head, that's all. I'm okay."

"You rest a minute then," he said, running the beam of his light over the ground around the truck. Moving behind, he must have crouched to examine the rear of the truck, she thought. He stood and finished circling around, ending up back where he started, standing next to her.

"There are some dents in your bumper, but it's hard to tell if they're fresh." A moment of silence passed. "I'll need to see your license, vehicle registration, and proof of insurance, please."

Nodding absently, she eased herself around to reach for her purse on the seat beside her. When her fingers met only age-softened upholstery, she slid her hand down and searched the floor in front of the seat. There was something there, but it didn't feel like her purse.

She let her fingers curl around it, cold and smooth and unfamiliar. Bewildered, she lifted it and could only stare. Her jaw dropped.

When the officer eyed the half-empty bottle of whiskey gripped tightly in her fist, his demeanor changed from detached civility to accusation.

"Now, Doc. You told me you hadn't been drinking."

"I . . . This . . . I'm . . ."

"You want to step out of the vehicle for me, please."

"This . . . This isn't mine," she stumbled. "I swear . . ." Her voice trailed off as she realized her doors were open, both of them.

"Officer, did you open my doors?"

"No ma'am," he replied. "They were open when I pulled up. I'd like you to step out of the vehicle, please, and show me some ID."

"Listen," she said in a firm voice. "I know this looks bad, but I don't have my purse. It *was* on the seat, and now it's gone."

"Mm-hmm. Okay. Would you kindly step out

of the vehicle?" He was still smiling, but his eyes narrowed and his stance shifted. He took a step back to give her room.

As she went to unclasp her seat belt, she realized it had already been undone. She always wore her seat belt fastened. Always. No exceptions, and she never forgot.

What in the hell was going on?

She looked up at the police officer again and took a deep breath. In as steady a voice as she could find, she said, "I'm Dr. Hunter, Claire Hunter. I live in Port Henry and was on my way to Seattle. My seat belt was fastened, I had identification, and this bottle is *not* mine."

Leaning to the right, she reached in to the open the glove compartment and felt around inside it. When her fingers met only empty space, she turned again to the officer.

"Um . . ."

"Let me guess," he said without intonation. "You've misplaced the vehicle registration and insurance card, too."

"This is my aunt's truck," she explained, "but I'm sure she kept the papers in the glove compartment. I was obviously robbed while I was unconscious."

That gave her the major creeps. While she'd been blacked out, activity had gone on around her. Somebody had been near her, touched her things, maybe even touched her. He'd unfastened her seat belt. Stolen from her. Incriminated her. She had been vulnerable to . . . anything.

"You sit tight." The officer sighed, extending his hand, palm up. "Set the bottle on the seat and hand me the keys from the ignition, please."

She did and he took them and walked to his cruiser, angled in behind the truck. His door was open, allowing her to hear the dispatcher's droning voice and the various calls.

Around her, the trees were bathed in flashes of blue and red light. A few minutes later, the officer returned to the truck.

"Step out, please, ma'am." He moved back a little, edging his right hip away. She'd seen her father do that, and Zach, too. Keeping their holstered weapon out of reach in case somebody made a grab for it. Cops always kept a physical distance around them for the sake of safety. Sometimes they kept an emotional one, too.

Gingerly, she got out of the truck, afraid her legs wouldn't support her. Clinging to the door, she stood and looked up at the officer.

"I was run off the road and robbed. I have not had anything to drink. Not a thing, Officer, uh . . ."

"Darling."

"Wh-what?"

He glared at her, his blue eyes all but snapping

in challenge. "Officer Daniel Darling. Don't make the mistake of laughing, ma'am."

"I won't, Officer . . . Darling."

He ran the beam over her face and body, holding the light in his left hand at shoulder height as though it were a knife he was about to plunge through her heart.

"Okay, here's the deal," he said calmly. "You have no ID, no registration, and there's an open container in your possession. Now, I'd like to believe your story, but we're going to have to take a trip down to the station and straighten this mess out."

"Am I under arrest?"

"Not at the moment. You wouldn't happen to have any outstanding warrants, would you?"

"Absolutely not."

He smiled, showing deep dimples. "Then you're probably okay."

As he spoke into the transmitter on his shoulder, requesting Aunt Sadie's truck be impounded, he opened the back door of his cruiser and Claire had no choice but to slide in.

At the North Precinct of the Seattle Police Department, Detective Robert Aranca, a middle-aged Hispanic man with wiry gray hair and sharp, seen-it-all black eyes, seemed no more sympathetic.

He'd requested that Claire take a BAC Verifier DataMaster Test, the official drunk test, which she did. And since she had no alcohol in her system, she passed.

Detective Aranca took her statement in his cluttered office. Between questions, she gazed at framed photos of what were obviously his wife and two young children, while she tried to stay calm.

"Your photo ID checks out," he said, appearing just as weary as she felt. Leaning back in his chair, he tapped the end of his pen on the desk. "You are who you say you are. Got a little problem with the open container, though, Doc."

"I was set up."

"Okay," he said. "Let's say everything you told me really happened. You got any enemies?"

"I didn't think so, but now I'm not sure."

What if she hadn't passed out? What if the guy had come back to take her stuff, and she'd opened her eyes, seen him? Would he have killed her? Why would somebody plant incriminating evidence? Had she been selected at random, or was this someone she knew?

It had to be random. It *had* to be some . . . weirdo.

Detective Aranca looked at her paperwork. "The vehicle's owner is your aunt, one Sadie Lancaster. Why does that name sound familiar?"

Claire took a long, steadying breath. "She used to be an actress." When Aranca didn't immediately respond, she said, "She was nominated for an Oscar three times. *Lady Beware.* Um, *Sunset Street*? *Magdalena Mercy*? Her last movie was years ago, but—"

"Oh, right, right, right," he said, nodding enthusiastically. "Yeah, Sadie Lancaster. Sure, I remember her. Hey, she was big."

"It was the pictures that got small."

"Excuse me?"

"Never mind."

"And just where is the famous Sadie Lancaster now?"

"She and her fiancé went away for the weekend to Victoria."

Aranca's eyes narrowed. "She got a cell phone?"

Claire wrinkled her nose. "You have to understand, my aunt considers modern technology suspicious. She thinks cell phones are evil, and that aliens use them to control human thought." When Aranca lifted both his brows, she explained, "She's from California."

"Ah," he said, nodding knowingly. "Listen, is there anybody we can call who can vouch for you, maybe give you a ride home while we check this out?" His voice was gruff, but not unkind. "You told Officer Darling you were on your way to your house here in Seattle. Anybody there who can come and get you?"

"Unfortunately, no."

"What's your specialty, Doc?"

"Internal medicine," she said. "But the hospital in Port Henry is small. There's a lot of overlap."

He nodded, then leaned forward as though to impart a secret. Softly, he said, "So, Doc, what's it mean when you got a constant pain right here?" He pointed to the back of his neck. "At the end of the day, it's just about killing me. The wife, she says it's stress, but I'm a real laid-back guy. You're a doc, what do you think it means?"

She smiled. "It means you need to see a physician for a thorough examination."

He pursed his lips. "Yeah, yeah. Okay. I might just do that." Rolling his pen between thick fingers, he said, "Look, I don't feel comfortable just letting you walk out of here, especially without ID and a bump on your head. It'd be a good idea to have a friend or relative drive you to the ER."

"Really, my head's fine, and I don't know anyone who . . . *oh*," she said suddenly. Relief rushed through her, and she began to relax a little.

"Detective McKennitt," she said. "Of course. God, where has my brain been? He's my best friend's husband, you see. I was their maid of honor. You might know him. He's still attached to Seattle, but mostly works in Port—"

"Whoa, whoa, whoa. Hang on a minute." Aranca put his hands up in the air, interrupting her outburst. His eyes squinted on her in obvious suspicion. "You know Detective McKennitt?"

"Yes." What in the world had happened to her mind? Maybe she should stop by the ER after all.

Aranca shook his finger at her. "Okay, Doc. You wait right here."

As he rose and left his office, Claire glanced at the clock. Twelve-thirty. No wonder she was exhausted and brain dead. She'd been up since dawn, had driven a hundred-plus miles today, and had been in a horrible car accident. Her eyes ached, her body was sore—and she was facing trouble with the law for the first time in her life.

After a few minutes, Detective Aranca returned with what appeared to be a genuine smile on his face.

"Dr. Hunter," he said, with more punch than when he'd left. "As we say here at the Seattle PD, all's swell that ends swell. Detective McKennitt is on his way to pick you up. I'm going to release you into his custody, which will make both you and me feel much better."

Soldier was on his way. Thank God. Relief eased her muscles, and she slumped in the chair. Finally, this ridiculous, wretched nightmare would be over.

"Thank you, Detective," she said, smiling wearily up into his eyes.

Aranca excused himself and left her alone.

Exhausted, she folded her arms on the desk and lowered her head. She'd rest and wait for Soldier to arrive.

But the moment Claire closed her lids, images began playing behind her tired eyes. Time drifted, she drifted . . . into brilliant, blinding light, the blast of a horn, the screech of metal scraping metal, tires squealing as she spun out of control. She tried to glimpse her pursuer's face, get a look at the man who had done this to her, but all she could see was . . .

". . . honey blond hair, brown eyes. About five-six, one-twenty. Claire Hunter, M.D. In. The. Flesh."

Her eyes snapped open. Lifting her head, she blinked and slid a glance toward the open door of the office.

And her heart seized.

Laser blue eyes met hers, direct, probing—but they were not Soldier's eyes.

A masculine mouth twitched at one end into a wry grin—but it did not belong to her best friend's husband.

She tried to keep her eyes locked on his face, but they drifted over his body anyway. Running shoes, jeans, jacket over an open-collar white shirt.

He seemed a little rumpled, a little sleepy, as if he'd just climbed out of bed—satisfied. Though he needed a shave, on him, stubble looked . . . oh, man.

"You know," drawled the man who was not Soldier, his voice sending vibrations deep into the core of her body. "Usually, I'm just called on to serve and protect. There's a special form for bailing doctors out of a jam in the middle of the night."

"Taylor." If she'd made her voice any blander, she would have sounded bionic.

"Actually," he continued, "I won't really mind filling out the form because I just had to see for myself if it was really you, Doc. You know, before you disappear again."

Claire stared across the room at him. She'd forgotten how good-looking he was.

That was a lie. She had never forgotten.

Taylor McKennitt stood with his hip resting against the doorjamb. He grinned, like a wolf might smile at the furry, timid, terrified forest creature it was about to toy with, then devour.

Rubbing her eyes, she peered past Taylor to Detective Aranca standing behind him. "Excuse me?" she said sweetly. "There's been a mistake. This is the wrong Detective McKennitt."

"I get that a lot," Taylor said, sighing deeply. "Good thing I have such a healthy ego." His grin widened to show his white teeth. Charming and predatory, all in one perfectly constructed bundle.

Claire's brow furrowed. "Detective Aranca," she insisted, a little louder now. "Really. This is the wrong Detective McKennitt."

Aranca snickered and nudged Taylor with his elbow. "You said she'd say that. What, you two have a big fight or something?"

What does that mean?

"Yeah. *Or something*," Taylor drawled, his eyes never leaving Claire's.

Aranca laughed. "Hey. Kiss and make up, okay? You two'll have beautiful babies. Listen, Mac. I'll call you tomorrow."

"Thanks, Bobby," Taylor said, his blue eyes still locked on Claire's.

Detective Aranca sauntered off down the hallway, whistling a happy tune, leaving her alone with the wrong damn McKennitt brother.

His gaze touched her forehead, and he frowned. "How'd you get the bruise? Are you all right?"

She reached up, her fingertips pressing lightly on her tender skin. "I played crash-test dummy with my aunt's truck. I'm okay."

"Do you have any other injuries?" His gaze

raked her from head to toe and he curled his fingers as though he wanted to check her out personally.

"No."

"You sure?" He narrowed his eyes, gauging whether she was telling the truth. Flattening his mouth, he said, "You're going to the hospital."

"No," she rushed. "I'm fine. I just want to take a bath and get some sleep."

For a moment, neither of them spoke. Claire looked away, but she felt his scrutiny just as though he were running his fingertips along her cheek, and down her body, low, across her belly.

Taking a reinforcing breath, she pushed herself to her feet, fighting a wave of dizziness that weakened her knees. Taylor lowered his arms and looked as though he wanted to help steady her, but he stayed where he was.

"Thank you for bailing me out, Taylor. I appreciate it, but I haven't done anything wrong. I was set up."

He smiled sympathetically, sort of. "Yeah. We've got a whole jail full of innocent bystanders. But in your case, I guess I'm willing to keep an open mind."

"In my case?" She raised her eyes to meet his. "An open mind? But you *know* me."

He lowered his voice. "Yeah, if the biblical sense counts for anything. You know, Doc, I must have been a few beers short of a six-pack to have gotten involved with you. But, live and learn."

He clamped his jaw tightly closed and stared at her.

She lifted her chin. "Well, sorr-ree. It was my best friend's wedding. It was fun and romantic. You and I, well, we drank champagne, danced way too close, and one thing led to another. It *happens*." That's as much as she would ever confess to him about that night, about how she'd felt, and what had really driven her into his arms.

"One thing led to another three times." He arched a brow.

"You're being unfair—"

"I think I'm being damn fair," he interrupted. "More than fair, considering. I've heard it from my brother that his wife told him that you don't particularly care for my line of work."

"What's your point?"

"My point *is*," he said, leaning forward to glare into her eyes. "My line of work seems to be coming in pretty frigging handy tonight, getting your delectable little ass out of a jam, wouldn't you say?"

She took in a full breath, and let it out slowly.

"I've already said thank you, Detective." Attempting to moderate her anger was like trying to put out a fire with an ice cube.

He made a sweeping motion with his arm. "I should probably leave you here. Let them toss you into holding so you can see how the other half lives, but my brother would have my nuts on a platter if I did that."

She scowled. "If that's the case, maybe I'll stay. I think I'd like to see your nuts on a platter, even though I'd probably need a microscope to find them."

"If memory serves, you had no trouble with my anatomy eight months ago."

"Taylor—"

"If we're done discussing my nuts," he said, his voice dripping with sarcasm, "can we go now? I was in bed having a really hot dream, and I'd like to get back to it."

"Fine," she snarled.

"*Fine,*" he snarled, louder.

She glared at him. How *dare* he show up here instead of Soldier. How dare he have mutated from the nice, easygoing guy she'd met a year ago into this surly, overbearing, macho jerk simply because she'd . . .

Dammit. This *was* the millennium of casual, mutually satisfying, no-strings-attached sex, wasn't it? They had both been consenting adults that night. Words like *love* and *commitment* hadn't entered the conversation, what conversation there had been. So why was he so defensive?

Claire concealed her hurt with a mask of nonchalance. Though she wouldn't give him the satisfaction of knowing it, his attitude toward her stung. She had romantic memories of making love with Taylor. He'd been a caring and generous lover, tender, endearing, and it had torn her to pieces to leave him in the morning, to decide never to see him again when what she wanted with all her heart was to stay wrapped in his arms night after night.

What did a woman do when she found a man like Taylor, and realized she had to give him up? The only thing she could do was go, and not look back.

As she stood there, her knees gave out and she slumped back into her chair. He was beside her before her bottom hit the seat, his hand gripping her arm, concern in his eyes.

"You're not okay. Dammit, I knew it." He crouched in front of her. His worried gaze flitted over every inch of her face and body. "I'm taking you to the hospital, whether you—"

"Not necessary," she groused. "I'm fine. It's been a long day, and I'm exhausted." She eyed him. "What did you say to that detective? He sure treated me a lot nicer after he talked to you."

With a broad and charming grin, he said, "I told him you're my fiancée."

She blinked about a thousand times and widened her eyes to stare up at him.

"You *what*? *Why*?"

He shrugged. "Felt like it."

"That is so stupid."

"I know. But I thought it might be easier to convince him I wasn't going to let you out of my sight until I got you home, safe and sound. They're still checking out your story, so you're not clear quite yet."

He grinned into her eyes, and her anger melted just a teensy-weensy bit.

"So when we leave," he instructed, "keep your mouth shut and your eyes adoringly on me—at least until we get to my truck."

"I think I'm going to be sick."

"You need to use the bathroom?"

"Not really," she said dryly. "It's just the thought of being engaged to you has had an adverse effect on my digestion."

Tilting his head, he eyed her and sighed. "Damn. And to think we used to be so close."

Enema
Unfriendly female.

Chapter 3

Taylor stood over Claire, assessing her condition. Her posture told him she was beyond exhaustion. Her beautiful brown eyes were red and swollen. The bump on her skull had to be throbbing.

Maybe he should carry her.

Yeah, and maybe he'd like a knee to his groin, he thought. Unless she was unconscious, he'd be wise to proceed with caution.

But the thought of Claire's body in his arms again sent his heart knocking against his ribs. Even after all these months, he was attracted to her as strongly as if she were magnetic north.

"Can you make it out to my truck?" he ventured. "Maybe I should carry you."

She sent him a miffed glance, fiddled with her hair, and straightened her shoulders.

"Detective, there are only two conditions under which I'd let you carry me anywhere."

"Okay." He sighed. "I'll bite."

She held up her index finger. "One involves a toe tag . . ." She closed her fingers into a fist. "And the other a white dress and a threshold."

"Dead or wed, huh?"

"Mm-hmm." She pressed her lips together, then smiled far too sweetly. "And since neither event is likely to happen, lead the way. I'll be right behind you."

She still looked woozy to him, so he reached for her arm. She shook him off. Jesus, she was as stubborn as a premenstrual mule, and would probably rather die than let on she was hurting.

"Dammit, woman," he snapped. "Lose the attitude, put your weapons away, and relax a little. Let somebody who has *not* been in a car accident, who has *not* had a head injury tonight, and who *may* be thinking more clearly than you, take *care* of you."

She blinked up at him and raised her brows. "Dammit . . . *woman*? That is so eighteenth century."

"Yeah, well I would have said dammit *pain in the ass*, but I'm nothing if not frigging progressive!"

"Taylor," she bit out between clenched teeth. "I'm a doctor. I would know if I were symptomatic. My reactions to the trauma are typical, and nothing more. The adrenaline rush left me shaky, but my pulse is normal now, my vision is clear, there is no headache or nausea present, and no broken bones. Worst-case scenario, I might need a sedative and bed rest."

"Physician, heal thyself?"

"If I thought I needed treatment, I'd get it."

"No you wouldn't," he said flatly. "You're afraid this'll leak to the press and your reputation will be dog food."

She looked like she wanted to scream. "I know you think I'm a real tight ass—"

"It would be ungentlemanly of me," he said, leaning near her ear, "to comment on how tight your ass is, because it might raise a question as to how I came by such intimate knowledge."

He cocked his head in silent challenge for her to pursue the issue at her own risk.

She set her jaw and stared at him. Man, if looks could kill, she'd need a permit for those eyes.

Slipping his arm around her waist, he said, "C'mon, Doc. Enough of this BS. Time to go. And remember, you love me."

"Oh, right," she drawled sourly. "We're engaged."

"You say it like you don't worship the ground I walk on. I'm crushed, sweet cheeks."

"Enough to break our engagement?"

He smiled at her like he knew a secret she could never begin to guess.

As they made their way through the crowded station to the door, they received wry grins and curious stares. He tightened his arm on her waist and tugged her just a bit closer.

"Opportunist," she muttered under her breath.

Through clenched teeth and a frozen smile, he said, "Shut up or I'll kiss you."

She pressed her lips together.

He didn't release her until they'd exited the building and crossed the lot. Nodding at the officers who had parked their unit next to his truck, he helped Claire into the passenger seat.

"Buckle up, hon."

Clicking her restraints in place, she gave him a sad little smile. "I've changed my mind, stud muffin. I don't want to marry you after all. I think we should break up."

"Ah, hell," he said dismissively. "You say that now, but you'll feel better after you've had a hot meal, a good night's sleep, and some top-quality, grade-A sex."

Behind him, one of the officers mumbled something to the other, and both men chuckled.

"Oh? Did you finally pick up that prescription?"

His eyes widened innocently. "The one for your spells? Sure did, funny face. We wouldn't want you to have another unfortunate episode, would we? Next time they might not let you out."

Before Claire could elbow him in the gut, Taylor shut her door and moved around to the driver's side. Sliding in, he buckled his own seat belt, cranked the ignition, and turned left out of the lot.

Beside him, Claire was silent. He saw her shoulders rise and fall, as though she'd taken in a big breath and let it out. Not facing him, she muttered, "You're an idiot."

"I've been called worse," he said, smiling. "So tell me what happened."

"I already gave my statement to Detective Aranca."

"I'm not asking for a statement."

"You're not involved in the case. Listen, I'm not trying to be difficult—"

"Honey, you're both trying *and* difficult. Now tell me what happened tonight."

She looked like she wanted to smack him, but instead said, "This isn't your concern. Thank you for coming to get me. I'll reimburse you for the gas and—"

"I don't want to be reimbursed. That's not why I did it." He studied her a moment. "But we can do a trade, like in the old days. You know, barter for goods and services."

Her eyes took on a suspicious glint. "What kind of . . . services?"

He shrugged. "You're a doctor. How about a checkup? I can't tell you how I've longed to get naked and hear you whisper those magic words."

"And they would be?"

"*Turn your head to the left and cough.*" He slammed his fist against his chest. "Oh, baby. Gets me right here, every time."

"Your aim is a little off, but that doesn't surprise me."

"You're such a fun date," he said lightly. "We really should do this more often."

She raised her chin and sucked in her bottom lip. It riveted his attention almost as much as if she'd taken off her blouse.

Checking his side mirror, he took the next left. "Tell me what happened."

"No."

"Claire," he growled. "Goddammit, tell me what happened."

"Well, when you put it that way . . . *hell* no."

He pulled over to the side of the road and let the engine idle. "We aren't going anywhere until *you* tell *me* what happened."

She clamped her jaw tight.

"I've cracked tougher nuts than you," he warned. "I'm not hungry, don't gotta pee, am not the least bit sleepy, and I'm as patient as a turtle. You, on the other hand, haven't eaten for hours, and as a woman, have a bladder the size of a lima bean, are obviously exhausted, and have the patience of a stick of dynamite." He sent her a sly grin. "I can outlast you, sweet cheeks, so you might want to reconsider the silent treatment."

"*God*," she choked, doubling her fists and glaring over at him. "You are really something. *Fine.*"

He smiled. "I love it when I get my way."

"And you're such a gracious winner, too."

Taylor pulled back into traffic, listening as Claire related the incident, flicking glances in her direction to check her movements, body position, facial expressions.

"Can you describe the car?"

"No. It was big, though, and had squarish tail-lights high off the ground. It was either an SUV or a huge truck with a camper shell on it."

He drove slowly, tuning in to the remaining notes of terror in her voice. She was trying to maintain, but her voice was a little thin, a little shaky. What had happened tonight had scared the hell out of her. He curled his fingers around the steering wheel, suddenly wishing it were the gonads of the guy who'd hurt her.

Cutting a quick glance in her direction, he said, "Could you make out anything about the driver?

"No."

He stopped for a red light, still gripping the gonads-cum-steering wheel, letting the facts tumble around inside his brain.

When the light turned green, Claire said, "Take a left on Roosevelt."

"It's actually faster if you go . . ."

Uh-oh. His own words hit him, and he let his voice trail off. Maybe she was too tired to pick up on—

"You know where my house is?" Her voice was cold enough to usher in a new ice age.

Silence, as thick as mud, oozed between them.

Taylor blew out a long, dramatic sigh. "I know I should be ashamed of myself," he said solemnly. "It's a compulsion, a disease. Surely you can understand. I deserve your pity, Doctor, not your scorn."

Claire burst out laughing, a sound that somehow managed to ride the fine line between joy and dementia.

"Of course," she nodded, wiping her eyes. "Sure. Absolutely. I should have known." She looked at him with a flat what-*am*-I-going-to-do-with-you? look in her eyes.

He took the next corner, pulled into her driveway, and turned off the ignition. "Oh, and by the way . . ." He tried his best to look humble and pathetic. "The apple tree in your backyard needs pruning."

"You used your position as a public servant to stalk me."

"*Stalk* is such an ugly word. I prefer . . ." He squinted, pretending to search for the right term. ". . . covert personal surveillance." If she only knew how covert and personal his surveillance had been at her aunt's farm.

He wouldn't confess to her how many times he'd driven by her house, hoping she was in the city, hoping to catch a glimpse of her. Or how he'd changed the route to his own house on the days he knew she was there, just so he could make sure the neighborhood was secure, that her car was in the driveway, that she was safe. He would never tell her how fast his heart beat, how wildly, when he did happen to see her walking to the mailbox or clipping the roses in the front yard.

"Covert personal surveillance," she repeated slowly, shaking her head.

"Let's get your stuff," he ordered, changing the subject. "I'm suddenly very tired and I've got a willing babe waiting for me in dreamland, and if you don't—"

"Oh, save your breath," she groused. "You'll need it to blow up your date." Grabbing for her seat belt, she froze in mid-unbuckle. "What do you mean, get my stuff?"

"Get. Your. Stuff." He enunciated the phrase as though he were speaking to a disobedient preschooler. "You're not staying here."

"I am so staying here."

"Are not."

"Am so."

Unable to keep the scowl off his face, he said, "You were released into my custody. I'm responsible for you, therefore I'm not letting you out of my sight until I know exactly what's going on here. It obviously hasn't occurred to you that a man you don't know has your ID, your credit cards, pager, and your cell phone, too, yes? And all the other stupid, lame, useless crap women keep in their purses. I didn't spot a tail, but he might have somehow followed us here. You'd be alone without even a phone in the house. Am I right?"

She blinked and cocked her head. "*Somebody* needs anger management ther—"

"I *assume* you have a spare key hidden around here so we can get in and pack a bag for you? After that, we are leaving. Got that, sweetheart?"

Claire shrugged and mumbled something under her breath, averting her eyes from his.

Ah, hell. He should probably cut her some slack. After all, she'd had a shock, she was exhausted, and all she probably wanted was to go inside the house, lock the door, and curl up underneath the covers until tomorrow brought sunshine to make the nightmare go away.

In a gentler tone, he said, "Listen, Claire, I—"

"There's a key under the flowerpot on the back porch."

"A *flowerpot*!" So much for good intentions. "As security systems go, that pretty much sucks, babe."

She crossed her arms; defiance shone in her eyes. "The flower has *gigantic* thorns."

Maybe it was the way her eyes widened and her voice squeaked when she said *gigantic*, but he felt his mouth curve into a smile, and his heart soften.

"Yeah, those would sure scare me off. Now, I figure, little thorns, they're simply for show. Medium-sized thorns, they make a guy think twice. They're saying, maybe I'll hurt you, maybe I won't. Big thorns, well, they're so in-your-face, I'd consider them a challenge. But *gi-*

gantic thorns? They say don't even think about it, pal, not without a SWAT team, special weapons, and a negotiator."

Her mouth twitched and her cheeks flushed.

"This is a very safe neighborhood," she muttered.

Opening his door, he went around to open hers. When she stepped out, she yawned, then said, "All right. You win. It's after two in the morning. I guess I can find a motel that's open—"

"You're staying with me." Slamming the door, he scowled down into her defiant eyes. "And don't give me any more trouble. I've got thorns of my own, sister, and I'm not afraid to use 'em."

Thirty minutes later, Taylor slid into bed and pulled the sheet over his naked body. Man, he couldn't remember the last time he'd been so tired. But as much as he wanted it to be, the day was not quite done.

Grabbing his cell phone from the nightstand, he momentarily considered how cruel it would be to awaken his brother in the middle of the night, but the thought quickly dissipated when he considered the situation Claire was in.

After three rings, he heard a sleepy, "Soldier McKennitt."

"Sorry, Jackson. Haul your ass downstairs so you don't wake up your wife. We need to talk."

In the background, Taylor heard Betsy murmur a question, and his brother's deep voice gently answer. He rolled his eyes, but grinned when he heard a soft smack, and knew Soldier had kissed her before climbing out of bed.

Moments passed, doors opened, closed. "It's nearly three in the morning," Soldier growled. "Who died, and it better be somebody I care about. Deeply."

The screech of chair legs echoed against Taylor's eardrum as his brother obviously made himself comfortable at the kitchen table.

"Betsy doing okay?"

Soldier groaned. "Hell, I don't know. By the end of the day, her feet look like puff pastries. She thinks she waddles like a carb-loaded duck, and she cries when she reads Victoria's Secret catalogs."

"So do I."

"Yeah, but for a whole other reason."

Taylor chuckled. "Sorry, big brother. Is there any upside to a woman being eight months pregnant?"

Pause. "Uh, yeah."

Taylor assessed his brother's evasive tone. "But you're not going to tell me what it is?"

"Uh, no."

"Okay, well, tell her I'm sorry I woke her."

"No problem," Soldier said. "She has to pee

every two minutes anyway, so she was about due. Besides, she's having trouble sleeping. The only time she can get comfortable is when I . . . uh, never mind. You were about to explain to me in intricate detail why you woke me up."

Taylor slipped one arm behind his head. "It's about Claire."

"Oh?" Soldier said, his voice suddenly wary. "What happened?"

"I brought her home with me. She's in bed."

A pause, muttering, blustering, cussing. "You're thirty-two years old and you called me in the middle of the night to tell me you scored with a girl? Just what am I supposed to say, way to go, dude?"

"Feign insult some other time, Jackson. Somebody tried to kill her tonight."

His brother's tone went dead serious. "Our guy?"

"I don't know yet." For the next five minutes, Taylor recounted what he knew of Claire's story. "She asked for you, but Bobby Aranca got a hold of me instead. They're going to do a drive-by of her house here in Seattle, and Sam Winslow said they'd do the same at the farm in Port Henry. Bobby's supposed to call me with anything they get off the aunt's truck."

"Anybody check out the scene?"

"She was too tired and shaken up for me to take her back up there tonight. I figured I'd do it tomorrow when I drive her back to Port Henry."

"I can meet you. What time?"

Taylor batted the question around in his brain for a moment. "Nah. You need your beauty rest. Until I find out more, I can do this solo."

"You think this is related to Mortimer?" Soldier didn't bother to stifle a yawn.

"What do you think I think?"

"Yeah, that's what I thought. The question is, what's the connection?"

"I don't know," Taylor said. "She was driving her aunt's truck. Maybe whoever it was didn't realize it was Claire until after he'd run her off the road. Maybe Sadie was the real target. Or, hell, I don't know. Maybe it was completely random. Some guy getting his rocks off scaring women."

"I don't like that scenario any better."

"Me, either." He scratched his stubbled jaw. "I'll let you know what I find tomorrow. In the meantime, I'm keeping Claire with me."

"Copy. I'll see you—"

"Hey, wait," Taylor interrupted. "Before you hang up, one last question. Has Betsy ever said anything to you about why Claire has a thing against cops?"

"No, not really," Soldier said as though he was considering the question. "Far as I know, she just thinks it's risky business."

In the background, a soft voice called Soldier's name.

Taylor heard his brother swallow. "Uh, gotta go."

Betsy's voice, closer now, laughing, purring something unintelligible yet unmistakable in its tone.

Soldier swallowed again. "I have to go, Tayo. Now."

"Is everything okay?" Taylor teased.

"Great. Uh, everything's great. Call me tomorrow."

The line went dead, and Taylor decided to try really hard not to imagine what was happening on his brother's kitchen table right now.

Artery
Place where paintings are displayed.

Chapter 4

Claire fought to free herself from the tangle of bed linens twisted around her like a shroud. With a final kick, she curled up into a sitting position. Hunched over her raised knees, she sucked in air, forcing herself to calm while she pressed two fingers against her damp throat and checked her heart rate.

Too fast, way too fast. Take a deep breath, slow it down, steady now.

Her eyes sought something familiar in the unfamiliar room, and she nearly panicked until she remembered.

Taylor's house. Taylor. The accident, the police, the wrong McKennitt brother . . .

Clutching the thin blanket to her breasts, she fought allowing her lids to drift closed. The dream—too vivid, too stark—might come back. Even now, violent images lurched obscenely inside her skull, reluctant to fade away though it was daylight, and her eyes were wide open.

A woman's scream still echoed through the air. Not hers, surely. She hadn't screamed out loud . . . had she? She didn't think she'd ever done that, yet over the last year, the night terrors had seemed so real . . .

Suddenly, her door flew open, revealing a half-naked man holding a gun. He glanced quickly around the room, then let his gaze slowly settle on her.

"You okay?" His voice was husky from sleep, his eyes laser sharp, his stance poised for pursuit, his jeans unbuttoned.

She nodded and put a trembling hand to her forehead. She didn't want him seeing her like this, emotionally ravaged, still shaking from the after-effects of the nightmare. Her brow was slick with perspiration, and she could feel cold sweat under her arms and trickling down her back.

Grabbing the water glass from the stand next to the bed, she closed her eyes and chugged its contents, nearly drowning herself getting it down her throat. When she opened her eyes again, he was staring at her.

"You didn't have to drink it all in one gulp," he drawled. "I have more." He set the gun on the table near the door.

Her heart tripped inside her chest, jabbing her ribs. She kept her eyes at chest level, which wasn't all that much better for her nerves.

"I heard you scream." His sharp gaze narrowed, assessing her. "Was it a man or a mouse?"

"Neither. I sneezed," she lied. "Sorry if it woke you."

They stared into each other's eyes for a moment. He didn't believe her, but, thankfully, didn't seem inclined to make an issue of it.

She considered telling him about the dream, sharing her fears. Even though it had been more than eleven months, he would understand her lingering terror. After all, the stalker who'd gone after Betsy had nearly cost Taylor his life as well. Then when Claire became the target, it was Taylor who had taken her home from the hospital, stayed the night with her, guarded and protected her from further harm.

Bottom line, she'd survived the assault and the stalker had been dispatched. If the incident wasn't completely out of her system, that was okay. It would be. She was on the mend, and in fact hadn't had an episode for weeks.

The accident last night, and seeing Taylor so unexpectedly again, must have stirred things up, and her psyche decided to trot out the trauma one more time.

"It's after noon," he said. "I'm going to get dressed. I'll wait breakfast until you're ready, so take as long as you need." He picked up his weapon and closed the door behind him. Claire let out a shaky breath.

Touching the swell just above the hairline on her skull, she winced. Tender, but not the goose egg it had been last night.

She showered, brushed her teeth, dressed. Then, plopping onto the bed, she picked up her comb, but before she could untangle the damp mess on her head, she noticed a large oil painting on the wall above the desk by the window. She'd been too tired last night to check out the place, but now, by the light of day, she realized the room was much larger than she'd realized, was wonderfully decorated, and what she had assumed was a dime-store print was, on closer examination, anything but.

Rising, she moved closer to the painting, drawn to the color and composition like nothing she'd ever seen outside a museum.

It was lovely in its understated power. An incredible interpretation of a storm at sea, exquisite in its detail, and beautifully executed. How had Taylor been able to afford such an obviously expensive painting on a detective's salary, and why on earth did he keep it buried in the guest room where very few people probably saw it? Perhaps it had been a gift. Maybe he hated seascapes.

Then she noticed a smaller painting on the wall near the door. This one was a portrait of an adorable little girl. She looked very serious holding a kitten and a balloon, as though she was terrified of losing one or both of them. Her brown eyes gleamed with youthful energy, and her shaky smile . . . was somehow familiar.

Claire compared the two paintings. They had to have been done by the same artist. Even though the topics were vastly different, both canvases were strong, painterly, vibrant with life.

She finished combing her hair, made the bed, and with one last glance at the wonderful paintings, closed the door behind her.

More oils lined the hallway upstairs and followed the staircase as it descended to the first floor. Splendid paintings on every subject imaginable, from a bowl of lavender hydrangeas, to a schooner sailing the sea. All were powerful, all breathtaking.

At the foot of the stairs, Claire glanced into

the living room and nearly dropped to her knees. Dear God, the room looked like a frat house on a Sunday morning. Empty bottles, crumpled cans, newspapers, and discarded neckties littered the coffee table. A pile of clean socks waiting to be matched and put away sat in a plastic basket next to the recliner, and books of every kind and color were scattered on the end table and floor. A pair of boots had been shoved under the coffee table, and a bowl stacked high with pretzels and chips rested on the floor near the chair facing the TV.

She was about to turn away from the clutter, when she raised her eyes to the fireplace, and her breath caught.

Above the mantel hung a large oil painting depicting a runaway cattle drive. Dust blurred the bawling cows while wranglers with ropes and rifles, atop galloping horses, tried to turn the herd. The colors, the movement, the enormous energy of the painting held Claire in thrall. She searched until she found it, then felt her lips curve into a smile.

Seeking out the kitchen, she entered and looked around. By comparison, the living room had been as clean as a hospital surgery.

"You are a slob," she said to Taylor's back.

He stood at the sink, rinsing out a couple of brown earthenware bowls. On the counter, amid the rubble of empty coffee mugs, teaspoons, stacks of plates, and a baseball glove and ball, the coffeemaker burbled and popped as the rich scent of coffee filled the air.

Without looking around, he said, "*Slob* is such a harsh word. I prefer creatively disheveled. Besides, only boring people have immaculate houses." He yanked a dish towel from an open drawer and began drying the bowls.

"Not into calling a spade a spade, I gather."

"Sure, when I'm playing poker. Other than that *sneeze*," he said, pronouncing the word as though he'd never heard it before, "did you sleep okay last night?"

"Great," she fibbed. "Like a baby."

With a barely concealed look of doubt, he opened a packet of apple-cinnamon oatmeal and poured it into her bowl.

"Thanks," she said sarcastically, placing her open hand over her heart in a dramatic move she'd seen Aunt Sadie perform a hundred times. "You're going to make some woman a *wonderful* husband."

"Was once."

Claire immediately regretted her remark. She looked up at him, but he avoided her gaze. "Right. Sorry. I'd, um, I'd forgotten. You're divorced."

He shrugged and opened four oatmeal packets for himself. "I'm working on forgetting it, too."

She gave a little sort of I-see nod, pressed her lips together, then slid into a chair.

To Taylor's credit, the table was clean and devoid of hazardous waste. He'd set down two fresh plastic placemats, and the fact his said "Merry Christmas" in elaborate script did nothing to diminish the realization that he had obviously tried to make things nice for her.

Straightening her blue and green plaid placemat, she ventured, "If you don't mind my asking, do you think you'll ever get married again?"

"Sure." He went to the cupboard and pulled out some paper napkins, tossing them on the table in a fluttery heap.

"But wasn't the divorce hard on you?"

"It was a walk in the park compared to the marriage." Reaching for the steaming copper kettle on the stove, he poured boiling water on her oatmeal as she stirred it with a spoon. "Besides, I don't plan on getting divorced again."

He caught her gaze and held it until she had to look away.

Angry at herself for her inability to remain as detached as she'd like, she pushed herself up from the table and went to retrieve two mugs from the hooks under the white pine cabinet.

"Did you . . . like being married?" She avoided his eyes by pretending to check the mugs for spots.

"You don't have to get out your disinfectant, Doc," he said, his brows snapping together. "They're clean. Everything's clean, it's just that everything's everywhere. And, yeah, I liked being married well enough. The good parts. The unfaithful-slut part didn't set too well with me, but I plan on being a lot more selective next time."

He doused his own oatmeal with boiling water and stirred the contents of the bowl into a steaming glop. Adding milk and brown sugar, he sat down while Claire poured hot coffee into both their mugs.

As he watched her sit and stir milk into her oatmeal, he said, "What about you, Claire? You ever plan on getting married?"

"My aunt would like it if I did," she said lightly.

He took a sip of coffee, set the mug down, leaned back in his chair. "That's what we law enforcement types call an evasive answer."

She lifted a shoulder. "I'll get married when the right man comes along."

At her words, he arched a brow. He was wearing jeans and a T-shirt the color of slate that fit his athletic body like a second skin. Rubbing his open palm over his flat abs, he said, "How do you know he hasn't already come along, but your nose was so high in the air, it blocked your line of vision?" He took his thumb and flicked the end of his own nose, then grinned.

"I don't think you know me well enough to judge me, Detective."

His blue eyes bored holes into her brain. Shrugging, he drawled, "Well, I guess I know you well enough to have made love to you for hours the night of my brother's wedding. I guess I know you well enough to get out of bed in the middle of the night to help you out of a jam. I guess I know you well enough to bring you to my house for your own protection."

Claire set her spoon on the table. In her sweetest tone, she said, "You never let an argument end until you've won, do you?"

He leaned toward her. With a grin Claire would have considered charming on any other man, he said, "Were we arguing just now? And more importantly, did I win?"

Claire eased herself back in her chair. "You try to be a bully, but I know for a fact you have a sensitive side."

He sent her a wary look, as though he was trying to figure out where she was going with this. Finally, he said slowly, "I cry at sad movies, if that's what you mean. You know at the end of *Homeward Bound*, when that old dog comes limping over the hill, and the kid runs—"

"That's not what I mean, but thank you for

sharing." She pursed her lips. "I'm talking about the paintings."

He blinked. "What paintings?"

"The two oils in the guest room, the paintings along the second floor hall and down the stairs, and that magnificent Remington-esque over the fireplace."

His eyes downcast, he fiddled with his spoon. "You . . . think it's magnificent?"

She nodded enthusiastically and sat forward in her chair. "Really, Taylor, I do. *All* the paintings are beautiful, stunning."

He took in a deep breath. Was it her imagination, or was he blushing?

"You have an amazing talent," she went on. "You must have had art teachers who told you so. Why didn't you pursue it? Why didn't you become an artist instead of a police officer?"

Taylor still didn't look at her. With a casual shrug, he said, "It's just a hobby. Helps me unwind." He raised his eyes to hers. "How'd you know I painted them? They're not signed."

"Yes they are."

He lifted his chin. "Yeah?"

"In the bottom right-hand corner," she said, "there's a tiny *TSMc* scribbled into the oil. A person could miss it if they didn't know what to look for."

"And you know."

Picking up her empty bowl, she walked to the sink. "There is no way you would ever paint anything so awesome and not want to take credit for it. Soldier said something once about you being a good artist, but I thought he was just being kind."

Tossing his spoon onto the table, Taylor leaned back in his chair. "If you think that shows you know me, Dr. Hunter, think again."

Claire rolled her eyes. "Well, excuse me, Mr. Macho Arrogant Keep Away From Me Hotshot Typical Stupid Male. Complimenting your talent was _not_ a come-on."

Fuming, she turned, scrubbed the bowl and spoon she'd used, dried them, and put them in the cupboard. "There. Now you only have four hundred and ninety-nine things to wa— What are you doing?"

He rose from the table and began stalking toward her.

"Okay, fine," she stated flatly, lifting her hands as a barrier against him. "Your paintings suck, you no-talent dilettante. Happy now?"

He stopped two feet in front of her, grasped her by the wrists, and held her in place. The heat of his body kept coming, though, wrapping her in warmth like an invisible embrace.

"I like that you like my paintings," he whispered.

Though she wanted to speak, words wouldn't come. The strength of his fingers gripping her wrists, the aroma of his soap coupled with the muskier scent of his clean body, the fiery blue of his eyes, combined to render her mute.

He released her, stepping away, and she felt suddenly cold, as if the sun had left the sky.

She realized she wanted to touch him, call him back, but he moved beyond the reach of her outstretched hand. She thought to call his name, but before she could speak, he said, "Finish up and get your stuff. I have a few hours' work to do, then I'll take you back to Port Henry. On the way, I want to check out your accident scene. And we can talk some more about what happened."

She furrowed her brow and nodded agreement.

We can talk some more about what happened. Which what happened? she wondered. What happened between them eight months ago? What happened yesterday when she was forced off the road? Or what was undeniably happening between them right now?

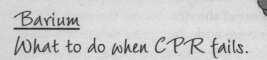

Barium
What to do when CPR fails.

Chapter 5

"It started here," Claire said softly, gesturing with her hand. Though she hid it well, Taylor was certain her fingers trembled just a little. "About here, I think. It was dark, and I was . . ."

Terrified, Taylor finished in his head.

He downshifted, slowed, and took the next bend in the road. "This is where he first made contact?"

She nodded absently, as though reliving the incident inside her head. "Yes. He hit my bumper a couple of times. His high beams were on so I couldn't see anything in my rearview mirror but glare. Then he laid on the horn. At first I though he just wanted by me, but he kept ramming my bumper until . . . *here*. Here's where he started shoving me off the road."

Her eyes were wide, her voice thin. She leaned forward with one hand on the dashboard as she described the accident. Since there was no place to turn out and stop, Taylor checked his mirrors and slowed as much as possible, examining the road ahead and the rocky incline to his right. Ahead of him, the road curved sharply, allowing no view of oncoming traffic.

"Around this corner," she said, then swallowed. "I—I saw this bend coming and knew I was going too fast to make it. He shoved me hard. I slammed on the brakes and at the same time, pulled the emergency brake, but I had too much momentum going, couldn't stop, and couldn't hold the turn."

Slowly, Taylor took the same turn that Claire had been forced to take last night. Thick black skid marks lay like dark ribbons on the pavement where she'd tried to stop. The road curved, the tracks did not. She'd headed straight across the oncoming lane. Anything could have been coming up that hill last night, from a motorcycle, to a semi, to an old farmer in a produce truck, to a family.

He felt his jaw tighten as he fought down all the what-ifs and how differently this story would have ended if Claire's guardian angel hadn't been perched on her shoulder.

She must have been panicking like hell, wondering what would happen. Even now, her skin had drained of color, her eyes widened and filled with unshed tears. She kept her lips pressed together, her spine straight.

He knew she was tough, now he knew she was brave.

"But you made it, Claire," he said gently. "You kept your head, and you made it."

Without looking at him, she nodded. "Um, the turnout's right around this corner. You'll be able to see—Oh, no."

If Taylor hoped to find a single shred of evidence at the turnout where Claire had been run off the road, it was all blown to hell when he rounded the bend. A logging truck stood parked on the gravel. Between the front fender of the shiny red cab and the length of cut timber filling its extended bed, the eighteen-wheeler took up about fifty feet, and not an inch of turnout to spare. On top of that, last night's summer drizzle had morphed to muck whatever tire or footprint evidence might have existed.

"Shit," he muttered under his breath. "Not even room enough for me to pull over."

He took in as much of the scene as he could, asking Claire questions. Behind the rig stood the bent metal barrier that had saved her from going over, but there was no way he'd find any footprint or tire evidence at this point.

Waving to the gray-haired driver relaxing in the cab, munching on an enormous sandwich, Taylor shifted gears and rounded the next bend, looking for the spot the driver must have used to park in order to come back and rob Claire just minutes after the accident.

But there wasn't one.

"He must have taken the chance this road is seldom used," he said. "Probably pulled over, left it idling, jumped out and ran back to your truck. Maybe he wanted to see if you were hurt, but when he got there, and you were unconscious, he decided to take your stuff."

As Taylor spoke, a car came up behind him. Dammit. There was no way he could pull over, so he had to keep going. Since this part of the road was paved side to side, he wouldn't be able to get any tire tread evidence anyway.

Blowing out a frustrated sigh, he sped up and said, "Robbing you couldn't have been his plan all along, because there was no guarantee you'd hit your head and pass out. Taking your things must have been a crime of opportunity."

"Okay, but what about the bottle?"

"You got me. My guess is, he was drinking and he just brought it along when he came to check on you. Set it down when he gathered up your stuff, and forgot to grab it when he saw the lights from the cruiser coming down the hill. Or he left it on purpose to put you in hot water."

Easing back into her seat, she said, "I guess. I'm just glad it's over."

He shot her another glance. "You've been coping okay, right?" he ventured, as certain puzzle pieces began clicking into place. "Being assaulted by Betsy's stalker, and now this. Heavy-duty traumas, even for a doctor who—"

"I'm coping just fine," she interrupted. "Thanks for your concern, Detective, but I'm right as rain."

No you're not.

The realization struck Taylor with the force of an ecclesiastical epiphany. Not only was she not all right, she was doing her best to mask her true feelings. He wondered if she'd let down her guard with anybody over the last eleven months. Her aunt? Her best friend?

He'd bet even money she hadn't.

When he'd first seen her at the station last night, he'd assumed her up-tight attitude was a result of the accident, not to mention unexpectedly running into him again. She'd been scared and tired, true. But he'd been viewing her though a combined filter of frustration, anger, and, yeah, unwanted attraction.

Now that he'd had a chance to talk to her and

let his emotions dissipate a little, he was beginning to suspect there was a lot more going on inside her head than she was willing to admit.

She'd had a nightmare last night, and had screamed.

I sneezed, she'd said. *My ass*, he'd thought.

Had her nightmare been related to the car accident, or was this new trauma too close on the heels of the old one?

Claire was a doctor. She'd survived medical school and internship and boards and whatever else doctors had to go through to get to be doctors. She was used to being in charge, the one others looked to for answers, for strength.

What had happened nearly a year ago had undoubtedly shaken her confidence, but because she was supposed to be tough in the face of adversity, she probably fought to maintain her image even though her mind and her heart were still coping with such a brutal attack.

It gnawed at him a little that he hadn't seen it sooner. His very presence must be a reminder of the night she'd nearly been killed. She'd needed him then, and he'd been there for her—as a cop, and as a man.

Now she was shutting him out. Whatever had caused her to scream in her sleep was obviously something she didn't want to talk about. Not to him, anyway.

"I don't think you're right as rain," he said. "In fact—"

"I'll make a deal with you," she said, her tone dry. "I promise not to play detective with you if you won't play doctor with me." Placing her fingertips at her temples, she closed her eyes and muttered, "I can't believe I just said that. Talk about an opening . . ."

"Oh, yeah." He grinned. "Playing doctor with you sounds like a whole lot of fun, bunny hugs."

"Stop calling me by those fake endearments. We don't have an audience, so there's no need for it."

"What makes you think they're fake?"

Her mouth flattened. "And stop pretending to be so charming."

"Who's pretending? I *am* charming. *Everybody* says so." He smiled at her, just to drive the message home.

"So insufferable," she muttered. Louder, she said, "Take the next right, please."

The chickens and the goose flapped and squawked and scattered as Taylor pulled to a stop in front of the farmhouse at the end of the long gravel drive.

He gave a quick glance around, pretending he'd never laid eyes on the place before. It was closing in on five in the afternoon. Sunshine glistened off the pond just beyond the barn, while graceful trees shaded the house. Agatha lay sprawled under a rocking chair on the porch, trying to escape the heat. Other than the animals, the place seemed quiet.

He turned off the ignition. Time for a little subtle interrogation.

"I've seen some of your aunt's old movies," he said. "She was really beautiful."

A smile tilted the ends of Claire's mouth. "I think Aunt Sadie is still beautiful."

"Does she miss Hollywood?"

Her smile broadened. "Probably. She talks about the old days a lot. Sometimes it seems she has a little, um, difficulty letting go of the grandeur."

"You mean, like Norma Desmond?"

Claire snickered. "Nothing so dramatic as in *Sunset Boulevard*, but it must be hard to have been so famous, so glamorous, the toast of the town, and then one day give it all up to—"

She stopped herself. Licking her lips, she said, "Basically, I think she's pretty grounded in reality. Mostly anyway. I know she misses the old days."

"That's not what you were going to say. Why did the fabulous Sadie Lancaster leave Hollywood?"

Shrugging, she avoided his eyes. "Long story. Emotionally, I don't think she's ever left. She's virtually memorized every line of dialogue she ever heard." With a lopsided grin, she said, "Sadie and Hitch make quite a pair."

"Is that her boyfriend?"

"Hitch?" She laughed at that, her eyes closed, her neck arched, and he found he wanted to grab her, say something, do something, anything to keep her laughing. The Claire he'd known once upon a time.

Shifting her body in his direction, she said, "Sadie's fiancé's name is Mort. Hitchcock is Aunt Sadie's African Grey parrot. She brought him with her when she left Hollywood twenty years ago. She keeps him in his cage in her room when she's gone, but when she's home, Hitch has the run of the place."

"A parrot, huh. Does he talk?"

She chuckled. "Getting him to talk is easy. It's shutting him up that's the trick."

"What about Mort?"

"He talks, too."

"Very funny."

"You won't think so once you've met Mort."

Jumping into the tiny opening she'd given him, he said, "Don't you like this Mort guy?"

Claire tilted her head as she unfastened her seat belt, taking her time to consider his remark. Her brow furrowed slightly.

"I think it's nice Aunt Sadie's involved with a

man her own age. She's been a widow for twenty-five years. I'm sure there are times when she's been . . . lonely. Mort is somebody she can talk to, share common generational memories with."

Her words were supportive, but her tone and body language told a different story.

"But . . ." he drawled, waited.

As though deciding what to share with him, she nibbled on the corner of her bottom lip. He let himself watch her. Just . . . watch her. It was easy to do. Claire was one of those rare women who was beautiful without being obvious about it. Everything about her was understated, which was why, the first time he'd looked into her eyes, he felt like he'd been zapped with a stun gun. Now, at this moment, it was all he could do to keep his mind on business and his hands to himself.

"Mort owns a funeral home and a crematorium," she said slowly. "Mortimer's Mortuary, downtown." She smiled. "Now, I know it sounds judgmental of me, and I'm sure most funeral directors are regular people just like you and me . . ."

"Yet . . ."

"He gives me the creeps." She slapped her thigh with her open palm. "There. I've said it. I'm a bad person, I know, but I swear, Mort could be a grocery clerk or a jet pilot or a stockbroker, and he'd still give me the creeps."

"Mort the mortician gives you the creeps?" Taylor chided. "Other than the fact his name is Mort, how do you mean?" He kept it light, casual, simple curiosity, that's all.

She smiled at him as though she had a secret. Her eyes sparkled like mellow sherry, and long dimples appeared in her cheeks. She looked more like the woman he'd met a year ago, the one he'd found so irresistible, the one he'd danced with half the night, and made love to the other half.

"Yeah, Mortie the mortician," she snickered. "He doesn't seem to mind, though. Apparently it's a longstanding family trade, passed from father to son."

"Hmm. I guess when his dad told him to grab a cold one, he wasn't talking about beer."

Laughter bubbled from deep in her throat. It was a thoroughly sexy sound, and he felt himself respond.

"Maybe it was his mother who passed along the trade," she said wryly. "What would you call a lady mortician?"

Taylor paused for effect. "Mummy?"

She let her head fall back on the seat as she laughed until her eyes were moist and her cheeks rosy. "I hate it when you do that," she said to the ceiling.

"Bowl you over with my wit?" he ventured. "Captivate you with my humor? Impress you with razor-sharp retorts?"

"I don't know that I'd call them razor-sharp," she drawled, "but, well . . ."

She let her words trickle off. Sitting up again, she studied her fingertips, fiercely avoiding eye contact. "Listen, Taylor. I . . . um, we . . . what I mean is . . ." Finally, huffing out a long breath, she said, "Oh, hell. Never mind."

"Yeah," he said lightly. "Me, too."

She looked over at him, her expression unreadable. Apparently, they'd leave things at that. No use rekindling a dead fire.

"You were telling me about Mort," he said, shoving the conversation back in the direction he wanted it to go. "What is it about him that bothers you?"

She relaxed her shoulders, obviously relieved to let the topic shift into more neutral territory. Reaching up, she fiddled with her earring.

"Aunt Sadie told me that he has very extravagant tastes and spends money like a drunken sailor. The engagement ring he gave her is over three carats."

"Is that a lot?"

She shook her head and looked at him with pity in her eyes, as though he'd just asked whether the Earth was round.

"Yes, Detective Tiffany, three carats is a *lot*. He wears imported silk suits, owns several high-end automobiles, travels to Europe all the time, and throws catered parties that rival celebrity victories on Oscar night." She lifted a shoulder. "Of course, he has a steady supply of, um, customers, if you will, but Port Henry isn't that big, and his isn't the only mortuary around. He just seems to spend a lot more money than he makes."

Taylor feigned minor enthusiasm over Claire's remarks, but the reality was, everything she said fit the profile of a man who was using his legitimate business as a front.

Before he could ask another question, Claire laid her hand on the door handle. "Well, nature calls," she said. "I need to go in now. I'd offer you some iced tea or lemonade, but—"

"Great!" he interrupted. "I could use some."

Before she could protest, he'd already jumped out of the truck and was halfway around to her door. She climbed out, glared up at him, and seemed to resign herself to inviting him in and fixing him a cold drink. "I guess it's the least I can do after all you've done for me."

Silently, she trudged up the steps to the

kitchen door. Agatha looked up sleepily from under the rocking chair, yawned until her tongue curled, shifted position, and dozed off again.

Taylor nearly bumped into Claire as she stopped dead in her tracks.

"Great," she muttered, patting her pockets. "The Seattle PD still has my keys."

Bending, she picked up the edge of the straw door mat and picked up the shiny brass key lying there.

"Tell me I didn't just see you do that," he scolded. "A key under the mat, Claire? Why don't you just leave the doors wide open with a big sign that says, *Intruders welcome. Steal me blind!*"

Her mouth flattened as she opened the screen door and curled her fingers around the door handle. "Aunt Sadie and I trust—"

She stopped. The handle turned, but she hadn't unlocked the door yet.

Taylor straightened his spine. As he nodded for Claire to step back against the wall, he moved in front of her, reaching under his jacket for his .38. Grasping the butt of the weapon, he turned the brass doorknob.

"You sure your Aunt Sadie isn't home?" he whispered.

She nodded.

His heart hammering inside his chest, he slowly shoved the door all the way open. It creaked on its hinges as it swung into the room and banged against the wall. The hollow sound echoed for a moment, then all was silent.

The square room was large and airy. Sunlight spilled in from two lace-covered windows onto the wood and glass cabinets, blue tile countertops, mellow hardwood floor. The rose-striped wallpaper was pretty, and copper pots in a variety of sizes hung in a neat row above the enamel stove. A calendar on a nail fluttered in the slight breeze made by the opening door. It was a typical country kitchen, cute and quiet and comfy.

Then he focused on the kitchen table, on what was on it.

"Houston," he said under his breath. "We have a problem."

<u>Secretion</u>
Hiding something.

Chapter 6

Claire placed her palms on Taylor's broad back
and peeked around his shoulder. When she saw
what he saw, her hands flew to her mouth to stop
a startled gasp.

Across the room, in the middle of the kitchen
table, sat her leather purse. Arranged in a circle
around it, like moons orbiting Jupiter, were her
wallet, cell phone, pager, hairbrush, comb, notebook, makeup case, a roll of postage stamps,
several pens, her prescription pad, business
cards, tissues, and the little Swiss Army knife
Betsy had given her for her birthday twelve

years ago. Loose change stood stacked like chimneys—one pile each for pennies, nickels, dimes, and quarters.

Taylor turned, curving his fingers around her arm, tugging her away from the open door. He reached into his pocket and withdrew his cell phone. Handing it to her, he murmured, "Get in my truck. The keys are in the ignition. Lock the doors. If I'm not back in five minutes, or if you hear shots fired, get the hell out of here, phone the PHPD, and request backup. Do *not* hang around, and above all, do *not* come in after me."

Though the words had been quietly spoken, his tone held an air of unequivocal authority. His blue eyes had cooled, sharpened, and gone deadly serious. His grip on her arm was firm, his muscles taut. He seemed poised, as though he might have to take off at a dead run at the snap of a twig. Every word, every movement emphasized how Detective Taylor McKennitt expected to be obeyed without question.

Toward the back of her heart, hidden among the shadows of grief and loss and uncertainty, where, a year ago, she'd locked away her tender feelings for Taylor, she felt the deadbolt softly rattle.

"Could he still be in there?" she whispered.

"I doubt it, but I'm not going to assume anything."

He released her arm, and she did as he asked. Once she had snapped the locks inside the truck, he nodded and turned toward the open kitchen door. His weapon in his right hand, he eased himself inside the screen door and into the kitchen.

In Claire's hand, the cell phone grew warm and sticky. She could feel her pulse in her fingertips. Rolling her wrist, she checked the time. Five thirty-three. He'd said five minutes . . . three hundred seconds . . . three hundred heartbeats. An eternity.

Her gaze glued to the empty kitchen doorway, she tried to keep her breathing steady. Where was he now? Probably through the dining room, and on into the living room. He'd check the closet in the foyer, stop and look in the office, then go up the stairs to the bedrooms.

Her bedroom was first, he'd go in, open the closet to find the pile of underwear to be laundered she'd left on the floor. But he wouldn't notice that, would he? Then into her bathroom. She cringed again. She'd hand washed two bras and left them hanging over the shower stall door to dry. But he wouldn't notice those either. Probably.

He'd move down the hall to Aunt Sadie's room. Hitch would be in his cage. He'd blink and probably say something inane. Hitch, not Taylor.

Hmm. Then again . . .

After he'd finished with Aunt Sadie's closet, he'd move into the hallway and check the other two rooms. Then back to the hall, and down the stairs to the kitchen to the door and . . .

As she thought it, Taylor pushed the screen door open and stepped onto the porch. The door squeaked as it eased shut.

Her breath whooshed out of her lungs and tears stung her eyes. He was all right. No shots fired, no officer down. And whoever the guy was who'd broken into her house was gone.

Flicking the locks, she shoved the door and jumped out, hurrying to stand beside him on the porch.

She swallowed. "Everything okay?"

He nodded. A strange light shone in his eyes.

"What?" she choked. Was there a dead body in the parlor?

"Pretty underpants." He waggled his brows.

She made a gushing sound with her throat. "Pervert."

He shrugged. "A man's got to take his plea- sures where he finds them."

Glancing around the yard and up the drive, he blew out a long breath. "The gravel won't show any tire tread or shoeprints, even though I doubt he drove right up to your door. Nice of him, though, to put the key back under the mat."

His blue eyes bored into hers. Meaningfully. "Your prints on it probably obliterated his, if he left any."

Taylor extended his hand, palm up, and she placed his cell phone in it. Punching in a number, he put the phone to his ear. As he waited for the call to ring through, she said, "Are you calling for a CSI team?"

"I've got everything I need in the truck."

"Just you? Doesn't Seattle have a unit?"

"Sure, but we only use it on homicides or violent assaults. It appears any wounds to your purse are only superficial. So all you get . . . is me."

His words rumbled inside her skull as she tried to ignore their double meaning.

While Taylor reported the incident to the PHPD, she watched him as he stood, legs braced, head down, focused. Her own personal knight gallant.

Would that be so bad? she asked herself. Men like Taylor McKennitt didn't come along every day. But then, her Nagging Little Voice chimed in, men like her father and brother didn't come along every day, either, and look what had happened to them.

The lightweight leather jacket Taylor wore emphasized the breadth of his shoulders; his faded denims, the lean line of his hips. His dark hair was cut short, yet there was enough there to run her fingers through. It looked soft to the touch, and she knew for a fact that it was.

Taylor McKennitt was a very masculine man. The way he walked, his sexy baritone voice, the sharp look in his eye, his obvious strength, athleticism, and confidence all combined to make a woman feel safe, protected.

It was nature's design that a female respond to a male who displayed all the manly virtues. She was simply reacting to feminine programming, but that didn't make him any easier to ignore.

But you will, warned that Nagging Little Voice.

He finished the call, closed the cell phone, and shoved it into his pocket, but before he could say anything, the sound of squealing tires in the driveway made them both turn to see a silver Mercedes SLR McLaren roar down the driveway and slide to a stop behind Taylor's truck.

Immediately putting himself between her and the newcomer, Taylor shoved Claire behind him.

"Anybody you know?" he growled.

She looked around his shoulder as the car door swung open. "Yes," she said, feeling a little confused. "He's a colleague of sorts. An orthopedic surgeon. His name's Adam Thursby." But what was he doing here?

Without turning, Taylor said, "Your boyfriend?"

"No." She should say yes, just to see the look

on his face, but it wouldn't be fair to use Adam like that.

"Don't tell him I'm a police officer," he ordered in a low voice.

"I understand," she agreed, setting a smile of greeting on her face for Adam as he crossed the yard and approached the porch.

Adam Thursby was tall, toned, tanned. He appeared to be forty-something, had an athletic build and sun-streaked brown hair. He wore expensive dark glasses and a blue silk suit that made him look like a fashion model. As he stepped up onto the porch, he whipped off the glasses and sent her a brilliant smile—which faded considerably when he shifted his gaze to Taylor.

"Hello, Adam," she said, moving around Taylor to greet him. Halting in front of her, Adam slipped his arms around her waist and tugged her close. Her breath caught and she automatically put her palms on his chest to keep him at a distance.

"Hello, gorgeous," he murmured, giving her clothing the once-over. "Hey, you're not ready. You haven't forgotten about our date, have you?"

Taylor sized up Adam Thursby. So this was the competition, huh? Well, if Claire liked a guy who looked liked Plastic Surgeon Ken—emphasis on the *plastic*—she need look no further.

As she introduced them, Thursby granted Taylor a smile. His teeth were so white and straight, he looked like a baleen whale sucking in krill.

Thursby released Claire and offered his hand. Taylor shook it. Hard.

The two men smiled coolly at each other.

Thursby might look like the Used Car Salesman to the Stars, Taylor thought, but he had one hell of a grip.

"How do you know Claire?" Thursby said to Taylor. The question was innocent enough, but he heard the underlying message loud and clear.

Before Taylor could answer, Claire interrupted.

"Not that it's not nice to see you, Adam," she said with a rather iffy smile. "But what are you doing here? I'm sure I mentioned that I was going to be in Seattle this weekend."

Dr. Dingledick's face crumpled in disappointment. "Did I screw up? I thought you meant next weekend. Well, as long as I'm here, let's have dinner anyway, okay?"

"Oh, Adam," she said. "I'm so sorry you've gone to all this trouble, but the truth is—"

"Not a problem," he said magnanimously. With his hand at the small of her back, he guided her toward the kitchen door. "I can wait while you change. I promise it will be worth your while."

Taylor moved to intercept them, but Claire put her hand on Thursby's arm, stopping him as he reached for the screen door.

"There's been an accident, Adam. This isn't a good time." Was it Taylor's imagination, or did Claire look shellshocked by this guy?

"Accident?" A frown created no creases on Thursby's forehead. "Are you all right? What kind of accident? When?"

She slid her hands into her jeans pockets and briefly explained the situation. "And since Taylor lives in Seattle, he was kind enough to give me a ride back to Port Henry."

"Good God," Thursby said, placing his palms on her shoulders. "So that's how you got that contusion above the right orbital ridge. Are you *sure* you're all right, sweetheart?"

Sweetheart. Taylor's brain bent a little around that one. Did Dr. Bedpan always call her sweetheart, or was it simply for Taylor's benefit?

Claire's cheeks tinged pink as she smiled up at Thursby. "I'm okay . . . Adam," she said as she gently pushed the man's hands from her shoulders.

"I'd still like to take you out. It might help you to relax."

"Actually, I'm pretty tired. All the excitement. Listen, I haven't checked my voice mail since this morning. Why don't you and I go for a walk down by the pond. I can borrow your cell phone, if I may, to check my messages."

"Where's your cell phone?"

"Um, the truth is, my purse was stolen."

Adam looked thoroughly confused. "You were in a car accident, *and* you were mugged?"

"Yes."

Taylor watched as Thursby put his arm around her again and began leading her off the porch. "Obviously you're okay now, but I want to hear about it. I want to hear *all* about it."

"While you're taking your walk," Taylor said, "I'll do that job in the kitchen we talked about."

"Job?" Adam stopped and looked back at Taylor. "Are you a carpenter or plumber or something?"

"Or something," Taylor said, without elaborating.

"Wait here, Adam," Claire said as she stepped off the porch. "I'll be right back."

When she was out of earshot, Thursby turned to Taylor.

"So you're a sort of handyman, are you?" Intelligent gray eyes assessed Taylor as he waited for an answer.

"Handy enough."

"You got your toolbox with you?"

"Yep."

"Have everything in it, does it?"

"Crescent wrench, hammers, wire cutters, screwdrivers . . . the works."

"Well, while you're busy being *handy*," Thursby drawled, his eyes narrowed on Taylor, "just make sure you don't screw anything that belongs to me."

Taylor looked off across the yard to where Claire was closing the passenger door of his truck. Her hair shone like satin. Her movements were graceful, like a dancer's. And her mouth, plush and rose pink, looked ripe for a kiss—*his* kiss.

"Since I don't see anything here that belongs to you," he said casually, "I guess that won't be a problem."

Thursby visibly heated, but said nothing as Claire climbed the steps. Showing them a piece of notepaper, she said, "I'd made a list of calls I have to return this afternoon, and left it in the glove compartment. You ready for that walk, Adam?"

Claire led the way down the steps and out across the barnyard. They passed the chickens, strutting and bobbing as they searched with bright black eyes for leftover bits of grain. Gerty, the goose, flapped and honked, extended her neck as if to attack, then abandoned the strategy to waddle away.

Near the pond, plump bees, their dangling

legs heavy with pollen, rose and dove from clover to columbine to daisy, while butterflies floated on the wind like white gossamer bows. Claire looked on the familiar scene with fresh eyes. As a little girl, this place had been her summertime playground. Then, as a lonely teenager, her haven of love and safety and peace.

And now her sanctuary had been invaded. Why? And by whom?

She risked a quick glance back at the farmhouse, knowing Taylor was there, in the kitchen, doing everything he could to find some clue to who had hurt and robbed her. Rubbing her temples, she tried to settle her frazzled emotions.

Next to her, Adam seemed thoughtful, too. He'd flipped the edges of his jacket back and slid his hands in his pants pockets. Though his shiny black shoes had accumulated a patina of brown dust, he seemed not to notice.

"Are you sure you're really okay?" he said as they reached the wooden arbor bench Claire's grandfather had built decades ago. A profusion of wild red roses stretched up one side of the trellis and tumbled down the other, creating a shady spot from which to rest and enjoy watching the mallards drift like bathtub toys across the flat surface of the pond.

Claire edged onto the bench and folded her hands in her lap. Adam settled next to her, close enough for her to feel the heat from his body. Leaning forward, he rested his elbows on his knees.

"I'm sorry you were hurt. I care about you, Claire . . . care *for* you. I don't think you realize how much."

Studying his handsome profile, Claire bit her lip. She liked Adam. He was fun to be around, and they'd had some interesting conversations, but that was about as far as it went. Since her brief interlude with Taylor eight months ago, she'd dated a few men, but none had turned her inside out, the way he had. Not even Adam.

"I appreciate your concern," she said, the trite phrase the best she could do at the moment. He was obviously interested in her, but she didn't want to lead him on, so she chose her next words carefully. "I truly enjoy our friendship." Okay, so it wasn't exactly original, but it worked.

"Ah. I see. We're *friends*." He smiled. "Code words for *Sayonara, baby*. I know the drill, Claire."

"I'm sorry, Adam. Listen, I . . ."

Flicking a glance toward the distant farmhouse, he said, "Is there somebody else?"

"No," she said, but she knew in her heart it simply wasn't true. Whenever she'd considered becoming involved with a man, an image of Taylor had shoved itself right into her brain and hung out there, as if he owned her.

It wouldn't be fair to commit to a relationship with Adam, or any man, when she knew she was capable of much stronger feelings. Until she'd met Taylor, she hadn't even been aware she could have such intense feelings, but now that she was, she'd be cheating any man she didn't feel at least as strongly for.

"How much longer until you get your license?" she asked in an effort to divert the conversation.

He shrugged. "Any time now. I passed the boards of course, but there must be some foul-up with the paperwork. I hate not being able to practice medicine, but until the State of Washington grants me a license, I'm on an extended vacation. Not that I'm complaining," he said, sending her a charming grin.

Claire raised her gaze to look past Adam's shoulder. Still no Taylor.

Plucking a red rose from the vine, she cupped it in her palms. Leaning back against the white lattice, she said, "Will you be able to get your kids soon?"

Adam brightened considerably. "God, I hope so. I miss them so damn much, but I need to finish getting the house fixed up and arrange for school for them, of course. As soon as that's done, I'll drive down to Oregon and pick them up. Then we'll be a family again." He grinned and nodded his head, glowing with happiness.

She smiled, twirling the rose in her fingers. A sharp little thorn caught on her thumb, leaving a small dot of blood behind. She wiped it away with her free hand.

"You must miss them terribly," she said. "Your kids."

His smile faded, and a stark look crept into his eyes, altering his entire demeanor. Suddenly, he looked . . . broken.

"My kids are my reason for living," he said quietly. "They're the reason for everything I do, everything I think or feel. I hate being parted from them." He straightened, brightened. "But soon. Just a few details to work out, and our separation will all be a faded memory. So, tell me all about the accident."

In as few words as possible, she related the incident, then glanced at the house again. Still no Taylor. Why was he taking so long?

"Is there anything I can do?" Adam offered. "Get you a guard dog? Camp on your doorstep? Camp inside your doorstep? Camp at the foot of your bed? Camp in your bed—"

"I get the picture." She laughed. "Thanks, but the police are handling everything."

He reached in his pocket and pulled out his cell phone, handing it to her. "You needed this?"

In the time it took Claire to check her messages, return three phone calls, and confirm her rotation at the hospital, evening had begun to creep across the sky, elongating the garden's shadows, bringing up a cool breeze from the sea. One by one, frogs joined to form a throaty chorus, and high overhead, a hawk shrieked. The butterflies were gone, and most of the bees had begun to disappear as day meandered quietly into night.

Returning Adam's cell phone to him, she said, "I don't know how serious this guy is about hurting me. I don't want anybody else becoming a target, including you, so maybe it would be best if—"

"Don't worry about me."

Leaning forward, he scooped up a pebble from the garden and flung it into the pond. A plunk, a splash, and tiny waves rippled across the surface like an opening blossom.

"I don't give a shit about some weirdo targeting me," he scoffed. "Have dinner with me tomorrow night."

"Adam, I—"

"Come on, have dinner with me, Claire," he

coaxed. "I promise I'll behave. I won't tell you how attracted to you I am. I won't tell you how special you are. I won't even mention how crazy you'd be to pass up a great guy like me."

He slid her a grin, and she smiled.

"I don't want to give you a false impression—"

"No problem. But hey, everybody's got to eat." He blinked innocently at her. Yes, Adam Thursby was a very nice guy.

"All right," she said, laughing. "On one condition. I pay for my own. This is not a date."

"I'll take it." On Adam Thursby's face, a smile was more than just a smile. With his movie star good looks and athletic build, that charming grin really was gilding the lily. "I'll pick you up at eight. Wear something . . . special."

He didn't go back to the house with her, but walked directly to his car. By the time she reached the kitchen door, the Mercedes was already speeding up the driveway where it turned onto Puget Road, and disappeared.

Claire crouched down to rub Agatha's tummy, wondering if she had made a terrible mistake. Dinner with Adam, tomorrow night. She would keep it platonic, friendly. Their conversations were always lively, he seemed to have a fairly even disposition, and they had a lot in common.

Yet, as her fingers idly slipped through Agatha's soft fur, when she tried to envision Adam sitting across from her tomorrow night, it wasn't Adam's face she saw. It was Taylor's.

Doctrine
Physician's restroom.

Chapter 7

He stood in the kitchen, watching through the window as Adam Thursby roared off up the driveway. Checking out the crime scene—and finding little viable evidence—had left Taylor in a sour mood, but the thought of that arrogant ass in a relationship with Claire set his teeth on edge. Something wasn't right about the guy, although Taylor certainly couldn't find fault with the man's taste in women.

Claire walked toward the house, her arm lifted in a wave of farewell to Thursby, a friendly smile curving her lips. She jogged up the steps, then bent to pet her cat. From behind the lace curtain, Taylor watched as she stroked Agatha's fur and spoke in a low, soothing voice. The kind of voice a man longed to hear from a woman in the wee hours of the night.

He turned back to the table, cursing a blue streak, then checked to make sure the evidence bags were labeled. Closing the lid of his case, he snapped it, hard, envisioning Thursby's jaw.

Shoving thoughts of the irritating surgeon out of his mind, he focused on the evidence he'd collected.

There were prints everywhere, but he had a sinking feeling none would belong to Claire's attacker. He'd gotten other bits of trace evidence, too, including a light-colored hair, probably Claire's.

That was it. Their perp had been very careful not to leave a thing behind.

Crossing the room to the kitchen door, he unlocked and opened it. She stood and faced him, her lovely brown eyes wide with curiosity.

"Did you find anything?" She nibbled nervously on her bottom lip, a trait he was beginning to appreciate very much.

"We'll see," he said, then gestured to his leather case sitting on the tile counter by the sink. "I've got to run this into the lab for processing. First I need to get a set of your prints and obtain a hair sample. Since Sadie isn't here, I picked up some latents and hair evidence from her bathroom. If we eliminate the two of you, I may have lucked out and gotten something on our perp." He gestured toward the door with his chin. "I see Dr. Armani took off."

She folded her arms under her breasts in a typical gesture of defense. He followed her movements, admiring what he saw, then lifted his gaze to her eyes.

"I think you made it pretty clear you don't like Adam," she said in an admonishing tone. "You needn't resort to name calling."

"You're absolutely right. He's not around to hear it, so what's the point? I'll hold off until he's within earshot."

"You're being juvenile."

"Like I care. He's a prick."

She made a sound of exasperation. "You don't even know him."

He shrugged. "I'm a cop. Trained to observe and assess people and make quick decisions about them all the time. I've observed and assessed. Friday's a prick."

"It's Thursby, and he's not a . . . God, you are infuriating!"

"It's a gift. I'd advise against seeing him again until we've figured all this out."

"Too late," she said, watching him closely.

"I'm having dinner with him tomorrow night."

He glared into her eyes. "Wrong answer, dumpling. Until we get this house secured and find out exactly who's behind the attack on you, and whether he plans more fun and games, you're going to keep a low profile, and have police protection."

"Meaning you, I suppose."

"Meaning me. Strictly business, by the book."

She straightened her arms by her side and doubled her fists, but before she could verbally tear into him, the sound of yet another car interrupted them.

"I thought the country was supposed to be so damn quiet," he snapped. "Hell, this place is like Grand Central."

As Claire preceded him out the kitchen door, the black Cadillac Deville skidded to a noisy stop, sending plumes of dust and gravel chips ten feet in the air. The driver side door flew open and a man bolted out, his bald head shining like a beacon in the waning light of early evening.

Though Taylor recognized him instantly, he said to Claire, "Who in the hell is *that*?"

She frowned. "It's Mortie, Aunt Sadie's fiancé. But I don't see Aunt Sadie . . ."

By the time she'd stepped down from the porch, the old guy had come panting across the yard to halt in front of Claire. She wasn't that tall, but she and the mortician stood eye-to-eye.

"Mort?" Claire said, sending a worried glance at the car. "Where's Aunt Sadie?"

Mortimer dabbed at the perspiration beading his brow, then shoved his handkerchief haphazardly into his breast pocket. It hung over the edge like a wilted flower. Rubbing the back of his neck with one pudgy hand, he swallowed. "Well, gadzooks, ain't she here? Figured she'd come straight here."

Claire's eyes narrowed. "I thought you two were going to spend the weekend in Victoria. Why would she be here?"

Taylor watched as Mort lowered his head, shaking it slowly and jutting out his bottom lip like he'd been a very bad boy.

"We had a . . . difference of opinion, you might say," he said with a sniff. "She got agitated. Came back early. You know how difficult Sadie can be, big movie star and all."

Claire fisted her hands on her hips.

"Aunt Sadie's the most even-tempered person I've ever met," she accused, her tone one of irritation mixed with frustration. "If she's not with you, and she's not here, then where in the hell is she, Mortie?"

Taylor moved down off the porch and went to stand at Claire's side. She glanced up at him, worry darkening the color of her expressive brown eyes.

With a helpless shrug, Mort said, "Okay, we're on our way home when we stop at the Arco a few miles back, you know the one I mean, on the corner there by the senior center? And Sadie goes into the ladies' room to splash a little cold water on her face, but . . . well . . ."

"But what?" Claire demanded. "*Out* with it, Mort."

The mortician's dark eyes shifted to the right, then the left. He blinked a few times, and stuck that lower lip out once more.

"The way of it is," he mumbled, "she goes into the ladies' room, but never comes the hell out. I wait a while, then go and knock, then take a peek inside. But she ain't there! There's not a soul around getting gas, so I ask the guy in the office, and he says he ain't seen no lady. So I'm thinking she might have taken off to hike home." The look on his face was one of a defiant hog. "Expected her to be here. Didn't see her on the road. If something bad's happened to her, for Pete's sake, it sure as hell ain't my fault!"

Former screen idol and disinclined senior citizen Sadie Lancaster trudged along the side of the road, furious with herself.

"Of all the gin joints in all the world . . ." she

muttered as she took another step. She'd intended to call a cab as soon as she got clear of the service station where she'd left Mortie stewing in his own juice, but so far, she'd been unable to locate a pay phone.

She kicked a small stone out of her way. "Love means never having to say you're sorry. Lies. The old poop."

Except for the irksome arthritis in her knees and hips, she was in fair-to-middling shape, and home was only a few miles away. If the stiffness got the better of her, she would just curse Mortie's misogynistic hide all the way back to the farm.

What had she ever seen in the little pipsqueak, anyway? "He's not *worthy*," she scoffed to the toes of her shoes.

Behind her, a car slowed, then rolled past her to stop a few feet ahead. A woman with short brown hair leaned out the passenger window.

"Ma'am?" the woman called. "Are you all right? Would you like a ride?"

Smiling sweetly at the nosy nincompoop, Sadie said, "Thank you for your concern, my dear. However, I am fit as a fiddle and simply out for a little stroll."

The woman said something, gave her a thumbs-up and a wave. The car moved away from the curb to continue on up the modest incline.

Didn't recognize me, Sadie mused in mild irritation as the car disappeared over the crest of the hill. *Well, nobody does anymore. I guess that's just the way of it.*

She straightened her shoulders and trudged on.

Puget Road was narrow and winding and mostly uphill, unless you were going down to town, which, of course, she was not. There was no sidewalk to speak of, so she stayed as far to the right as she could without getting lost amid the thick stand of Douglas firs that stood like mute soldiers along the road.

The walk would do her good. Nothing better to clear away the cobwebs or mend a broken heart. Not that her heart was actually broken. Mortie had *never* had the power to do that.

"I'm walking here," she mumbled in defiance. Then, a little more gusto, "I'm walking here!" She'd built up quite a head of steam listening to Mortie's ranting and raving, and no better way to vent her anger than by walking away from him, leaving him in the proverbial dust.

He hadn't loved her after all. He'd only wanted to use her to advertise his funeral home. He'd even come up with some wretched slogan: *When the Director yells cut and I take my final bows, I'll rest in peace with Mortimer's.*

Mort wasn't only vile, he was . . . well, he was sure no Raymond Carver!

She heard another car slow, and watched as it

moved a bit past her and stopped. From the looks of them, a passel of teenagers in a faded blue VW camper. The window squeaked as the passenger cranked it down.

"Dude." A freckle-faced, red-haired boy stuck his head out. "You want, like, a lift or something?"

Dude? She was a sixty-five-year-old woman, for cripe's sake—though she would never admit to that age in public. And she was walking, briskly for the most part, not crawling along like a one-legged slug! What was wrong with these people?

"No thank you, young man," she stated, though her breath was a bit harder to catch this time. "I'm doing quite well."

The kid shrugged, said something to one of the other boys in the car, and they sped off up the hill leaving a whirl of dry leaves skittering behind them.

Kids these days. *They* most certainly didn't remember her. She could say her name outright and they'd simply blink at her like one of those vapid MGM script girls, or one of the pimply-faced teens who asked if you wanted your meal super-sized. Bah!

She shifted her shoulder purse to keep it from banging her thigh as her thoughts returned to Mortie. What an annoying little turd. It would serve him right to sit in that gas station for hours waiting for her to come out of the restroom.

She hadn't taken the road he'd assume she'd take, either. No sir. She'd cut over to Puget and would follow it all the way back to the farmhouse. And when he did finally show up? Well, she would refuse to speak to him!

Another car buzzed past her, then another. One going up the hill, one coming down. They'd both had their headlamps on. She raised her face to the sky. My, was it that dark already? Must be close to eight.

She stopped to catch her breath. Funny, she'd driven this route for years and never realized how steep it was until now. It wasn't that she was old and her muscles and bones weren't what they'd once been. No, no, no. Why, in the old days, she could dance all evening, make mad love all night, and still be able to put in a full day at the studio with her lines memorized and her marks down pat. It was Spencer Tracy who'd taught her about professional behavior. Such a dear man. Gone now, like so many others.

She eyed the hill before her. Well, she'd just take it slow. Slow and steady won the race.

By the time she was halfway up the hill, the sun had dropped close to the sea far behind her, painting the Northwest sky a brilliant red. But soon the light would be gone and she still had a mile or so to go.

Cursing her stubborn pride for not accepting

one of those rides, she took a deep breath and soldiered on.

Another car behind her slowed, then moved up and kept pace with her. Late-model station wagon of some kind. While she watched, the window lowered. The passenger side was empty, but she saw the man behind the wheel lean toward her. She stopped walking—huffing to catch her breath. The car stopped, too.

"You trying to prove a point, Sadie, or you want to get in?" His voice was deep, almost melodic. A little Gable with a touch of Mitchum. She didn't recognize it, but she liked the sound of it.

Bending a mite, she looked into the open window.

Nice-looking gent, plaid flannel shirt, crooked smile, light eyes, maybe blue, gray hair, and plenty of it. Around sixty or so, fit, and handsome, too. Joel McCrea with a hint of Sean Connery.

She considered him for a moment, then said, "Have we met?"

"No, ma'am."

"Are you a serial killer, sir?"

"No, ma'am."

"Do I appear to be in difficulty?"

"No, ma'am," he said, smiling. Yes, definitely Sean Connery. "But daylight's about gone and you're wearing dark clothing. Another fifteen minutes, and you're going to be invisible. Hate to see the first lady of the silver screen reduced to roadkill."

She narrowed one eye on him. She was flattered, but suspicious. "You recognize me?"

"Like they say in the movies, I am your number one fan." His eyes twinkled and he grinned. "I mean that in the nicest way possible, Miss Lancaster. Now, you gonna yammer all night or get in?"

In the time they'd been talking, clouds had moved in, darkening the sky considerably. She eyed the crest of the hill once more—what she could see of it in the waning light. Softly, she drawled, "I suppose I shall be forced to depend on the kindness of a stranger."

Opening the door, she slid in, but sat very close to it, with her fingers on the handle.

Pulling back into the road, the driver said, "Where to?"

Sadie clutched her purse to her bosom and looked over at him. "About one mile past the crest of this hill, there is a mailbox on the left. I shall show you when we arrive."

He nodded. "Name's Corrigan. Flynn Corrigan."

Flynn? As in Errol? Yes, the name certainly suited him.

"Mr. Corrigan," she said with a polite nod.

"Call me Flynn. Your car break down or something?" he asked casually. "This doesn't seem like the best place for a hike or evening constitutional."

She thought of Mortie, the things he'd said, how angry and used he'd made her feel. He was a disgusting excuse for a human being, and besides, he was up to no good, she just knew it. She'd developed a feel for those kinds of things. After all, she'd appeared in seven crime dramas, *two* of them with Jimmy Cagney, by God.

"I was with someone," she said. "But I decided to walk home."

He arched a bushy brow. "Have a fight with your boyfriend, did you, Miss Lancaster?"

"Well, aren't you the Nosy Parker." She clutched her purse hard against her breasts.

He smiled over at her again, but remained silent.

They reached the crest of the hill, and he shifted gears, keeping the wagon at an even speed. It was close to dark now and Sadie was thankful he'd come along when he had. In her black pants and navy sweater, she would indeed have been invisible to cars on the narrow road.

Feeling a bit guilty at having snapped at him, she said, "You live on the Olympic Peninsula . . . Flynn?"

"No, I'm a stranger here, myself."

She couldn't help but grin at the old movie line.

"Just visiting for a while," he added. "Fishing, mostly. I'm retiring in a couple of months, and I'm on the lookout for a decent place."

"If a happy retirement is your goal, then Port Henry is your place."

"Must say, I like the scenery."

And couldn't *that* be taken two ways, she mused. She liked this Flynn Corrigan. Oh, yes. She liked him a lot. Today might not turn out too badly after all.

His hands were on the steering wheel, but she couldn't sneak a peek at his ring finger without being obvious, so she contented herself with gazing out the window, counting the number of stars that had winked on in the last few minutes.

"Lovely evening," he said, taking another turn. "We getting close to your place?"

"Not far now," she assured him, tucking a strand of hair behind her ear. She was suddenly not all that anxious to be rid of Flynn Corrigan. It had been a long time since she'd been in the company of such an attractive fellow, and she rather enjoyed basking in the glow.

"This it?" he said, gesturing to the old-fashioned lamp post illuminating a large mailbox at the entrance to a long gravel drive.

"It is. You can let me out here, if you like."

He flicked on the turn signal, then headed left into the driveway. "Wouldn't be very gentlemanly of me to leave you up by that mailbox to make your way down to the house in the dark. I was raised better than that."

As they rounded the barn, she saw Claire's car next to hers in the double carport, but no sign of the pickup. In the yard sat a truck she didn't recognize.

And Mortie's effing Deville.

She must have made some kind of noise, because Flynn let the wagon roll to a stop, then turned to her. "Somebody you don't want to see?"

She gave a little snort and a curt nod.

He gazed out at the shiny Cadillac, then over at her. "Maybe you'd like to thank me for the lift by inviting me in for coffee. Of course, a cold beer would be better."

She locked gazes with him. Oh, my. He had such nice eyes. Like a winter sky reflected in chips of ice. And about as sharp, too. Very Paul Newman.

Shaking her head, she said, "I appreciate your giving me a ride, and I would very much like to invite you in. But the evening may turn a bit . . . uncomfortable."

"The boyfriend."

"Not as of about an hour ago."

With a tilt of his chin, he said, "Miss Sadie

Lancaster, first lady of the silver screen, you owe me a beer, and I aim to collect."

As Taylor and Claire ran for his truck, a station wagon she'd never seen before began making its way down the drive.

Over his shoulder, Taylor drawled, "Like I said, Grand Central. Stay put until we see who *this* is."

As soon as the car stopped, the passenger door flew open, and Aunt Sadie stepped out. Her silky, shoulder-length hair—once blond but now an eye-catching silvery gray—slid over one eye, á la sultry screen siren Veronica Lake. Sadie raised her chin and glared across the yard at the gaping Mort.

"Well, aren't you a parasite for sore eyes," she snapped. "What are you doing here, you repugnant lump of snake entrails?"

Mortie rushed toward her, but before he could get far, the driver's door opened and a man emerged. He was as tall as Taylor, rangy, and had a no-nonsense look about him that said he was accustomed to taking charge.

The mortician skidded to a halt, cutting worried glances between Sadie and the stranger.

"My God, are you all right, Aunt Sadie?" Claire said, moving to give the older woman a hug. Since she was nearly a head taller than

Sadie, hugging her aunt always felt to Claire as though she were embracing a delicate bird. "Mort said there'd been some kind of trouble?"

"No trouble at all, my dear," Sadie said wistfully, patting Claire's cheek. "Besides, Mortie was just leaving." Addressing the mortician, she said, "Good-bye, Mr. Chips!" She stepped away from Claire, raised her arm, and, with a theatrical wave of her hand, dismissed him.

Mort rubbed his chin with his short fingers, a look of anger in his eyes. "Well, by jingo, Sadie, I think we should talk about this."

Sadie looked down her nose at him. "Sorry, Mortie. You *are* the weakest link." She removed her engagement ring and handed it to him. "Good-bye."

"But Sadie," he whined. "Let me explain. We've been through so much together—"

"And most of it was your fault."

"Sadie," Mort pressed, his eyes gone big and pleading. "Remember what you said when I asked you to marry me? Remember how it was between us? We can have that again. Tell me I ain't blown my chances with you, dear lady."

Sadie looked wistful for a moment, then said softly, "Things change, Mortie. It's best this way. We'll always have our memories. We'll always have . . . Spokane."

He drew his mouth into a thin line across his

face. "Well, if you won't marry me, then at least go through with the endorsement, for pity's sake. You need to reconsider—"

The stranger stepped forward and Mort clamped his jaw shut. "I believe I heard the lady ask you to leave," he said. Though the words were softly spoken, there was an underlying steel to them that Mort would be a fool to ignore. He shot a glance at Taylor, then over to Claire, finally to Sadie. Obviously outnumbered and outgunned, Mort finally took the hint.

"Okay," he barked, sweet pleading replaced in the blink of an eye by red-faced fury. "I'll go. But you're makin' a mistake, Sadie Lancaster." He shook his finger at her as he backed toward his car, nearly tripping over his own feet. "A *big* mistake."

Muttering something under his breath, he opened the trunk and set a blue suitcase on the gravel. Then flinging himself into the Deville, he tore off up the driveway leaving a cloud of dust behind him, and a very bad feeling in the pit of Claire's stomach.

When Mort had gone, the man who'd driven her aunt home said, "Guess I'll take a rain check on that beer, ma'am."

Before Sadie could make introductions or explanations, he slid behind the wheel of his car and was gone.

Staring after him, Claire sighed. "Who was that masked man?"

Taylor stepped forward, a quirky grin on his face. "I kind of expected him to say hi-ho Silver, away."

Sadie scoffed. "You're both too young to remember the Lone Ranger!"

"Not when you've got cable, ma'am."

Sadie chuckled, then took a good, long look at Taylor. Smiling, she nudged Claire's arm.

"Claire," she all but purred. "Where are your manners? Who is this handsome young man?"

Before she could answer, Taylor extended his hand and said, "Taylor McKennitt, ma'am."

"McKennitt? Like Claire's friend Betsy?"

"Betsy's married to my brother."

Sadie's eye widened. "Are you a policeman, too?"

"Yes, Miss Lancaster, but I'm on . . . vacation, so I'd appreciate if you'd keep it to yourself."

"Aunt Sadie," Claire said, taking the woman's arm and escorting her to the porch steps. "I want to hear what happened between you and Mort. He hasn't mistreated you, has he? Because if he has—"

Patting Claire's hand, Sadie said, "No, no. Nothing like that. It's just, well, something strange is going on with Mort, and I don't like it." Shaking her head, she said, "For one thing, he broke faith with me, out-and-out lied about his feelings for me just so I'd do an endorsement for his business!"

"Oh, Aunt Sadie. I'm so sorry. Are you okay with the breakup?"

Gazing up the darkened driveway, Sadie said grandly, "Frankly, my dear, I don't give a damn."

Fraud
Sigmund's felonious brother.

Chapter 8

After a long night hanging around the crime lab in Seattle, catching a few Zs at home, then tackling the drive back up to Port Henry, Taylor walked through the door of the PHPD around noon on Sunday, in search of his brother.

Sam Winslow, mid-thirties, squared-jawed poster boy for stalwart law enforcement officers everywhere, leaned over the counter, his tanned face contorted in concentration as he worked the *New York Times* crossword.

As the door closed, Winslow raised his head and smiled. "Would you look at this. Two McKennitts in one day." Anticipating Taylor's question, he stabbed the air with his pen. "The other one's in the green room. Hey, what's a six-letter word for barb-tailed dragon? Begins with W."

Taylor pushed through the swinging gate that separated the public area of the station from the police-business-only section. "Wyvern," he said, spelling it out as he passed.

Sam penciled in the letters, then laughed. "It works. Hey, how'd you know that?"

Taylor shrugged. "Busted one once for starting a fire without a permit."

As Sam's deep laughter trickled off, Taylor walked past the three presently unoccupied desks, all of which sported computers, toppling stacks of file folders, and an array of coffee mugs. Wanted posters, information bulletins, and flyers for local events were tacked to the message board on the far wall. On a beige Formica side table sat a blackened glass coffeepot, its acrid contents having boiled away hours, maybe even centuries ago.

He passed through the doorway and into the green room—so named for the pastel mint paint somebody had mistakenly thought would look attractive. Soldier sat at a square oak table, his back to the wall, a bottle of water in one hand, a cell phone in the other.

As Taylor dropped into one of the empty

chairs, Soldier covered the phone with his palm. "Go take a leak or something while I finish with this."

Since Taylor didn't feel nature's call, he decided to stay put and simply stare out one of the two bay windows that allowed massive amounts of natural light into the room.

The Port Henry PD was a brick building that had begun life as a cannery. Built on Water Street about midway into town, it boasted views of both the docks and the busy downtown. Out across the bay, past Heyworth Island, mile-high clouds feathered over the blue horizon, while sailboats skimmed across the windswept surface of the water. On the nearly empty sidewalks, tourists casually made their way down the street looking for antiques and souvenirs, while hungry gulls hovered over the nearby shoreline like stringless puppets.

"But, honey," Soldier cajoled as he shot Taylor a get-lost look. Taylor smirked and made himself more comfy.

"You look beautiful," his brother insisted to the phone. "Well you don't remind *me* of a Macy's Thanksgiving balloon. Uh-huh. Uh-huh. No, your feet are just as cute as ever, and in no way resemble overgrown marshmallows. Uh-huh. Uh-huh. No, you don't waddle like a duck and even if you did . . . Uh-huh. Uh-huh . . ."

Taylor bit down on his tongue and diverted his gaze to his fingernails. He felt his brother's eyes on him, a silent warning he'd better keep his trap shut or suffer the consequences.

"Tell you what," Soldier coaxed gently. "I'll be home in about an hour. We can go out for a late lunch. I hear there's a special at Ilsa's. All you can eat sauerkraut and ice cream. God, no, not together . . . oh. Okay, yeah, together, I suppose, if that's what you, uh, really want."

She said something, and Soldier's features softened. His blue eyes—so like Taylor's own—gleamed with emotion as he spoke to his wife.

"Hey, it's okay. No, you're not being overly emotional. Just a few more weeks to go. You're doing great."

That Soldier loved his wife, Taylor thought as he watched his brother, was like saying the Earth went around the sun, or that kittens were soft, or that rain on the roof was romantic. Common knowledge, no-brainers, givens. In fact, they were so in love, it came close to making Taylor sick. And might have if he wasn't so happy for them. It almost hurt to watch them, sometimes, especially since his own marriage had been such a complete failure.

But the brother he'd admired and even idolized since they were kids had become a caring and devoted husband, and was about to become a terrific dad, just like their own had been. How cool was that. Life was coming full circle, like the seasons, and in the quiet moments of the night when he woke up in his bed alone, or when he stood in front of a fresh canvas trying to capture some universal truth in broad strokes or delicate patterns, he sometimes wished that circle included him. Maybe things would've been different. Maybe Paula would have settled down. Maybe if he'd given her a baby . . .

Soldier nodded and nodded and tried to end the call, but Betsy must've really been worked up.

"Okay, honey," he soothed. "I'll see you in an hour. Yeah. You know I do. Yes, I *do*." He flicked a glance at Taylor, then turned his head away. Hunched over the phone, he murmured, "I love you, too. Take care of our baby."

He folded the phone closed, set it on his desk, and stared daggers at Taylor.

"That was the most painful thing I have ever witnessed," Taylor drawled. "I'd put you out of your misery, but I left my gun in the car."

"Shut up," Soldier grumbled. "She's . . . hormonal, that's all." Rolling his eyes, he said, "You think PMS is bad? Pregnancy is like they have it for nine solid months."

"My heart's breakin' for you, pal." Taylor sighed. "Pretty wife, kid on the way. Life's tough."

Soldier beamed and leaned forward over the table, his eyes eager and shining. "We don't know for sure, but Betsy thinks it's a girl." He rubbed his knuckles against his jaw. "Shit. I don't know anything about little girls. What if I drop her or something? They're so tiny when they're born, you know?"

Taylor laughed. "Just nerves, Dad. You're not going to drop her."

Soldier nodded thoughtfully, then burst out, "And what about college? Do you think she'll want to go to the UW, or maybe—"

"Jackson!" Taylor choked. "She won't be born for almost a month. Cut the kid some slack. Let her slobber and burp for a while before you send her off to college."

Soldier shook his head and relaxed back into his chair. "Sorry. I can handle a perp with a knife without breaking a sweat, but the thought of holding a baby, my baby . . ."

"Yeah," Taylor said without looking at his brother. "I hear ya."

He stood and walked toward the window that faced the sea. His hands on his hips, he said, "I met Mortimer yesterday, up close and personal."

Soldier became suddenly alert. "How? Why?"

"I was there when they got back from their weekend trip. They'd had a fight and Sadie broke off their engagement. She thinks he's doing something, but she doesn't know what." Running his fingers through his hair, he said, "For their own safety, I want to bring Claire and her aunt in on this sooner rather than later."

Soldier opened the bottom drawer of the file cabinet behind him and pulled out a cellophane bag. From the mini fridge, he grabbed a plastic container of salsa. Tearing open the bag, he reached in, grabbed a large chip, scooped up about a quart of salsa, and stuffed the whole thing in his mouth. Cheeks bulging, he turned the open bag toward Taylor. "Chrp?"

Food. Great. He was starving. Reaching into the bag, Taylor grabbed a handful of triangular tortilla pieces.

Soldier swallowed, then took a swig of water. "We've only been on this case a couple of days. We still don't know if Mortimer is the brains, or if he's just a willing dupe." Another chip, another glop.

"Having met him," Taylor said, scooping salsa onto a chip the size of Arizona and bringing the dripping mess to his lips, "I vote for dupe." Shoving the heavily laden chip into his mouth, he mumbled, "Wrr drn't rven knrr ff arr whrstle-blwrr rs trlling thr trrth."

Soldier stared at him. "We don't even know if our whistle-blower is telling us the truth?"

Taylor nodded and crunched. "Tht's whrt er sdd."

"Well, if she was, then there's a lot at stake. I agree. Talk to them. Maybe the aunt has seen something." Then, "How do you think Claire's going to feel when she finds out we've had the farm under surveillance?"

"Ptthd," Taylor said past the chip in his mouth. He swallowed, then sucked a blob of salsa from his thumb. "But her being pissed at me has sort of become a tradition between us."

Cellophane rustled noisily as Soldier crammed the bag into the drawer. "You talked to Bobby Aranca yet?"

Taylor nodded and turned back to the window. Out across the water, white sails bobbed and tipped in the wind like paper boats on a pond.

"Sadie's truck offered up no viable evidence. Some dents. Scrapes of black paint. The lab's analyzing it now. The officer on the scene made a few notes, but it was too dark for him to get much. By the time I got there yesterday, the turnout had been compromised."

"You find anything at the farm?" Soldier scribbled away on a notepad.

"I checked the perimeter of the property. No tire tread, no shoe prints. He either beamed directly into the kitchen from the mother ship, or he obliterated his tracks. The only prints in the kitchen were Claire's and Sadie's."

"You said you found a light-colored hair."

Taylor nodded. "Not Claire's. Not Sadie's."

Soldier rolled the water bottle between his palms. The thin plastic made a popping sound. "Since Mort was with Sadie, he couldn't have run Claire off the road, but he could have hired it done."

"Except for an apparent lack of motive, that's got my vote. There's a connection," he said. "There's gotta be."

"What about Mort's partner?"

"Could've been." Taylor sighed. "If we only knew who the partner is and where they're actually performing the harvesting. Maybe Sadie's seen something. Any description, no matter how vague, will give us a hell of a lot more than we have now."

Soldier nodded. "Go for it." A moment later, he crossed his arms over his chest and sent a meaningful look toward Taylor. "Now that that's taken care of, you want to tell me what's bugging you?"

"I've told you all I know in terms of the ongoing investigation."

Soldier flattened his mouth. "C'mon. Out with it."

"This may come as a major shock, big brother," Taylor said, "but I stopped telling you everything when I was ten."

"And here I thought we had no secrets between us."

"Yeah, well," he muttered. "Okay. Actually, I do have a little . . . thing I wanted to discuss with you."

"I don't want to discuss your little thing."

"You're a frigging comedian," Taylor said dryly. "You want to cut me some slack here, or what?" Then, thinking better of it, he said, "Ah, hell. It's Claire. She's having dinner tonight with some hotshot doctor."

"Do you care?"

"No," he scoffed. "Hell no. She's way too stuffy for me. Pushy, arrogant . . . *always* has to have the last word . . . *always* has to be right."

Soldier's eyes narrowed as though he was trying to remember something. "Sounds vaguely familiar. I think I know somebody like that."

Taylor's mouth flattened as he glared at his brother.

Solider picked up his pen and clicked it. "So, you two really are finished, huh."

Taylor remembered her hasty exit eight months ago, the unreturned phone calls. It hadn't taken him long to figure he was getting the brush-off.

"Yeah, we're finished," he said to Soldier, and left it at that. "I want to run a background check on this Adam Thursby." He scribbled the name on his brother's notepad. "I think that's how you spell it."

Soldier looked at the paper. "I think 'dick-head' has two Ds."

"Yuk, yuk. Just run it, will you?"

"Is this just because Claire's having dinner with him?"

"Absolutely not," Taylor scoffed. "That would be childish." As he headed for the door, he said, "Anyway, she says he's not her boyfriend. They're just acquaintances. It's just dinner. Everybody's gotta eat."

Soldier scribbled some more notes, then let his pen plop onto the desk. A slow grin spread over his face. "Well, she's right about one thing."

"What's that?"

His smile widened. "Everybody's gotta eat."

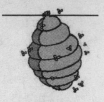

Detonate
What _Deton_ did at dinner.

Chapter 9

Claire reminded herself—for the umpteenth time—that intense sexual attraction had nothing to do with long-term compatibility. But, oh, the short-term benefits could sure cure what ailed you.

As she brushed her hair and applied blusher and lipstick, she thought about how simple it would be to slide into a physical relationship with Taylor. She'd tried to convince herself—and him—that the night they'd spent together had simply been sex, but in reality, it had been the closest thing to contentment she'd known since her parents had died. And it had terrified her.

Dammit, she thought as she tossed the brush onto the dressing table. Why did he have to be a cop? *Why* a cop?

In the mirror's reflection, she stared into her own eyes. Did she see truth there, or only excuses? What did he see when he looked into her eyes? Confusion? Determination? Fear?

Dammit, she should never have slept with him. But, oh, how she had wanted him that night. *Him.* Not just sex, but *him*, Taylor McKennitt with his blue eyes and broad shoulders, his charming grin, smart-ass comebacks. He could be a royal pain, but when she was with him, every nerve tingled as though she were standing on a live wire. All her senses became aware of him at once. She could taste him on her lips, simply by catching his scent. She could feel his fingers on her skin, just by the look in his eyes, or hear the thrum of his heart by touching his hand.

Sleeping with him again, being that intimate, would mean betraying her parents' memory, and Zach as well, and opening herself to more pain. Loving him physically could only lead to loving him emotionally, and she knew it.

Once had been enough, and she'd spent the

last eight months trying to get her stubborn heart to move on . . .

Shifting her thoughts, she shoved Taylor aside with a mental nudge of her hip, and ushered Adam into her mind.

Walking to the closet, she tugged her ivory silk dress off its hanger. Sleeveless, scoop-neck, slim skirt, the dress was perfect for a summer evening. As she zipped it up, she stepped into her matching heels. Choosing a simple gold bracelet, she struggled to single-handedly fasten the clasp on her left wrist.

Now for the best part of getting dressed— choosing which pair of earrings to wear. The gold dangles were cool and classy, and they moved when she walked, almost brushing her shoulders. Elegant, sophisticated, just right for a platonic dinner with the Olympic Peninsula's handsomest soon-to-be-licensed orthopedic surgeon.

Abruptly, an image of the Northwest's handsomest detective edged its way into her mind, drop-kicking poor Adam right off a cliff.

She tapped her foot. How like Taylor, even in her imagination, to be so arrogant.

As she neared thirty-five, she was coming more and more to the conclusion she'd like to find a great guy and get married.

What if that guy was Taylor? What if . . .

An image of her mother's face at Dad's funeral stung her brain. A year later, another funeral. Mom's. And a few years after that, Zach coming out of surgery, torn to pieces, barely hanging on to life. The memories pressed themselves into Claire's skull like a doubled fist.

Bad luck, they'd said. Father and son, both cops. Such bad luck.

You make your own luck, Claire thought. *Some places just aren't safe to go.*

She blinked at her image in the mirror as her dour thoughts were interrupted by the screech of a bird. Then Aunt Sadie's soothing voice drifted up the stairs and through Claire's open door, grounding her once more in reality. Over Sadie's words, Hitch squawked again.

"... farm ... had a farm ..."

"What did you have, Hitch?" Aunt Sadie asked. "Tell me what you had."

"... had a farm in ... Africa," Hitch muttered in parrot monotone. "... a farm in ... Africa."

"Good boy, Hitch," Aunt Sadie praised. Then, louder, "Claire, dear?"

Aunt Sadie's sweet voice trilled up the stairs like musical notes carried on the wings of a butterfly.

"Yes?" she answered, switching off her bathroom light.

"Your Dr. Thursby is here."

As soon as Aunt Sadie spoke those words, Claire felt herself react.

Not mine. Not interested. Nice guy, but that's all.

Well, at least her truthful inner voice was still working.

"I'll be right down," she called, making a grab for her handbag.

With a silent vow to enjoy herself this evening, she closed her bedroom door and pasted a polite smile on her lips.

Adam was waiting at the foot of the stairs, leaning against the banister.

"You look great," he said, appreciation glowing in his eyes. "Claire—"

". . . excuse me while I whip this out . . ."

Adam jerked his head around to glare at the parrot sitting on the newel post behind him. Hitch glared back, tilted his head, and muttered softly, ". . . be afraid . . . be very afraid . . ."

"And . . . cut!" Aunt Sadie laughed. "My, aren't you inventive tonight, Hitch."

As Claire came down the staircase, Sadie urged Hitch onto her forearm. Smiling at Adam, she said, "I'll just take him with me into the kitchen."

". . . whip this out . . ."

"That'll do, Hitch."

". . . whip this out . . ."

"Shut up, Hitch."

The bird muttered something about badges and not needing any, as Sadie retreated through the door and into the kitchen.

When they'd gone, Adam returned his attention to Claire, letting his gaze move from the tips of her shoes to the crown of her head.

"To tell you the truth," he said, "that bird took the words right out of my mouth."

"Adam!" She felt her cheeks heat.

He arched a brow. "Do all your patients fall in love with you, Doc?"

Claire's breath snagged on a dry spot in her throat, and her step faltered.

Do all your patients fall in love with you, Doc?

Taylor had said those words to her the day they'd met. He'd been injured; he was her patient. And later, when he'd recovered, he'd been fun and flirty and charming . . .

Stop it! For God's sake, she was going to dinner with Adam Thursby. She *had* to get Taylor off her mind, had to quit measuring every man she met against Taylor McKennitt. *Really, girl. Get a grip!*

She brushed past Adam to retrieve her coat from the closet in the foyer. Without a word, he took it from her fingers and helped her slip into it. The blue silk lining felt cool against her bare arms. When his hands lingered a little too long on her shoulders, she stepped away and turned, giving him a big smile.

"Ready," she said on an exhaled breath.

Adam looked down at her, his brow furrowed in concentration.

"You have a beep on your nose."

"A what?" She lifted her hand to her face, but he circled her wrist with his long fingers, stopping her.

"A beep. Here," he said. "I'll get it."

With his thumb and forefinger, he lightly pinched her nose and said, "*Beep.*" Then he laughed, leaned down, and kissed her.

As kisses went, it was a nice one. A gentle tugging on her lips, sweet, inoffensive, nonthreatening.

Even so, she wasn't sure if she felt flattered, charmed, or annoyed.

He lifted his head and smiled down into her eyes. Adam had gray eyes. She loved gray eyes. They were almost her favorite color. Who needed laser blue eyes when you could have smoky, foggy gray?

He wore a charcoal suit and silver silk tie. He'd shaved and obviously taken care to look especially nice. When he offered her his arm, she slipped her hand through the crook, becoming instantly aware of his muscles under her palm. It was hard to ignore the warmth of his body, the clean smell of his soap, his height, his good looks. People seeing them together would think they were a couple. His attire and attitude seemed designed to perpetuate that assumption.

She wasn't sure if she felt flattered, charmed, or annoyed.

"There's a table with an ocean view waiting for us at Vittorio's," he said. "And a bottle of very expensive wine."

"Sounds great."

Vittorio's Restaurante occupied the floor above The Crow's Nest, a cozy bookstore built on the docks near the ferry landing and marina. As Adam seated Claire, she glanced out the window at the crimson sun, settling for the night into the wrinkled sea. Just below, harbor lights began to wink on, illuminating sailboats, fishing trawlers, small yachts, all rocking gently in their moorings. Through the glass, she could hear the rhythmic *tink-tink-tink* of the wind slapping ropes and tack against bare masts.

The young tuxedoed waiter arrived to pour the wine, and as they lifted their glasses, Adam said, "To everlasting friendships." Tapping the rim of his glass against hers, he smiled.

Sipping the wine, she let the rich taste flow across her tongue and down her throat.

As another waiter began clearing the table behind Adam, she turned and gazed for a moment out the window, listening to Adam chat on about the superb menu choices. Conversation turned to shop talk, and they discussed patients, procedures, policies.

Their waiter returned, then departed after taking their orders.

Her wineglass in one hand, Claire felt herself begin to relax a little. This would be okay. A nice dinner with a man she liked. Nobody and nothing could throw off her equilibrium tonight.

Until she caught a glimpse of the man they were seating directly behind Adam: Taylor McKennitt.

The wine in her mouth went down hard, and she choked, covering her lips with her napkin.

Adam's brow furrowed. "You okay?"

She nodded enthusiastically, set her glass down, picked up her water goblet, and chugged the contents.

Glaring into Taylor's bemused eyes, she scooted her chair to the left, hoping to use Adam's body to block her view. It didn't work. Taylor scooted his chair to the right. She scooted again, so did he. If she scooted any farther, she'd be on the other side of the window.

"Is something wrong with your chair?"

"Not at all," she said lightly. "The, uh, view was getting on my nerves."

Over the top of his open menu, Taylor winked.

Fury sizzled her brain. Her nerves felt like

somebody had gone at them with a steel scouring pad. How *dare* he follow her . . . and sit facing her . . . and position himself to hear their every word.

Adam glanced out the window. "The view?" he mumbled around a bite of breadstick. "I can have them lower the blinds if you like. I didn't know you hated boats so much."

Redirecting her gaze to Adam, she said, "No need. I'm fine now. Really."

Silently, she cursed Taylor's parentage and lineage and ancestors and even their belongings and pets, and vowed to get even with him for this if it took the rest of her life.

While Adam tried to engage her in conversation, knowing Taylor could hear every word they said, Claire kept her responses to nods and brief yeses and nos.

Adam set his wineglass on the table and tilted his head. "You seem a little distracted tonight, Claire. I know you've been through a lot this week. I'm here for you, if you'd like to talk about it."

In her line of vision, Taylor broke a breadstick in half and glared at the back of her dinner companion's head, subtly sticking out his bottom lip in an isn't-that-sweet pout.

"It's been a very trying few days, Adam. That's all."

At the demon table behind Adam, Taylor grinned, then quietly gave his order to the waiter.

"So, Claire," Adam said as their waiter returned to set their plates in front of them. "Tell me more about that handyman I met at your aunt's place."

All too handy, if you asked her.

Taylor took a sip of wine and sat back in his chair, thumbing the rim of his glass as though he didn't have a care in the world.

She set her jaw and glared at him just beyond Adam's shoulder.

"He's a former patient," she snapped. "Victim of a hit-and-run. Cerebral trauma. Prognosis poor. Not long to live. Down to minutes, I'd say." Her eyes locked with Taylor's, she grabbed her fork and stabbed her herbed chicken breast, then sliced it in half. Violently.

"Really." Adam leaned forward over his plate as if to confide a secret. "He seemed okay to me, even though I thought he was a bit of a prick."

She curved her lips in an appreciative smile. "You're very astute."

Taylor took a bite of his salad and chewed it, watching her intently.

"He's fine during the day, nearly normal," she said, making sure Taylor could hear every word. "But, according to his team of psychiatrists, his personality undergoes a dramatic change when his meds wear off and he forgets his second dose."

Taylor stopped chewing.

"And this manifests how exactly?"

She bit into her chicken, baring her teeth. "Multiple personalities."

"Well, one of those personalities is definitely a prick," he drawled.

"Oh," Claire hastened, "he was like that before the accident. But since the trauma, when he's under stress, a secondary identity apparently emerges."

Taylor tilted his head as though he was dying to hear what she'd say next.

She leaned forward as if to divulge a secret. "He believes himself to be a Cassanova, and thinks every nubile woman he meets a potential conquest."

Taylor raised his brows, grinned, nodded, and gave her a thumbs-up.

Adam scowled. "Does he consider you a potential conquest?"

She shrugged. "Oh, I'm sure he does. I mean, I am a woman, and he is wholly indiscriminate. *Any* nubile female will do. The file from his psych eval says that when he's pursuing a woman, he exhibits pronounced disfluency and agitation. Yet he persists in the belief that, if he can just find the right pickup line, he can get any woman into bed."

Adam laughed. "He stutters, gets pissed, and thinks he can score?"

She slid her gaze from Taylor's eyes to Adam's, and smiled serenely. "It's been known to happen."

Taylor pursed his lips and slowly shook his head as if to say, *Is that the best you've got?*

"The fact that he's impotent compounds the problem, of course." Picking up a breadstick, she snapped it in half.

Taylor straightened, blinked, then scowled.

Adam raised his head. "Yeah?" he smirked. "Well, I sure had that one pegged."

The waiter appeared to refill their wineglasses. As he picked up the bottle, Adam's cell phone rang and he reached for it, accidentally bumping the waiter's arm and splashing the dark Cabernet all over his shirt and tie.

"I'm sorry, sir!" the waiter choked. "Here, let me get a nap—"

"Never mind," Adam growled, jumping to his feet. He pressed his napkin to the saturated fabric as he thumbed a button on the cell phone. "This is Dr. Thursby," he said quietly. "Yes. One moment." Turning to Claire, he said, "I'm sorry. I have to take this. A patient in Portland. You understand."

"Certainly," she said, partly rising from her chair. "The wine stain. Is there anything—"

Moving away from the table, he said, "No, I'll be fine. I'll take the call in the men's room while I try to wash some of this wine off my shirt."

"Of course."

Taylor's blue eyes bored holes into the back of Adam's skull as he retreated to the bathroom. When Adam had gone, Taylor downed his wine, then tossed his napkin on the table like a gauntlet thrown at her feet. He shoved his chair back, stood, and began walking toward her.

Claire froze in place, locking eyes with Taylor.

Stay away you self-serving jerk! Don't come any closer!

He ignored her telepathic order and stopped when he reached her table.

"W-w-well, I'll be d-damned," he stammered loudly. "Look at this. A n-n-nubile female."

"Go. Away."

"N-Nice dress," he said. "Do you know what would look good on you?"

"No," she sighed wearily.

"Me."

"My," Claire drawled, looking into Taylor's glittering blue eyes. "That *is* an old line."

"Hey, b-b-baby. Should I call you in the morning, or just n-nudge you?" He waggled his brows.

"Taylor . . ."

"Do you believe in the hereafter? Then you know wh-what I'm here after."

"Taylor," she warned. "You've gone far enough."

"My name's not Taylor. It's Haywood."

"Haywood?" she said dully.

"Yeah. Haywood Yakissme."

He smiled down at her, and their eyes met, and for a moment, it was as it had been a year ago when things were fresh between them, uncomplicated, and the possibilities had seemed endless.

In spite of herself, she felt the ends of her mouth curl into a smile.

"Haywood Yakissme?" she snickered.

"Yeah," he said softly.

His lids lowered a bit, and his eyes sparkled like fireworks on a clear July day. He leaned forward. Without thinking, she lifted her chin.

A large, masculine hand appeared out of nowhere, a barrier between them. Claire looked up the length of arm to see Adam staring daggers at Taylor.

"Not on my watch, pal. What in the hell are you doing here, McKlintock?"

Taylor shoved his hands in his pockets and rocked back on his heels, shaking his head. With a smile, he stuttered, "Mc-Mc-McKennitt."

"You sound like a frigging chicken," Adam mumbled. "What do you want?"

Taylor's eyes assessed her companion. "A place in the country. A good home-cooked meal. Warm socks on a cold day. Oh, and world peace." Turning to Claire, he said, "Nice seeing you both again." He glanced at Adam. "Except for you."

"Hey," Adam said. "What happened to your stutter?"

Taylor cocked his head and considered Adam for a moment. "It took a hike, right along with your humility, pal."

With a quick nod to Claire, Taylor turned on his heel and returned to his table, where he threw down some bills, then left.

Another young waiter appeared at their table, dabbing at the wine stain on the white cloth. As he worked, he slid narrow glances at Adam.

"Where's our other waiter?" Claire asked. "Is his shift over?"

The boy turned to her, but before he could say anything, Adam interrupted. "Oh, I saw him in the restroom. Seemed to not be feeling well. A stomach thing, I think. Isn't that right, boy?"

Without a word, the waiter nodded, gathered up the soiled napkins, and left.

Taking his seat, Adam fumed, "Did you know McKennitt would be here tonight?"

"Adam," she laughed. "I didn't know *we'd* be here tonight. You picked the restaurant, remember?"

"Sorry," he said, his eyes dark and troubled. "This has gone so badly. I'm sorry."

"Adam, it's okay. Things hap—"

"No. That stupid son of a bitch ruined everything."

True, Taylor had obviously followed them and intruded on their dinner, but he'd been harmless enough, even funny, and she didn't like hearing Adam refer to him that way.

Relaxing back in her chair, she smiled again. When it was clear Adam was going to continue behaving like a little boy who'd been denied dessert, she said, "Well, he's gone now. No harm done. There was no *everything* to ruin, was there?"

He huffed out a long breath, eyed her for a moment. Reaching into his breast pocket, he pulled out a small black box. With his thumb, he snapped it open.

And there it sat. Moonbeams on velvet, snatched from the sky, resting on a band of gold.

Her heart stopped. Slowly, she lifted her gaze to his.

"Everything," he murmured, "was me . . . asking you . . . to marry me."

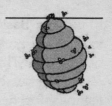

Dilate
To live a long time.

Chapter 10

Claire stared at the ring, then at Adam, then back at the ring, then back at Adam. Searching his shining and eager eyes, she tried to find some kind of rationale for his proposal.

The truth was, she barely knew the man. He'd appeared one day at the hospital, asking about staff positions. It had been a slow day, so they'd had a chance to chat for a while. Since then, they'd met for drinks or dinner a few times. He always mentioned his kids and how much he missed them. Beyond that, they'd never held hands, strolled in the moonlight, even kissed until tonight. Basically, they'd never been intimate in any way.

Yet Adam Thursby wanted to marry her?

Apparently he had quietly developed deep feelings for her—much deeper than the ones she'd developed for him.

"Adam," she said with a nervous laugh. "We hardly know each other. I don't know what to say."

"Say yes." He grinned sheepishly at her and set the ring on the tablecloth by her wineglass.

It was uncomfortable, even a little embarrassing, to have a man invest in a diamond ring the size of a doorknob and propose marriage when you didn't return his affections. She didn't want to hurt his feelings, but this was so out of the blue . . .

"I'm afraid I can't." She gently moved the ring box back to his side of the table. "We barely know each other."

With his index finger, he slid the box back across the table. "So let's get to know each other."

What on earth had happened to his hand? "Your knuckles, Adam. They're red and swollen. How—"

He shoved his hand under the table. "Nothing," he said in an airy tone. "Banged 'em on the bathroom door. I was in such a rush to get this damn wine off my clothes."

That's not what it looked like to her, but why would he lie about hurting his knuckles? It wasn't as though he'd been in some kind of fist-fight, which was what the redness, scraping, and swelling suggested to her.

Glancing down once more at the box, she set it on his side of the table. "I like you, Adam. But I think that's as far as it will ever go."

His friendly eyes went a little dull at that, and he cleared his throat. Quirking his mouth into a charming grin, he picked up the box and set it firmly in front of her.

For a moment, she wasn't sure if she felt flattered, charmed, or annoyed.

Clasping his hands together, knuckles curled under so only the index fingers protruded, he aimed them at her. "I don't think you've given me a fair chance, Claire. When you know me better . . ."

Annoyed won by a landslide.

"I'm sorry, but the answer is no. I think I'd better go. I can take a cab home, if you prefer."

His handsome features suddenly seemed distorted. Too angular, too hard. The gray eyes she'd thought attractive had gone dark, flat, accusing. Then he shrugged and gave her a smile.

"My fault," he said apologetically. "I rushed things. You're just so . . . well, perfect for me. And for my kids." His cheeks flushed. "I'd love for you to meet them when they get here. Really, they're terrific. You have no idea how much I miss them."

Guilt at hurting his feelings flooded her heart. Reaching over, she patted his arm. "I know you miss your kids, Adam. I wish I were the woman to make you happy, but I'm not. I'm sure you'll meet someone soon."

Claire wanted to pay for her meal, but Adam insisted on picking up the tab. To make up for upsetting her, he said. He drove her back to the farm, and though he'd been cordial the whole way, some niggling thing had begun eating its way into her mind. Something was off about him. Perhaps it was his body language. His actions and unconscious movements didn't match his words. She was no psychologist, but she'd studied human behavior enough to know he wasn't being entirely truthful with her. Maybe it was as simple as fear of rejection; maybe it was more.

When he'd pointed at her after she'd rejected his proposal, he'd used the "gun" posture with his index fingers. Though he was smiling, that action indicated he was angry—very angry— and possibly thought she should be made to pay for infuriating him.

Whether that was true or not, however, she had no way of knowing. She only knew she never had to see him again. She wished him well, of course, but considered their relationship had run its course.

When she finally fell into bed, she found sleep as elusive as vapor. She dreamed of Taylor, but whenever he was close enough to kiss, Adam's angry face would intervene, startling her into waking.

Curled under the covers in the big bed she'd used since she was a kid, she inhaled a cool breath of the morning air that tickled the hem of the curtains at her open window. Down around her feet, Agatha stirred, stretched, blinked at the new day, and raised her back leg straight up to begin her morning ablutions.

Shoving the covers aside, Claire decided to push thoughts of Adam and Taylor away, too.

After a quick shower, she dressed and checked her messages. There were seven—three from patients, three from other physicians, and one from the pharmacy. Since she wasn't on call, her pager had been pretty quiet for the last few days, which was a blessing, considering what had been happening in her life.

She glanced out her bedroom window to see Aunt Sadie working down in the vegetable garden at the side of the house. Beside her, Agatha had taken a position in the shade of an enormous tomato plant, its ripe fruit shiny and red in the late morning sun.

Sadie loved her garden and would probably spend all day out there, losing track of time the way Claire did when she was working with the bees.

Well, Claire decided, since her aunt was occupied, she may as well go downstairs to her office and get caught up on her patient files. After grabbing a quick bite to eat, she sauntered into the office, sat at her grandfather's big old mahagony desk, and began shuffling through the stack of notes and folders she'd been neglecting since the accident.

By the time she was finished, it was nearly five o'clock. The aroma of brewing coffee curled up the stairs as she was coming down, luring her into the kitchen. Just as she arrived, Aunt Sadie shrugged into her peach-colored summer sweater.

"Now, you be a good boy while I'm gone," she said to Hitch, who was doing a two-step back and forth across the back of a kitchen chair.

". . . come back . . . Shane . . ." Hitch finished his recital, then squawked and began screaming for Shane all over again.

"So dramatic." Sadie sighed when the noise

had died down. She nudged the parrot under his beak. "Where *do* you get it?"

"I couldn't begin to imagine." Claire laughed.

"Anything you need from the store? Thought I'd make a quick trip, now that the Seattle Police Department has been nice enough to return my truck."

The truck in question had been delivered last night while Claire was out to dinner with Adam. If they'd found any evidence that might lead to the identity of the perpetrator, they were apparently keeping it to themselves.

With a shake of her head, Claire said, "Thanks, Auntie, but I don't need anything."

"When's your next shift at the hospital?"

"Tomorrow."

Sadie's delicate gray brows arched as she said, "Are you sure it's safe to go to work? How do you know whoever hurt you won't try it again?"

And wasn't that the million-dollar question.

"I don't," Claire answered, trying not to let the worry show in her eyes. "But I can't let what happened interfere with work, Aunt Sadie. Trite as it sounds, life goes on." She went to the cupboard and pulled out a mug. "The police assured me they're going to keep an eye out for more trouble. The security guy is coming tomorrow to change all the locks, so we shouldn't be bothered by any more intruders."

Sadie's gentle eyes were filled with worry. "This whole thing is most disturbing and I fear for your safety. Do me a favor, and stick close to home for a while. No more trips to Seattle until this is settled."

Claire gave her aunt a gentle squeeze. "You have my promise I'll be careful." Time for a change of topic. "I think I'll go to check on the hives now. Some of the supers are probably full enough to be harvested."

Instead of answering, Sadie pursed her lips, shifted her slight weight onto her other leg, and jangled her car keys in her hand. Claire knew her aunt well enough to know when something was on her mind, and Sadie obviously wanted to say, or ask, something, but didn't know how to approach the topic. Finally, "How did your date with Adam go last night?"

Behind them, Hitch hopped onto the table, chattering nonsense, filling in the silence with chirps and mutterings.

"It was fine," Claire said vaguely. "The food was wonderful."

She thought of Taylor and the antics he'd pulled. "It was entertaining."

Then she thought of Adam and the small velvet box. "It was filled with surprises."

And then she thought of the answer she'd given Adam. "It was over early."

Sadie narrowed one eye on Claire. "Have you slept with Adam?"

Knowing Sadie as she did, Claire wasn't at all shocked by the question.

"No."

"Do you plan to?" Sadie lifted her head, and her silky hair slid back, allowing Claire to see the intense concern in her aunt's eyes.

Letting the empty mug dangle from her index finger, Claire said, "No."

"Never?"

"Well, he asked me to marry him . . ." Hesitant to go into the whole thing, she let her voice trail off.

Sadie frowned, deepening the lines between her eyes. "He's very handsome. Reminds me of a young Bill Holden."

"Who?"

Sadie smiled wistfully. "Before your time, dear." She sighed. "Adam simply oozes confidence."

"Surgeons generally do. It's a part of the job description. They can't do what's required unless they are very self-possessed."

Fiddling with her keys again, Sadie said, "Call me a big buttinski, but I don't think you know that fellow well enough to marry him."

"You've been a big buttinski all my life, darling." She chuckled. "Why stop now?"

Settling her hips against the sink, Claire considered her feelings about Adam, not that they mattered anymore.

"Adam and I have similar goals. And he's reputed to be an excellent surgeon on his way up. But, the truth is—"

"The higher a monkey climbs, the more you see of its behind." Sadie flattened her mouth and shook her head. Her eyes closed like those of an empress about to bestow the wisdom of the ages.

"Aunt Sadie, I . . . you didn't *like* Adam?"

"How *I* feel about him's not important. You seem to feel you know him, but you don't. Not if you haven't slept with him, you don't."

"Oh, it's okay," Claire said. "Listen, I should explain. See, last night—"

"Other than teaching you how to protect yourself, and trying to impart some wisdom into yours and your brother's heads about making smart decisions, I've pretty much kept quiet about sex." A tiny smile tilted her mouth. "I know you've probably had your share of beaus, and you've probably slept with some of them, and that's fine." She gave a sharp nod. "I'd think it a mighty sad turn of events if a woman your age had never enjoyed what the bedroom has to offer. But . . ."

Her voice trailed off as she gazed directly into Claire's eyes.

"When I ran off to Hollywood at sixteen, I was a virgin. First thing I did was get rid of it." She let a singsong sigh past her lips, and smiled wearily. "Virtue was a burden that became too heavy to bear. Besides, undue importance has been placed on keeping it. Life is hard enough, Claire. Dispatching of one's innocence lightens the load considerably, frees a person to tend to other, more important things. If knowledge is power, then knowing how adult physical relationships work takes the edge away from the males and gives it to the females. A man can't take advantage of a girl who's figured a few things out."

"You were a woman ahead of your time, Auntie."

"Unquestionably," she said, lifting her head in a manner befitting royalty. "What I am trying to say, Claire, is that it has been my experience a woman doesn't really know a man until she's been at his mercy, flat on her back, with his hands on her. In other words, until she's had sex with him."

Claire's mind went immediately to Taylor, and this time, she did nothing to stop it.

"Some men," Sadie continued, her eyes downcast, "some men treat you like you're no more than baggage for them to use any way they wish. Those men are known as selfish bastards."

". . . bastards . . ."

"Shut up, Hitch. Some men will take much more than they're ever capable of giving. Those men are known as selfish sons of bitches."

". . . sawfish . . . sonsabbats . . ."

"Good boy, Hitch." She smiled sweetly at her pet. "He's so quick." Returning her attention to Claire, she said, "And then there are some men who will idolize you, cater to your every whim, and generally overwhelm you with affection to the point of being cloying. While that may sound appealing, it gets quite tiresome."

"And what are those men called?"

"Boys." Sadie shook her head. "The goal in a relationship is mutual passion. You give, he takes. He gives, you take. When all's said and done, it's good for everybody, nobody feels cheated, everybody's satisfied, and you've got yourself one hell of a sex life."

A sad look entered her eyes, and her voice faltered a little. "Of course, that can't be all there is. You've got to have love and compatibility going for you, too, as I had with my darling Phillip, brief though our marriage was. Essentially, until you've seen how a man treats you in bed, Claire, you don't really know him at all."

"I didn't accept Adam's proposal, Auntie. Our relationship is over."

Sadie gave a sharp nod as if to say, *Perfect!* Then, she seemed to have an afterthought.

"And that other young man I met," she said. "The studly dark-haired one?"

"Taylor."

She looked into Claire's eyes for a long time, then said, "You have slept with him, haven't you."

"Yes."

Pursing her lips, she gave Claire a steady look. "Are you going to marry him?"

Claire felt her throat close up. Her cheeks warmed, and her eyes stung a little.

When she didn't respond, Sadie reached up to tenderly stroke Claire's cheek with her thumb, and whisper, "I see."

With a watery smile, Claire choked, "Have I told you today how much I adore you, Aunt Sadie?"

The lady smiled. "Why yes, dear. I believe you have. I saw it, just there, in your eyes, when you came into the kitchen."

Claire wrapped her arms around the delicate woman and gave her a squeeze.

"Thanks for everything you've done, all you gave up for Zach and me. I probably don't say it enough—"

Sadie pushed herself to an arm's length. "Pah! I gave up nothing. I'm basically a very selfish woman. I got what I wanted, you and your brother. What's that compared to the adulation of millions of moviegoers?" Her eyes sparkled, and she winked.

The kitchen door creaked and slammed shut behind the little dynamo as she headed to her truck. A few moments later, the old green Ford ambled up the driveway and out of sight.

Claire let out a long, slow, deep, disturbed breath.

It was as though Aunt Sadie had snuck into her subconscious and discovered Claire's most intimate thoughts about Taylor.

He had not used her like baggage. He had not taken from her and given nothing in return. And he hadn't worshipped her, either. He had been sweet, and passionate, and tender, taking a little, giving more. He'd held her close and caressed her, whispering soft words in her ear, nuzzling her neck with his smile, making her want him all over again. Making her want him forever.

Men had satisfied her desires before Taylor, but none had become a part of her the way he had.

Surely, she could find that kind of connection with another man. It didn't have to be Taylor, did it?

Turning to Hitch, she said, "You be a good boy. I've got to go work with the bees."

". . . wax on . . . wax off . . ."

"Yes, you're a very smart bird. Now shut the hell up."

With a shake of her head, Claire pushed open the kitchen door and went outside.

Though it was late August, September was making its presence known in the bite of the breeze as it tumbled a whirlwind of dry leaves across the yard. Soon the trees would begin changing, turning yellow and burnished orange and crimson. Already the apple orchard stood with outstretched branches heavily laden with ripening fruit, and the hive combs were filled with waxy amber honey. The evening air would cool and carry a subtle, smoky scent. Lazy summer days would become a memory, as long winter nights took their place.

As she crossed the yard to the barn, her muck boots crunched over the gravel, dirt, and leaves.

"Henrietta, Hermione, Hebsiba," she said to the trio of brown leghorns as they chuckled and flapped and scurried out of her way. She made a mental note to gather eggs from the henhouse once she was finished at the hives.

In the barn, she tugged on her leather work gloves, pulled the ancient wheelbarrow from its place in the last stall, and pushed it into the yard.

Over the decades, trips out to the beehives had worn ruts in the dirt from the yard to the field, and though the wheelbarrow was heavy, it was worth the effort because it invariably reminded her of her visits to the farm when she was a little girl.

From the time she'd been a toddler, her grandfather, Sadie's brother, had let her ride in the wheelbarrow. Claire had bounced and laughed as he purposely hit every bump in the trail, then pretended to lose control, threatening to dump her out into the tall grass that lined the pathway. When the wheelbarrow was filled with honey-heavy combs, he let her help push it back to the barn.

The hive bodies were a good hundred yards from the house, so by the time she arrived, she was panting from the exertion.

"Maybe I need to get one of those new, lightweight plastic jobbies," she mumbled as she eyed Grandpa's handmade version. The paint had long ago chipped off the enormous sheet metal bed, and the wooden handles had splintered in places, but she didn't have the heart to replace the thing. After all, her fingers curled around the handles in the same place her grandfather's had. When she touched them, she was touching him—and then she didn't miss him quite so much.

Claire approached the hives and began looking for evidence of mice or other infestations. Around her, the bees hummed and hovered and generally ignored what she was doing.

"Hey, b-b-baby," came a masculine voice from behind her.

Claire spun around, nearly losing her balance. He stood there, legs braced, hands on his hips, his mouth tilted in a cocky grin.

"You!" she snapped. "I can't believe you have the nerve to show your face after last night. What a jerk!"

His eyes sparkled with mischief. "No I'm not."

"Do you know every cheesy pickup line in the book?"

"Yes." With a smug look, he said, "If I c-could rearrange the alphabet, I'd put U and I together."

"Puh-leeze."

"D-do you believe in love at first sight," he stumbled, "or sh-should I walk by again?"

"You should walk in front of an oncoming train!"

"Hey," he said, shrugging. "You made up the rules when you told Dr. Doodledick about my so-called medical history."

"You left that door wide open when you barged in on my dinner date." She marched over to the first hive body and removed the lid.

"Can I help?"

"No."

His blue eyes locked with hers, and she felt her skin warm. "How did you know I was out here, anyway? You can't see the hives from the yard because of the apple trees."

He gestured to the wheelbarrow. "I just followed the noise-mobile there. I figured it was either you or somebody torturing the Tin Man."

Indignant that he would insult a treasured family heirloom, she huffed, "It used to belong to my grandfather."

"Looks like it used to belong to Noah."

He smiled at her then, a warm, sort of sleepy look that sent ripples of awareness all the way down to her toes.

You don't know a man until you've been at his mercy, flat on your back, with his hands on you.

She swallowed past the wad of cotton suddenly stuck in her throat.

Glancing at the beehives, he said, "I didn't realize you had bees."

"One does not *have* bees," she managed. "One *keeps* bees." Rubbing her chin, she said, "I learned how from my grandfather. It's a pleasant, gentle hobby."

"I don't know a thing about them," he said, widening his incredibly blue eyes like a little boy who'd been overlooked for dodgeball. "Maybe I can help you and you can teach me—"

"About the birds and the bees?" She scoffed and tugged at her gloves. "I have a feeling you wrote the book."

Smiling down at her, he said, "Are you going to collect some honey?"

With a sigh of reluctance, she said, "I'm not getting rid of you until you're ready to be gotten rid of, am I?"

"I'm such a pest. It's a curse, really."

"Seems to me you have more than your share. Don't you have any detecting to do?"

"I got off shift at five."

She shifted her weight to one leg. "Well, in answer to your question, yes, I'm collecting honey. If you want to stay and watch, I guess I can't stop you, but you'll be bored, and with any luck at all, your manly pheromones will piss off the bees and they'll all sting you."

"You make it sound so appealing, this *gentle* hobby of yours."

Ignoring him—or trying to—she turned away again. A moment later, she felt him directly behind her, the intimate waft of his breath on the back of her neck.

"Stand over there," she ordered in a desperate attempt to keep him at a distance.

He moved to where she had indicated. "Why here?"

"Because you were in the bees's approach to

the hive. They have flight patterns. If you stay out of their way, you're less likely to get stung. Are you allergic to bee stings?"

"Nope."

"Okay. Here." She carefully removed a comb from the first hive, and handed it over to him. Several dozen bees swarmed to it and began crawling over the wax cells. Taylor didn't flinch.

"How long do these guys live?" he said as he placed it in the wheelbarrow.

"Those guys are all girls," she corrected. She stopped what she was doing and smiled up at him. "In the world of bees, the males are good for one thing and one thing only."

He blinked innocently. "Bees can change flat tires?

"Once their duty has been done," she continued, unaffected by his meager attempts at humor, "those males who survived the mating flight are not allowed back inside the hive. They're a liability since they can't create honey or support the hive. They are *useless*."

She eyed him meaningfully.

"*If* they survived the mating flight?"

As she pulled another comb from the hive body, she said, "When a queen matures, she leaves the hive and mates in the air with whatever drones can get to her. All the sperm she will ever need to lay eggs for the rest of her life are collected at that time. When each male is through," she said slowly, arching a brow, "she kicks him away, disemboweling him and leaving his testicles and mating gear inside her. Of course, he dies."

Taylor turned a little green. She was certain if he could have cupped his hands protectively around his crotch, he would have.

"Just where does the *gentle* part come in again?" he said with a sly grin.

She carefully set the lid back on top of the hive body. "Time to earn your keep."

He gave her a mock salute, gripped the handles of the wheelbarrow, and began effortlessly pushing it back to the barn. He was wearing jeans and a jacket, and as Claire walked along behind him, she watched his backside in tormented appreciation.

Inside the barn, the air was cool, the light dim, as though someone had draped a dark cloth over the sun.

He set the wheelbarrow down, turned to her, and smiled. "I like honey."

"Imagine that," she drawled. "Okay. If I give you some honey, will you go away?"

"Probably not, but I'll take the honey anyway."

Before she could react, his hands spanned her waist and he tugged her into his arms, his open mouth claiming hers. He moaned, deep in the back of his throat like a hungry animal finally settling down to feed.

Slowly easing out of the kiss, he gazed into her eyes. "Thought you hated me."

"I don't hate you," she breathed.

"That why you kissed me back?"

"You caught me by surprise. Kissing you back was a reflexive action having nothing to do with—"

He lowered his head and kissed her again. This time, she moaned. Oh, God, oh, *no*.

Ending the kiss, she quickly stepped away from Taylor, out of arm's reach. "We're not doing this," she snapped.

"We just did. And what's more," he said lightly, "we liked it. Why are you so mad? It was just a kiss."

Maybe to you . . .

Engine noises, tires crunching over gravel, a car radio blasting an old swing tune—the arrival of Aunt Sadie's truck intruded before Claire said or did something truly stupid. She was having enough trouble controlling her breathing as it was.

Taylor rubbed his chin with his knuckles. "If that's your aunt, I need to talk to you both about a police matter."

A police matter? "A police matter?"

He gently grasped her wrists and tugged off

her gloves. Taking her hand, he began walking her toward the barn door. "Yes," he said. "It seems your Aunt Sadie's former fiancé has been a very bad boy."

Racketeer
Large-breasted swindler.

Chapter 11

One winter, when John Quincy Mortimer was a kid, he'd seen a ball of snakes under his father's house. Shiny and writhing, they'd squirmed over the dirt like a living tangle of black wire. He'd never seen anything like them since, but he felt them now, in the pit of his stomach.

He tilted back in his executive swivel chair until it squeaked like an angry hamster, nearly toppling him ass end over teakettle. Quickly righting himself, he remembered how often he'd heard that phrase growing up.

Mind how you go, you clumsy little good-for-

nothing, or you'll trip over your own feet and fall ass end over teakettle!

His face heated. Father would be ashamed of what his only son was doing, lying, cheating, putting the time-honored Mortimer name at risk. Gripping the armrests, he righted himself and cursed out loud, the harsh words bouncing off the walls of his spacious office as though the very air around him condemned him for his misdeeds.

But they weren't misdeeds, not really, not when you stopped to consider the good he was doing. For a higher purpose. For *humanity*. After all, the donors *were* already dead; *they* didn't care. He was doing the world a favor, truth be told. Sure, he made a little money at it, but that was simply his due, for the contribution he was making to science and medicine.

Mort adjusted his perfectly knotted tie and wiped the sweat from the back of his neck.

Bloody hell, why had he let himself get talked into this? At first, the money was nice, and there was so much of it! But now, things were getting complicated. Too many people were involved, and his partner wanted to go national. *National*, for Pete's sake! That meant the big boys. Guys with muscles and guns, long rides to the river in black limos, wearing cement overshoes. The *fuhgetaboutit* guys—except if Mort screwed up, they wouldn't *fuhgetaboutit*, *ever*, and he'd be in it cheek deep.

In order to keep those boys happy, the take was going to have to increase a thousandfold, maybe ten-thousandfold for all he knew. This was all getting too rich for his blood. He was small-time all the way. Small-time worked, the risks were minimal, the take modest but safe.

Leaning forward, he fiddled with his rose-wood desk set, rearranging the two pens until they stood at right angles to their hand-carved holder. There. Perfect.

Maybe he should get out now, he thought, if he still could, if his partner would let him. He had more money than he knew what to do with, and he sure wasn't gettin' no younger. He could retire, go traveling, maybe take Sadie with him—if she was nice to him again.

Normally, he wasn't a violent man, but Sadie dumping him like that—and in front of three other people, including that lumberjack who'd driven her home—that was enough to make even a pacifist double his fists.

A quick rap on his door had him straightening in his chair. He folded his hands in his lap, blew out a breath, and called, "What is it, Min?"

The door opened, and his secretary peeked in. Mindy Ketterer, forties, loyal, hardworking, greeted him with a polite mouth-only smile. Her dull brown hair was short, her too fair skin not at all flattered by an unbecoming cut. Behind thick glasses, her equally dull brown eyes swam and blinked. She opened her mouth to speak, but before she could say anything, a man shoved past her, and she retreated behind the door like a shy turtle closing up shop.

Mort shot out of his chair. "It's all right, Min," he rushed, keeping his instinctive fear under wraps.

When she peeked around the door, he gestured for her to close it. She cast a wary glace at the visitor, then did as Mort asked.

As soon as she'd gone, he said, "What in the hell are you doing here, LeRoy? We agreed we should *never* be seen together, and now Mindy—"

"Forget what I said," the man bit out. "And forget that stupid wide-assed secretary of yours. We need to talk."

Mort's after-hours business associate invariably spoke to him as though he were an irritating child who must be put in his place. He felt his temper rise, but worked to keep it in check. Pursing his lips, he combed shaking fingers through the few strands of hair gracing his head. He had to tread carefully—Kevin LeRoy could be a real bastard. The one time LeRoy thought Mort had cheated him, the guy smacked him so hard, it had nearly broken his nose. He still couldn't smell the flowers in the viewing room.

Kevin LeRoy, if that was indeed the man's name, which Mort doubted, strolled to the mahogany wet bar by the room's single window and yanked the cabinet door open as though he wasn't a guest, but lord of the manor. In fact, he generally behaved as if everything belonged to him, from liquor to people. Retrieving a half-empty bottle of Glenlivet, he splashed a couple of ounces into one of the crystal tumblers sitting on the marble bar top.

"Little early in the day, isn't it, LeRoy?" Mort said, though his own throat was damn parched at the moment.

As he sipped the scotch, LeRoy turned toward Mort, one eye narrowed. "Tell me about your girlfriend, Mortie."

"Sadie?" Mort shrugged, shoved his hands in his front pockets, and walked over to the landscape hanging above a deeply cushioned sofa. Gazing at the tasteful and serene watercolor, he said lightly, "Ex-girlfriend. I ended our relationship. Broke it right off."

"Did you now." LeRoy seemed to consider this for a moment as he took another sip of scotch.

Turning from the painting, Mort tried to confront his partner head on, but ended up investigating the man's tie knot instead. Imported silk, no doubt. LeRoy had very expensive tastes.

"Why do you care about my personal life?" Mort asked as casually as he could. "It ain't got any bearing on—"

"The hell it doesn't." LeRoy slammed his drink down on the bar, causing the amber liquid to slosh over the sides of the glass onto the marble, then drip onto the imported carpet. He either gave no notice, or didn't care.

"You took her out there, Mortie. Didn't you. *Didn't you?*"

Mortie knew where *there* was, but it hadn't been any big deal at all, and she certainly hadn't seen anything. He was fairly certain she hadn't, anyway.

"Oh, that," he said with a relieved sigh and a falsetto laugh that bordered on nervous tittering. "We were out for a drive in the country and I realized I'd misplaced my cell phone." He shrugged. "You can't get a signal worth a damn out there, what with it being so far down in the valley, so I set it down in the lab and must have forgotten—"

"I don't give a shit about your cell phone, Mortie. How much did she see?"

Mort licked his lips and eyed LeRoy's glass of scotch.

"We were only there a couple of minutes," he

insisted. "She stayed in the car the whole time. I-it was nearly dark. I swear, she didn't see diddly." Pausing, he swallowed, more anxious now. "H-how did you know about—"

"Do you think you're the only moron I've got on the payroll, Mortie?" LeRoy bellowed, his eyes narrowing into angry slits. "Not a thing happens in this operation that I don't know about. It doesn't matter whether she stayed in the car or climbed right inside a cadaver drawer. Now she knows the place exists, and she can point the cops to it, and put *you* at the scene, you stupid bastard."

Mort's uneasiness grew and he loosened his collar. "She couldn't possibly remember—"

In less time than it took him to finish his thought, LeRoy crossed the room. The flat of his palm against Mortie's chest, he shoved him against the window and glared down into his eyes. At the back of his head, the glass cracked, and Mort felt a stab of pain. Fearing LeRoy would shove him through the window, he stumbled, "Wh-what do you want me to do?"

"You're not going to mess this up for me. I have a lot at stake here, and you are *not* going to blow this." Glaring into Mort's eyes, he rasped, "Make her forget. Make her forget, *everything*."

"Wh-what? Y-you mean . . . no, you *don't* mean . . ."

"I *do* mean," he snapped. "One word out of

her could ruin it all, and I've worked too hard, taken too many risks to have some old lady spoil it. This is my last chance, Mortie. Everything's at stake here." Lowering his voice, he whispered through clenched teeth, "You don't know. You have no idea . . ."

Apparently thinking better of his remarks, he let his voice trail off. A strange light came into his eyes, his brow creased, and for a moment he seemed to appear . . . desperate.

Slowly releasing Mort, LeRoy backed away, polished off his scotch, then moved to the door.

"If you fail," he said with a tilt of his head and a casual smile. "If I have to do it, I won't stop at her, I'll come after you next. Got that, partner?"

"Miss Lancaster," Taylor said, trying to keep the irritation out of his voice. "I don't want to be rude, but do you think you can put Hitch . . . elsewhere?"

Like, in the oven.

"I'm so sorry, Detective," Sadie said. "Is Hitch bothering you?"

Forcing a polite smile, he said, "A little."

Taylor stared at the bird; the bird stared back.

Sadie—and the loquacious Hitch—sat on the couch in the living room as Taylor attempted to explain the situation at hand. The problem was, whenever he tried to make a point, the parrot became loud and intrusive. The old lady must be so used to the chatter, she didn't hear it anymore, but the bird was driving Taylor friggin' nuts.

". . . McKennitt . . . McKennitt . . . men are such bastards . . ."

From her chair in front of the fireplace, Claire snorted.

Sadie touched her fingertips to her mouth and chuckled. "Men aren't really bastards, Detective McKennitt."

"I know," he said dryly.

Hitch eyed him as though he had his doubts.

"Hitch," Sadie admonished. "You're being a very bad bird. Hush up now, or I'll have to put you in your cage."

"Attica! . . . Attica! . . ."

Ignoring Hitch, Sadie smiled at Taylor as she clasped her thin hands in her lap. "African Grey Congos have the intelligence of a five-year-old child and pick up new words all the time. He should calm down soon. Please explain to me again the meaning of the term *disarticulation technician*, Detective McKennitt."

Even at her age, Sadie Lancaster's youthful beauty was still in evidence. While the passage of time had softened her features and added wrinkles to her brow, her skin remained flawless, her cheeks plump and rosy. Eyes that had once lit up the screen had faded to the brown of autumn leaves. She had been Hollywood royalty through three decades, and her manner indicated she believed she still reigned.

"Simply put, Auntie," Claire said, "a disarticulation technician harvests knee and shoulder joints, and sometimes spinal columns from human cadavers."

Sadie's eyes widened. "Whatever for?"

"To sell," Taylor said. "Medical schools use the joints to teach students how to perform surgery. It's the disarticulation technician who actually removes, or harvests, these parts, usually under the auspices of a Willed Body Part order from the deceased or his family. All perfectly legal."

Sadie lifted her chin, arching both brows as she put two and two together. "And Mortie is involved in doing this without a Willed Body Part order. That is to say, illegally."

Taylor looked at Claire, then back to Sadie. "We believe so, but we don't have any proof. Since he does this just prior to cremating the bodies, there's no way of knowing for sure. There is little legislation in this state regarding harvested body parts, and the process is not very closely monitored, so only a complaint gives the authorities a heads-up that this is happening."

"And you've had a complaint."

"A few days ago, we received an anonymous tip that Mortimer may somehow be involved. The investigation is still in its early stages."

"Why can't you just go in and bust the smarmy little creep?"

Taylor smiled. "Mortimer doesn't have the skills required to do the actual disarticulation himself. We don't know yet who's doing them, or where they're being performed. And we don't think this was his idea. We believe he has a partner."

"You're right," Sadie agreed, nodding her silver head. "Mortie doesn't have the brains or the cojones to do something like this on his own."

"If we simply bust him, he may not roll over on his partner," Taylor explained. "We think the partner has several operations going, even to the point of bringing bodies in from out of state, harvesting the parts, then disposing of the corpses either by cremation or by dumping. At the first sign of trouble, the partner could disappear and still be in business at another location, allowing Mortimer to take the fall. Mortimer probably doesn't even know his real name, and we don't want to risk losing the lynchpin of this whole operation by moving too quickly."

Hitch emitted a long, loud wolf whistle.

Taylor glared at the bird whose head seemed disproportionately large for its smoothly feathered body. It was mostly gray, except for a mask of white across its eyes, and some brilliant red feathers under its tail. Those unblinking eyes were the color of bleached lemons, surrounding a pinpoint black pupil that apparently took in everything.

"Shut up, Hitch," Sadie said absently. She seemed to be turning something over in her mind. With a quick nod, she said, "I would have to agree that Mortie is up to no good. Yes. That makes sense to me."

Taylor shot a glace at Claire, who was unusually quiet. To Sadie, he said, "How long have you known Mortimer, ma'am?"

She stood and slowly walked across the room, Hitch doing the sidestep up her arm to her shoulder. When she reached the opposite wall, she tipped up the edge of a framed photograph that had been slightly askew.

"I met him about six months ago. He was fun at first, we hit it off, and I sort of became attached to him. When he asked me to marry him a few weeks back, I accepted. It was on our trip to Canada this last weekend that I realized he's a chauvinist and an opportunist. I broke the engagement." She looked squarely into his eyes. "He cared nothing for me, but simply wanted to use my celebrity status to enhance his business."

Taylor leaned forward, set his elbows on his

knees, steepling his fingers in front of him. "Can you recall seeing him with anybody odd or suspicious? Has he ever bragged about making money on the side? Ever taken you anywhere outside of town, someplace remote?"

While Sadie considered his questions, Taylor let his gaze meander back to Claire. He could tell by her expression that she was worried about her aunt, and alarmed at this turn of events. As he watched her, she lifted her eyes to his, and his blood nearly boiled.

He remembered them together that morning in the barn, remembered kissing her, and how she had responded. She wasn't as distant and cold as she'd like him to believe. In fact, her reaction to his advances had been encouraging.

Mentally, he shrugged. Hell, maybe he should press the issue. Maybe he should do it soon.

"Okay, but I get to be on top . . ."

"Shut up, Hitch," Sadie said, absently tapping her finger on her cheek.

Turning her attention to Taylor, she said, "There was this one thing. We were on a drive through the rainforest a while back. Mortie said he needed to make a quick stop. I was surprised, because as far as I could tell, we were in the middle of nowhere." She scratched Hitch under his beak. "But we turned off the road and ran smack-dab into this enormous gate. It was locked electronically, like it was a millionaire's hideaway or something, but all that was behind it was a sort of old farm, with a big barn. Everything was closed up, though. I waited in the car, and when he came back out, we left."

"You didn't see anybody? Any cars maybe?"

She brightened at that. "Oh, yes. Now that you mention it, it does seem rather odd that such a broken-down old place, all dark and gloomy like, had, let's see . . ." Her voice trailed off as she closed her eyes. Her fingers moved in front of her as though she were ticking off numbers. "Three. Three cars. No, wait. Two cars and a big SUV-looking thing."

Taylor and Claire locked gazes.

"What color was the SUV?" Taylor's heart sped up. *Black*. She would say black. He *knew* she would.

"Black."

Claire cleared her throat. "Aunt Sadie, the SUV that bumped me off the road was black."

Sadie's eyes widened in alarm.

". . . alrighty then . . . well alrighty then . . ."

"Shut up, Hitch."

Taylor scrubbed his jaw with his knuckles. "Claire was in your truck when she was hit, but the driver had to have known it wasn't you behind the wheel, if not before, then certainly afterward, when he took her purse."

None of this made any kind of sense. If Mortimer was behind Claire's attack, why? If it was the partner, what was his motive for scaring Claire? Why Claire? Why not Sadie?

"Could you find the place again?" he said. "The road with the gate?"

Sadie considered this while Hitch nibbled gently at her ear.

"Honestly, I doubt it. We'd been driving all over the place and it was nearly dark as it was. I slept most of the way back. I'm sorry, Detective McKennitt. I'm not much help."

". . . Detective McKennitt . . . bastard . . ."

"Shut up, Hitch." Sadie smiled at Taylor, a flirty little grin that put a sparkle in her eye and must have set the boys' hearts to racing a long time ago.

Ignoring the frigging bird, he said, "On the contrary, ma'am. You've been a great deal of help."

He closed the notebook he'd been scribbling in and tucked it into his inside jacket pocket. "Have you heard from Mortimer since you broke your engagement?"

"No."

"Do you think he'll give up, or will he persist?"

Sadie pursed her lips. "I don't know. I was very angry, and he knows it. I gave him back his ring."

"Okay, look, I don't want you to call him, but if he should initiate contact, could you try to find out where that place was he took you in the country?"

She perked right up at that. "You mean, spy for you?"

Across the room, Claire's smile died. "Taylor, no," she protested, her voice thick with alarm. "You can't ask Aunt Sadie to do something so dangerous."

"If I thought there was any risk," he assured her, "I wouldn't ask." Turning to Sadie, he said, "I don't want you going anywhere with him. This is just if he calls and you can find a way to work it into the conversation. Your asking a lot of questions could arouse his suspicions."

Sadie clapped her hands together like a kid at a birthday party. "Oh, a new role! God, it's been so long." Her eyes narrowed and her voice lowered at least two octaves. "I know just how I'll play it," she emoted. "I'll get you what you need, Detective. You can count on me."

Taylor sent her a stern look. "We appreciate your cooperation, ma'am, but I want you to exercise extreme caution. If he calls, try to get him to talk about that place. Any information you can get out of him will be of great help."

"And if he doesn't call?"

Taylor's mouth flattened. "We'll find some other way. Don't initiate contact, ma'am. Promise?"

Sadie grinned. "I . . . promise."

Juvenile
Child–sized river in Egypt.

Chapter 12

"So," Claire said, her hands shoved deep into her pockets. "Now that you've done your good deed for today, you'll be taking off, hmm?"

Taylor's eyes snapped at her remark. "What in the hell does that mean?"

She flicked a glance at Aunt Sadie, who was deep into some private kind of stand-up routine with Hitch over by the window.

Keeping her voice low, Claire said, "Didn't you see how she responded when you asked for her help? She thinks this is like a movie role. Dammit, Taylor, I'm going to have to watch her every second to make sure she doesn't do something risky. It's not like I don't already have enough to worry about—"

"I'm old, not deaf," Sadie sang lightly, causing both Taylor and Claire to look her way.

". . . not deaf . . . Detective McKennitt . . . bastard . . ."

"Shut up, Hitch," Sadie admonished as she turned to Claire. "Don't worry dear. I'll be good."

Her eyes held a sparkle that unnerved Claire more than a little.

Urging Hitch up to her shoulder, Sadie said, "I'm going to my room now. I need to work a bit more on my memoirs. I'm stuck on my brief affair with . . . oh, never mind. You're too young to remember him." She slid a shrewd glance between Claire and Taylor, standing toe-to-toe, obviously ready to do battle. With a sly smile and the arch of a brow, she tilted her head as though confiding to the bird. "Fasten your seat belt. It's going to be a bumpy night."

As Sadie and Hitch disappeared up the stairs, the parrot muttered something about a failure to communicate.

Unwilling to let her concerns go unanswered, Claire curled her fingers around Taylor's forearm.

"I adore Aunt Sadie," she whispered. "If any harm comes to her because of this thing with

Mort, I'll hold you personally responsible. And I *mean* it."

For a moment, Taylor only stared down into her eyes, then he placed his hand over hers. "Claire. I'd die before I'd see any harm come to her. Or you. And *I* mean it."

They stood like that for a long time, long enough for Claire to realize something had shifted between them. The dynamics of their relationship had changed, solidified in some subtle way. She'd dropped her guard so briefly, yet it had given Taylor enough time to move past her defenses and into her life, into her thoughts, maybe even into her heart. She wanted to shove him back out again, resist her feelings for him, but she was weary from the struggle.

"What time is it?" she said, easing her hand from his arm. "I need to eat something."

In the cozy kitchen, they prepared and ate dinner together. Taylor talked about himself, his brother, their parents, what it was like growing up in Seattle. As he spoke, she watched him by the light of the candles she'd lit and placed on the table. During the day, Taylor's eyes were like twin blue flames, hot with intelligence and interest. Now, as they reflected the candles' glow, they smoldered like a banked fire. It would take only the softest breath to make them ignite.

As they cleared the dishes, he said, "I noticed

a little basketball court out behind the garage. Do you play?"

Setting a clean glass on the shelf, Claire closed the cupboard door. "Grandpa put it in for Zach and me when we were kids. We'd play after dinner on summer evenings."

"What a coincidence. This is after dinner on a summer evening."

"I haven't played for years."

Closing the silverware drawer, he narrowed one eye on her. "Then it's time you got a refresher."

"Some other time," she said, as she hung the damp dish towel to dry. "I'm really not very athletic. I'd probably break something."

Despite her protests, he took her by the wrist and urged her out the back door, dragging her around the house to the small basketball court. "Got a ball?"

It took a few minutes, but they found it in the garage. It looked more like a doughy brown pillow, but they pumped it up, and were back on the court a few minutes later.

Claire toed off her shoes. Beneath her bare feet, the short grass in the yard felt cool and damp, a contrast to the warmth of the smooth cement of the court. Although night had fallen, light from the back porch poured onto the yard, casting Taylor's handsome features in sharp contrasts and angles. From the open bedroom window above, she could hear Hitch begging HAL to open the pod bay doors.

"As you may recall," Taylor said, picking up the ball and twirling it on his thumb. "You try to throw the ball through the hoop, and I stop you. Then I throw the ball through the hoop while you try and stop me."

She raised a brow. "It sounds like you always succeed and I always fail."

"Well," he said with exaggerated shyness. "I am taller than you, stronger, very athletic, faster, and I do have a few trophies from college—"

"Oh, really," she said flatly. "Trophies."

He shrugged and smiled as though he was apologizing in advance for cleaning her clock.

While he was busy congratulating himself on his assumed victory, Claire grabbed the ball from his relaxed fingers, spun around, arched her arm toward the basket, and lobbed the ball through the hoop.

"Two points," she stated.

Taylor stood gaping at her. "Hey! You didn't give me a chance to—"

She bent and scooped up the ball, but as she went to throw, he stopped talking and blocked her. She ducked under his outstretched arm, and lobbed in another one.

"Two points," she huffed. "Puts me up four."

Flashing him a smile, she saw the fire light in

his eyes as he came after her. But she twirled around, stepped back, jumped and threw, and in it went.

"Two points. Six, zer—"

"I can add," he snapped.

Claire retrieved the ball, dribbling it away from him. Before she could get another one off, he snatched it away, turned and shot, and missed.

"Those trophies you have," she laughed, recovering the ball, bouncing it on the cement, "were for varsity hopscotch, right?"

Another lob, another score.

"Eight, zip," she sang.

"Basketball is about more than scoring," he growled. "There's strategy, and rules. This game does have rules, you know. Anybody can score poi— Hey!"

While he'd stood complaining, Claire turned, arched her arm, and lobbed in another one.

Suddenly, what felt like a steel band wrapped around her waist, lifting her off the ground.

"Personal foul!" she squeaked as he held her against his body. Though she squirmed and struggled, he held on tight. With his free hand, he bounced the ball, shot, and scored.

"Now we're even," he panted, laughing, still lugging her around.

"*Even?*" she choked, wrapping her arms

around his neck to keep from falling. "I'm clearly ahead. Clearly the superior player."

He tossed the ball and scored two more points. "Now *I'm* ahead."

"No you're not," she croaked. "I thought you said you could add!"

"Hey now," he said, his voice very matter-of-fact. "I'm handicapped by carrying around a luscious babe, so I get double points."

"No you don't," she growled. "I was winning fair and square and you—"

"My, my, my," he drawled, looking into her eyes. "You really hate losing, don't you."

Yes. "I can be a gracious loser, when I actually *lose.*"

He let her slide down his body until her feet touched the court once more. One arm still encircled her waist, while he held the ball against his hip with the other hand.

Claire pressed herself to him, letting her breasts rub against his chest as she moved her palms across the flat of his belly. Beneath her fingers, his muscles tightened.

"You really hate losing, too, don't you, Detective," she whispered suggestively. He swallowed. Those blue eyes went all sleepy. He lowered his head to kiss her.

She swooped in. Grabbing the ball, she spun

away and tossed in another perfect basket, clapped her hands and laughed.

Her arms out, fingers splayed, she went to capture the ball just as Taylor moved to block her. As they collided, her fingers smashed into the solid wall of his chest. The little finger of her left hand bent backward, and Claire let out a yelp. Gasping, she clutched her injured hand to her chest.

"Ouch, owie, owie, owie, damn!"

"Claire?" Taylor let the ball drop as he gently curled his fingers around her hand, tenderly prying it away from her chest. "Let me see."

She felt the tears well up in her eyes. Her little finger hurt like hell and it was all his fault. Damn him for being so smug. *Trophies*. Really. Men were so competitive.

"I won," she said as he took her injured hand into his warm palm. The finger had already begun to throb.

"Can you wiggle it?"

She did.

Lifting her hand to his mouth, he placed a soft kiss on the swollen distal phalanx. "I'm sorry your wimpy little finger got hurt when it smashed into my big manly chest."

Her jaw went slack. "You call that an apology?"

Shrugging, he said, "Well, if you'd let me keep

my points . . ." Before she could elbow him in the gut, he reached up and cupped her cheek.

"Claire," he whispered, looking deeply into her eyes. "I'm sorry. I didn't mean to hurt you. You going to be okay?" In his hand, hers felt warm and safe.

Examining the tender digit, she said, "The interphalangeal joint's a bit swollen, but I don't think the phalange is fractured." She looked up at him. "I won, you know."

His arm around her waist, he smiled sadly down at her. "If it makes you happy to delude yourself into thinking you won, then I concede. But if we'd played longer, I would have beaten the pants off you." His eyes took on that smoky quality again. "Figuratively speaking, of course. Let's get you inside and put some ice on that finger, Dr. Hoops." He smirked. "Or would that be Dr. Oops?"

Between the ice, the gauze bandage wrap, and the ibuprofen, Claire felt comfortable. The swelling wasn't that bad, and the sprain seemed minor. Mostly, she was embarrassed she'd injured herself during a silly backyard basketball game.

God, men were *so* competitive.

She sat in the living room, watching the weather report, her hand resting on her stomach. The kitchen door swung closed, and a moment later Taylor settled down beside her on the couch.

Evening had mellowed into a soft summer night, and a breeze wafted through the open windows, brushing Claire's cheeks. Even though her finger still throbbed, she felt more content than she had in years. Being with Taylor like this was familiar, even fun, and very, very appealing.

He slid his arm around her shoulders. "This wouldn't have happened if you'd acknowledged my athletic superiority and let me keep my points. You are so *competitive*." He sent her a wry smile, and when she raised her chin to tear into him, he kissed her.

And she forgot al-l-l about tearing into him, verbally anyway.

The moment his lips touched hers, desire flared deep inside her. He pulled back and looked into her eyes, then kissed her once more, cupping her breast in his palm.

"You're cheating again," she accused against his mouth. "Don't know how to play fair, do you . . . mmm?"

His tongue slipped inside her mouth, touching hers, coaxing. Easing her arms around his neck, she kissed him back, letting him do with his hands whatever he wanted.

And what he apparently wanted was to get her naked.

In seconds her blouse was open, her bra unclasped, and Taylor's warm, wet mouth was on her, licking, suckling. She felt her head spin as hard need took hold of her.

"Tell me what you like," he whispered as he bit the lobe of her ear. "Tell me what you want." His thumb rubbed her nipple, flicking it, sending a frisson of sensation throughout her body.

"Listen to me," she panted. "Please. I have to tell you . . ."

He pulled away, but said nothing, apparently waiting for the blood to return to his brain so he could comprehend that she was speaking. Finally, "What?"

"I had fun with you today," she said, her voice low and husky. "I enjoy your company—"

"Same here."

"But . . ."

He eyed her. "But we're not going to have sex," he finished for her. "Are we?"

Irritation and desire heated her blood and she smacked his shoulder. "This is about more than sex!"

He let out a sigh. "Well *that* confirms it. We're definitely not having sex." The look on his face was one of frustrated resignation.

"Not until we talk about it."

His lips quirked. "So we *are* going to have sex, but not until you talk it to death first."

"My God. You make open, honest, adult communication sound so—"

"It's okay. I pressured you. My bad."

"Taylor," she pleaded. "This *is* about more than sex. If I sleep with you again, I . . . God, I *hate* to admit this, but I'll fall for you. I like you way too much as it is, and I know myself well enough to know that making love with you would push me over the edge."

His mouth flattened. "Hmm. That would be terrible. I can see your dilemma."

"No, you don't understand!"

"Why in the hell are you so pissed? You're off the hook. No sex." Letting his gaze drop to her bare chest, he stared at her a long time, then murmured, "Sorry. You're on the hook again."

As his lips closed over one sensitive nipple, Claire let her head fall back, and she softly gasped. It had been too long since she'd made love, and her body was screaming for release. She felt her muscles tighten as desire warmed her to the core, making it difficult to push him away.

But she did.

"Okay, fine," he panted, resting his forehead against hers. "No sex. I get it. But you're sending me mixed messages here, Claire. You always have, and I need to know why. I think it's time you told me the truth."

Taylor moved away from her, distancing himself from her body, mentally preparing himself for whatever she had to say. His own body was practically convulsing with sexual energy, but he wasn't fool enough to think this conversation would have a gratifying outcome . . . no pun intended.

Women. They had to talk everything into the frigging ground. This was probably going to be about her needs versus his needs, her job versus his job, how a relationship between a busy doctor and a busy cop could never possibly work. Hell, he thought, they liked each other. A lot. Why couldn't they just sort of go with that and see where it led?

Licking her lips, Claire kept her eyes averted. "We've never shared family histories. It didn't seem important. The night of the wedding was . . . well, I never expected a relationship to come of it." She shot him a glance. "Did you?"

"Go on," he growled. Like he was touching *that* one with a ten-foot pole.

She took in a deep breath. "When I was a kid, we lived in St. Louis for a while. That's where my father was from; my mom was from here. Anyway, there were the four of us—Mom, Daddy, Zach, and me. We're twins."

"I see."

"Daddy was a police officer. He worked nights so he could spend more time with us during the day." Her eyes grew damp, her voice soft. "I remember saying good-bye to him that night. Just like any other night. But there'd been a thunderstorm and the streets were hot and wet and smelled of musty pavement. There were some kids riding their bikes. Old Mrs. Tully across the street was tending her roses, trying to keep them from wilting in the heat."

She swallowed, swallowed again, then closed her eyes. "I was asleep when the phone rang. I came wide awake and felt frightened. My heart beat so fast, it was like I'd been running from a monster. I don't think my heart has ever beaten so fast since."

Taylor's own heart crimped inside his chest and he turned toward her. "I'm . . . I had no idea. Claire, I'm so sor—"

"My mother screamed, you know," she continued softly. "She actually screamed. It was a long, high note that scraped along the edges of my brain, like the groove on a record album. I can replay the sound whenever I want, and sometimes when I don't. In the movies, a scream of shock and grief always seems so dramatic and overwrought, but when it's real, it seems too small, not nearly protest enough against the loss of a life. But my mother screamed, and I knew."

Reaching across the enormous chasm that suddenly gaped between them, he touched her cheek, slick with hot tears.

"Losing him like that," she said, "destroyed my mother. She died less than a year later. That's when Zach and I came to live with Aunt Sadie. She felt Hollywood wasn't a good place for a couple of grief-stricken teenagers, so she gave up her career, moved back here to the farm, and took us in."

"I can't imagine how terrible losing your father like that must have been."

"There's more. Zach . . ." She stopped, curled a lock of hair over her ear. "Zach followed in Daddy's footsteps. All the way down the line."

His eyes narrowed on her. "Meaning . . ."

"Meaning, he left Port Henry when he was twenty to join the St. Louis PD. Partly to honor Daddy, partly because it was all he ever wanted to do, to be. A police officer. Five years ago, he was shot during a routine traffic stop. The bullets did a lot of damage. He survived, but he's in a wheelchair. He will be, forever."

Silence thickened between them as her words sunk in.

"Jesus, Claire," he said, not entirely sure how to respond to the tragedies that had changed the course of her life. "I don't know what to say. I'm so sorry."

She finished buttoning her blouse. "The night you and I were together, I didn't think about the consequences of becoming involved with a cop. But the next day, it hit me hard. The truth is, I'm on the verge of falling for you, and if we keep seeing each other, kissing, if we make love, I'll go over. I can't afford to do that."

Of course, her story had only made him want her more, want to hold her, reassure her, comfort her. He was a very careful man and would not be hurt or killed in the line of duty, but since there was no way he could guarantee that to her, he'd only look like a fool making that kind of promise, especially when she had every reason to doubt it.

"Yeah, okay," he said quietly. "Yeah, well, I hear you. I mean, I haven't been divorced all that long. I'm not ready for any kind of *relationship* relationship. We can, well, we can just . . ."

By the front door, the grandfather clock chimed nine times. Agatha strolled into the living room from the kitchen, curled up on the footstool, and closed her eyes. Outside the open window, crickets played their creaky tunes.

Taylor battled within himself, not knowing how he should feel about Claire's news. Since he'd met her, she'd been a presence in his mind whether he'd wanted her there or not. The night he'd made love to her, he'd thought . . . Ah hell, what did it matter now what he thought, what he felt?

Pity mixed with anger in his gut. He'd nearly fallen for a woman who didn't want to have anything to do with him, and the fact of it was, he couldn't blame her. But, shit, if he'd only known sooner, he wouldn't have let himself—

A boom of thunder echoed through the hills, rattling the windows. Claire's eyes widened, Agatha looked up sleepily from her bed on the footstool.

"A thunderstorm?" he mumbled. Rising, he went to the window and pulled the curtain back, peering into the darkness. "Not a cloud in the sky. Some kind of explosion somewhere?"

The breeze ruffled the curtain, and he thought he caught the faint scent of smoke. Turning to Claire, still sitting on the couch, he said, "You smell anything?"

Wiping her eyes, she shook her head. He went to the kitchen and pushed the door open. Through the open window, he thought he saw a light flicker in the distance near the barn. Flinging open the back door, he stepped outside onto the porch. An unnaturally rosy glow shone through the slats of the ancient barn as smoke curled from the open window to twist like pale snakes around the branches of the overhanging evergreens.

"Claire!" he yelled over his shoulder as he began running toward the building. "Call 911! The barn's on fire!"

Arson
Not our daughter.

Chapter 13

He sat behind the wheel of his car, waiting. The summer had been a hot one, the barn was old; it would ignite like wood shavings on a campfire. Tender tinder. Ha. That was funny.

Somehow, he knew he should feel bad about what he had done, but hell, with so much at stake, he really didn't have a choice. She'd driven him to it. If she'd just seen reason, this little tragedy could have been avoided. Women. You couldn't live with 'em, and you couldn't kill 'em. Well, you could . . .

How long would it take the candle to do its

job? he wondered. An hour? Less? He wasn't an arsonist by trade, but he was pretty sure his gimmick would work; no reason for it not—

Whoa, he thought, jumping a little in his seat as the explosion caught him off-guard. There it went. Not bad. Not bad at all. Sort of like a clap of thunder or the pop of fireworks on New Year's Eve.

He yawned, stretched his arms, thought about all the trouble she'd been.

Plan A hadn't worked worth a damn. Running her off the road, leaving her stuff in the kitchen. Maybe Plan B would turn the trick. Maybe burning down her barn would light a fire under her, so to speak. From the moment he'd met her, he knew she was an independent sort. She'd need a reason to lean on a man, so he'd give her one. A woman in peril would always look to a man for strength. It was simply the nature of things.

Too bad he couldn't see the barn from where he'd parked, but he didn't want to be anywhere near the scene when the fire department and cops showed up.

He checked his watch. Not too late to call.

Pulling out his cell phone, he punched the autodial.

"Hello?" The young voice was soft, sleepy. Joy bloomed in his heart at the sound of it.

"Hi, sweetie," he cooed. "It's me, Dad."

There was silence for a moment, then "Oh."

He was used to her lack of enthusiasm. It didn't hurt. Well, it did, but he'd learned to steel himself against it. Besides, it wasn't the kid's fault. Brenda had done a top-notch job poisoning his kids' innocent minds against him.

"It's really late, Daddy. I was sort of asleep."

"I'm sorry I woke you, hon," he said. "I didn't know what time it was. Say, your birthday's coming soon, isn't it? I have a great surprise for you."

"Okay. Like, can I go now, Daddy?" There was a rustling sound as though she was putting the phone down.

"No, wait, wait, honey," he urged. "Don't go yet. Don't go."

Silence for a moment, then a soft "Okay."

He swallowed, grinned. "You know, it won't be long now, until you and your brother can come and live with me."

"But we live with Mommy, and—"

"I know you do, baby. I know." Sure, the kids lived with their mom. And why not? As the daughter of a wealthy businessman, she'd had money to buy the best lawyers in Portland while he'd barely scraped together enough to hire some yokel just out of law school. And the lies she'd told; he'd lost his kids because of that bitch's vicious lies.

"Wouldn't you like to live with me someday?" he said, trying to keep the hurt from his voice. "I'm working on it, honey. Daddy's working on that real hard. Pretty soon I'll have more money than your mom, way more, and the court will give you back to me. And the best part is, I'll have a new wife, a new mommy for you, and, guess what? She's a *doctor*. There's no way the court could ignore me then."

He heard the bitterness in his own voice and worked to mask it. "Won't that be fun, for you to live with us? I know you miss me as much as I miss you."

A quiet yawn, then "Can I go, Daddy? Mommy said she'd take my cell phone away if she caught me talking to you again. Anyway, we're moving soon and I don't think my phone will reach Europe."

"Wh-what?" He blinked rapidly and tried to collect his thoughts. "Europe? What in the he— What are you talking about?"

"Mommy's boyfriend is a zecutive or something in England." She yawned again. "He's going to be my new dad and we're moving there."

"When?" His voice was a stunned whisper.

"I don't know. Like two weeks or something. Can I go now?"

He swallowed. "Sure, thing, hon. Sure. I'll call

you again real soon, okay? Real soon. Give my love to your brother and tell him—"

But she'd already hung up. With shaking fingers, he pushed the cell phone back into his pocket.

Wiping the tears from his eyes, he forced his nerves to calm. His kids, his world, his fucking *everything*. All he was doing was for them. She couldn't take them away now. She couldn't! He'd get them back. Two weeks? Europe? No! No way!

He punched in Brenda's number, anger choking him. It rang two times, four, seven, ten. No answer. The auto voice mail droned out its usual bullshit.

"No!" he croaked over the recording. "Answer, you bitch. *Answer!* You're not taking them, you hear me? I'm getting them back! They belong with me! I . . . They belong . . ." His voice trailed off into a choking sob.

Ending the call, he gripped the phone in his hand, strangling it, squeezing the life out of it, picturing his ex-wife's neck.

Damn, life was unfair! His kids belonged with *him*. His little girl missed him, he could tell. She longed for him to come and get her and her brother, take them away from their wretch of a mother. Two weeks? He rubbed his temples.

He'd have to escalate his plans. He was close to having all the money he needed, the prestige, the clout. The courts couldn't deny him then. He could file before Brenda left the country. He'd get a court order, stop her. She couldn't take his kids to Europe where he'd have virtually no chance of getting them back!

As he wiped the sweat from his forehead and tried to calm his frantic thoughts, he heard the sirens coming up the hill.

By the time they got here, the damage would be done . . . not so much to the barn—though he expected it to burn to the ground—but to Claire's confidence.

Breaking down a woman's resistance. That was the name of the game. By the time enough bad things had happened to her, she'd be desperate for a real hero.

He got excited inside just thinking about it. He *would* win. There was still time. So much could happen in two weeks. His kids weren't lost to him, not yet anyway.

He felt his anger boil higher. He'd meant to step in the night he shoved her off the road, but that cop car had shown up and he'd been forced to hightail it. Christ, why was it there was never a cop around when you needed one, but when you didn't want one, the bastards always showed up too soon? Life was a riot, it really was.

He'd wanted to be the first man she saw when she came around, offer her his support, hold her hand, let her see the concern in his eyes. Concern, for her. Women loved that shit.

But he'd frightened himself a little, too, that night. He'd almost pushed too hard, and she'd nearly gone into the ravine. That wouldn't have been good. She'd have been too messed up, if she survived at all, to be any good to him. She was beautiful, an exquisite trophy. Scars on her face would never do. She might just as well have died, if that had been the case.

He was certain her finding her stuff inside the farmhouse would add another shock to her system, but she hadn't been alone then, either. That psychotic prick handyman patient of hers was with her.

But the barn fire, now, that would be different. While he couldn't just show up while there were firemen milling around, he'd go see her tomorrow. She had to still be reeling from the car accident, the break-in, and now the fire. She'd need a big, strong man to take charge, soothe her fears, show her she could depend on him.

I need you, she'd say, and he would stay by her side, show her how much he cared, how important she was to him, toppling any resistance. She would trust him, rely on him, and he wouldn't let her down.

He'd offer to help her take her mind off things, maybe go for a drive in the country, just the two of them. And she'd go because she wanted so much to be with him.

His eyes closed, he let the moment unfold. Her gaze would soften, and so would her heart. She would see him for the bold knight he was. She was basically weak, as were most women. They needed to be shown strength and then they would acknowledge it.

Claire was a real prize. He wanted, no, he *deserved* her. And she was a doctor, a respected member of the community. With his newly acquired fortune and his impressive doctor wife, the courts would be forced to reconsider the custody decree, and give him back his kids.

He let out a slow breath and smiled. His stomach unknotted and his shoulders relaxed. What with this new development with Brenda, he'd have to move quickly, but he could do it. He was nothing if not flexible. In the end, he'd get what he wanted. His heart ached to see his kids again. His arms felt empty. There was no way he'd let some other man take his place!

Claire was a hard one to pin down, but he'd made his choice and she'd realize soon enough they were meant to be. A true power couple. Heads would turn, jaws would drop. She was stunning, and on his arm, they would reign.

He scrunched down in his seat as the fire truck roared past, going up the hill. *Good luck, boys*, he thought. *Hope you brought some marshmallows, because that's all you're going to get for your trouble.*

He cranked the key in the ignition and headed slowly down the hill, back to town.

Yeah. He'd invite her for a drive, meander on out to the woods, show her how sorry he was for all her troubles. And then, when they were alone and she trusted him completely, he would make her his.

And if that didn't work, there was always Plan C.

By the time the Port Henry Volunteer Fire Department arrived on the scene, the fire was out.

Taylor surveyed the blackened interior of the barn. It was charred, but the walls and roof were still intact, soggy as hell, but sound. He smiled up into the rafters at the pattern of galvanized pipes hanging overhead.

"An automatic sprinkler system," he murmured.

Next to him, Claire said, "Grandpa was a very smart man. This is a wooden barn, filled with hay. If you look up the word *combustible* in the dictionary, there's a photograph of this very barn."

He grinned into her eyes. "Is there now?"

Her lips tilted. "I'm almost sure of it."

Their eyes stayed locked for a moment, then she looked away.

Gesturing to the pipes, she said, "Grandpa would be proud to know his hard work and foresight paid off."

Much of the smoke had dissipated, but the acrid stench of burnt wood and metal would cling for weeks and months to come. Through the haze, a man in a yellow slicker, helmet, and shroud approached them. He'd flipped up his Plexiglas face shield. The letters printed on his hat spelled out Captain Al.

"Here's your culprit, Detective," he said, holding out a blackened metal can—what there was left of it. "Smell that? Barbecue starter fluid. Probably stuck a lit candle in, then when it burned down level with the liquid, she went off."

"Not very sophisticated."

"Strictly amateur all the way," Captain Al said, "but effective. If the sprinklers hadn't engaged, you'd have lost more than just that old wheelbarrow."

Claire sucked in a quick breath. Her eyes widened as she searched the dark, smoky barn.

"Grandpa's wheelbarrow?" She looked like somebody had just cleaned out her bank account and fled to South America.

The fireman gave her a sympathetic nod. "Sorry, Doc." To Taylor, he said, "The arsonist set the can on a bale of hay to make sure the fire got a good start. The wheelbarrow was the only casualty, though. All the honey equipment in the adjacent shed is just fine. Gonna smell bad forever, though."

"Thanks, Cap," Taylor said, taking the burnt container from the fireman's gloved hand. "Do you have any idea how long ago he might have set this up?"

Captain Al rubbed the stubble on his chin. "Can's about ten inches. A taper just a bit taller would have given him thirty minutes to be somewhere else. Taller candle, more time."

Taylor nodded. So, while he and Claire had been playing basketball and discussing her family tragedies, somebody had set fire to the barn. Shit, right under his damn nose. God, that irked.

With his arm around Claire's shoulders, he walked her back to the house where Aunt Sadie sat in the rocking chair on the porch, her pink terrycloth robe wrapped tightly around her tiny frame.

"What'd they say?" she asked, her normally rosy cheeks pale, her eyes wide with worry.

"It was arson, Aunt Sadie," Claire offered. "But the good news is, Grandpa's sprinkler system saved the barn, and the trees, and probably the house."

"They know why?" she asked, her voice trembling. "I don't understand. Who would do such a thing?" The old woman tightened the robe and clasped her hands over her stomach.

"Not yet, ma'am." Turning to Claire, Taylor said, "Stay with your aunt. The scene's been badly compromised, but I still might be able to find something."

Claire glanced out across the yard as the fireman were busy coiling the hoses, loading up the truck, preparing to leave. "There's a big flashlight hanging on the wall by the fridge. Wait a sec, and I'll get it."

As the heavily laden truck lumbered up the gravel drive, Taylor flicked on Claire's flashlight, and began making a slow circle around the barn. He wouldn't find any usable prints this close to the building, but he might get lucky a little farther out.

Circling around to the back of the barn, he let the light play over the broad expanse of ancient wood. Then, *bingo*! A small door, still slightly ajar, led into what looked to be the tack room.

He shone the light onto the dirt just outside the door and found what he was looking for. Shoe prints. Not big boots like the firemen wore, not sandals like Claire or Aunt Sadie might have, but shoes. He followed the trail into the rhododendrons and azaleas behind the barn. Though he lost the prints amid the undergrowth, he kept climbing, crawling up the embankment, until he emerged onto Puget Road.

Wiping his hands on his jeans, he looked up and down the deserted road. The sides were grassy, not soft dirt as he'd hoped. But about a half a mile down, his patience paid off. More shoe prints, and—yeah, baby—tire tread.

As he walked back to his truck to get the glop he needed to make impressions, he let the facts assemble in his head.

First, Claire had been run off the road, probably by a black SUV. She'd been robbed, and her stuff positioned inside the farmhouse. An investigation of the kitchen had turned up a light-colored hair not belonging to either Claire or her aunt. The aunt in question had recently ended a relationship with a man the police were currently investigating, a man who drove the aunt to an isolated place where she'd seen a black SUV. Tonight, someone had set fire to the barn. But if he'd wanted to kill either or both women, why the barn? Why not the house?

Which woman was this guy after? What in the hell would he try to pull next? What exactly did he want, and what was he willing to do to get it?

GI Series
Baseball game between
teams of soldiers.

Chapter 14

"Have you changed your mind yet and decided to marry me?"

At the sound of Adam's voice, Claire looked up from her desk at the hospital. Her smile wavered. Adam Thursby was probably the last person on earth she expected to see today.

"Adam. Hello. Um, please come in."

Rising, she moved a short stack of file folders from the guest chair next to her desk and set them near her computer.

As he dropped heavily into the vinyl-padded

chair, a grin tilted his lips. "You haven't answered my question."

He was dressed in tan slacks and a white shirt with the sleeves rolled up. Perfectly groomed and gleaming, he looked as if he had just stepped off the jet from Palm Beach. "I overheard two nurses talking at the reception desk. They said there was a fire at your place last night." He leaned forward to touch her hand. "Are you all right?"

Claire nodded, withdrawing her hand and placing it in her lap. "I'm fine, Adam. It was just the barn, but the sprinkler system kept things from getting out of control until the fire department arrived."

His chin edged up a notch. "So the old barn's still standing, huh? Well. That's great." Smiling, he picked at a piece of lint on his pants.

With a quick glance at her watch, she said, "Listen, I'm a little short on time, Adam. Maybe this isn't—"

"The time to repeat my marriage proposal?" His eyes glittered with interest, and something else that struck her as being a bit deeper, and not quite as friendly.

She swiveled her chair to face him directly. "I gave you my answer at dinner the other night, Adam. I'm very flattered, but no."

His smile widened. "My fault. Sorry. I rushed you. But I'll keep the ring warm and we can take things a little slower if you like."

She swallowed, licked her lips. Why was he pressing so hard? "It's not that, Adam. I don't want to hurt you—"

"Not a problem," he interrupted, his tone just short of being sharp. He bent forward, resting his forearms on his knees. "I-I realize I was taking a risk by asking you to marry me so soon, but you have to understand, when I see something I want, some*one* I want, I'm afraid if I don't make my move right away, I risk losing out." He took a deep breath, as though he was preparing to deliver a speech. "Maybe I should explain a few things. Maybe once you hear me out, you'll change your mind."

She shook her head. "Adam, I don't think—"

"Remember my kids?" he rushed, his tone on the harsh side. Reaching for his wallet, he flipped it open. Two adorable faces smiled at her, both with blond hair, both with shining gray eyes.

"They're beautiful, Adam," she said, and meant it. "How old are they?"

"Crystal's almost ten, and Josh is eight," he said, his voice filled with pride. "They miss me as much as I miss them, if that's possible. Why, when I call, it's all I can do to get them off the phone. They adore me."

Turning the wallet in his hand, he gazed down at the photographs.

"I lost them in the divorce, you see," he said. "My ex-wife made up all kinds of lies about me. Horrible things. The judge believed them and granted her full custody."

"I'm sorry. I know how that must hurt."

He ran his finger around the edge of the picture, across the clear plastic, gently, as though he were caressing his daughter's cheek.

"Hurt?" His voice shook and his fingers trembled as he closed the wallet and thrust it back in his pocket. "Life is nothing to me without my kids. I can call them, but I can only see them once a month. And while Brenda has them at her mercy, she's been polluting their minds and hearts against me." His eyes sought Claire's.

"And they live in squalor," he continued. "Brenda takes my child support payments and squanders it on clothes and parties, jewelry, drugs for all I know, while the kids barely have enough to eat. Their clothes are rags. I'm worried about their health, their safety."

Claire's brow furrowed. "Surely there's something you can do. If the children are being neglected . . ."

"That's why I need you, Claire."

She sat straight up and blinked. "Me? What can I do?"

"You can marry me." He looked like a starving animal being teased with a morsel of food, a treat he would not be granted unless he performed the right trick. In the back of Claire's mind, warning bells began to chime ever so softly. "I have money and prestige," he said, "but I don't have a wife and home. You are smart and beautiful, a doctor. That would go a long way in influencing the court to grant me custody."

Claire shook her head and pulled away as much as she could. "Adam, I don't see how—"

"It has to be soon, though," he warned. "That's why I rushed you the other night. I'm so sorry. But you see, Brenda's getting married again. In just a couple of weeks. I've met the guy. He's . . . he's mean, brutal. He doesn't like kids at all. Crystal and Josh will suffer from living in the same house with him. He's sure to abuse them. So you see, I *must* get them back. I *must* convince the court to grant me custody."

Claire swallowed past a painful lump in her throat.

"I . . . I have to go, Adam," she murmured, shaking her head. "I'm terribly sorry for what you're going through, but I can't marry you. I'm sure if you talk to an attorney and explain—"

He jumped to his feet, startling her and nearly overturning the vinyl chair. His fists balled at his sides, he glared down at her, his eyes burning with fury.

"Can't marry me, Claire," he charged, his voice thick with emotion, "or won't. Time is running out, don't you see? Don't you *see*?" he pleaded. "Please, Claire. For God's sake, help me. Help me rescue my kids. *Please!*"

She had to get out of there. Adam Thursby appeared to be a man on the brink. His body shook with rage and his eyes stabbed her with accusation, and suddenly, she was afraid of him.

"I have to go," she said and brushed past him, feeling an enormous sense of relief when he did nothing to stop her.

Walking quickly down the short hallway to the reception desk, she tried to compose herself by looking over a chart, any chart—for all the good it did. She was so upset, she didn't see a word on the damn thing, but holding it helped buy a little time to settle her nerves.

When the door opened and closed behind her, she didn't look up. A moment later, through the open window on the other side of the waiting room, she heard the sound of a powerful engine revving in the parking lot. Adam's car sped by the window as he turned onto the street, tires squealing, the engine gunning. She listened until the sound faded into the distance.

Why did she feel like such a failure? Her heart ached for him, knowing now what he must be going through. There had to be some avenue he could pursue to ensure the safety of his children, or even be granted custody. Marrying her certainly wasn't the answer.

Adam was a physician, a well-respected orthopedic surgeon, at least, he apparently had been in Oregon. What kind of accusations had his ex-wife made that would prevent such a successful man from being granted at least partial custody of his own children? The woman must be horrible.

Claire let her gaze rest on the window while the scene in her office replayed in her head. Adam's behavior had been markedly different from anything she'd seen from him before. While his change in demeanor could be attributed to the fear and desperation he felt about getting his children back, still . . .

Before she could think more about it, Sally Beane, one of the volunteer nurses appeared at the door.

"Ready for you, Dr. Hunter," she said, handing Claire a pastel blue folder.

Claire gathered her thoughts and pulled herself back into the moment. "Um, great, Sally. What have we got?"

Sally was a cheerful brown-eyed brunette of forty-something. Perennially dressed in her own personal uniform of white sneakers, blue jeans, and a white knit top under a floral lab coat, she was a terrific nurse with a sweet nature.

"Second bed," she said. "Thad Kleinman, age twenty-two. Was in a fight a couple of days ago. Thought it was just a bruise, but he decided to come into the ER in case it's a cracked rib."

Claire flipped to the next page in the chart. Nodding absently as she read, she said, "Okay, I'll check him out, probably send him down to X-ray."

As she slid back the drape, she recognized Thad Kleinman as the waiter they'd had at Vittorio's, the one who'd accidentally spilled wine on Adam.

"Well, hello again," she said with a smile. "What happened to you?"

He sat on the edge of the bed, one arm wrapped around his middle. When he saw her, his eyes narrowed and his mouth flattened. Anger flaring from his hazel eyes, he said, "You were with him. Don't you know?"

What did that mean? "Know what?"

"Your boyfriend," he sneered. "Trapped me in

the john. Sucker-punched me in the gut. Told me if I said anything, he'd cut off my dick."

Two thoughts collided inside Claire's brain. The first was . . . *Adam? Adam attacked a kid in the restroom? That's not possible.* But the second was . . . *Adam. Adam attacked a kid in the restroom. Yes. He did.*

A week ago, she wouldn't have thought so, but now . . .

Her mind went to the scrapes and bruises on Adam's hand after he'd returned from the men's room. Dear God, was he capable of such brutality, simply because a waiter spilled wine on his shirt? The accident hadn't even been the boy's fault.

"I'm . . . I'm so sorry," she said with what little breath she had in her lungs. "Please believe me, I had no idea. Listen, you need to report this to the police. He shouldn't be allowed—"

"No way, Doc," the boy said, shaking his head, bending over the arm that still clutched his gut. "He's a big guy and he meant business. I like my dick right where it is, thanks."

"Thad," she argued. "If Adam assaulted you, you have every right to press charges. Think about it while I examine you and get X-rays, okay?"

While the young waiter was in X-ray, Claire tried to contact Taylor, but only got his voice mail. "Call me or come by the hospital when you get a chance, please." Then quickly added, "Police business."

As she slid her cell phone into the pocket of her white lab coat, she tried to fit the pieces of the puzzle that was Adam Thursby into some kind of picture that made sense. He'd always been considerate and solicitous of her, but since she'd refused his proposal, his demeanor had darkened considerably. And now this. Assaulting a mere boy, punching him in the abdomen, and then lying about it.

He said he'd scraped his hand on the bathroom door. An outright lie, if Thad Kleinman was to be believed, and why would *he* lie?

When Sally approached her with another file, she decided to set the matter aside until she saw the results of Thad's X-rays. If he went ahead and pressed charges, he might possibly need police protection. She wanted to talk to Taylor before anybody did anything.

Handing Claire the file, Sally said, "Ramon Sierra. Complaining of chest pains. I checked his vitals. Pulse is seventy, BP one-twenty over sixty. No fever." She gave a small shrug. "Seems basically healthy. Oh, and he speaks very little English."

Ramon Sierra raised his head and gave Claire a shaky smile when she entered the room. According to his chart, he was thirty-two, single, a migrant farm worker with no family in the area, no job at the moment, and no insurance. Sally was right, he looked fit and healthy, and since people who were sick generally looked sick, she took it as a good sign.

"*Hola*, Mr. Sierra," she said with a smile.

His head bobbed. "*Hola, Doctor.*"

She went to the sink and washed her hands. When she turned to him again, she placed her hand on her own chest. "You have pain here? *Dolor*?"

"*Si, si.*" He nodded enthusiastically, placed his fist against his chest and spoke in rapid Spanish. Claire's own hit-and-miss Spanish wasn't nearly good enough to follow everything he said, but she got the gist of it.

"Okay," she said, reaching for her stethoscope. "*Intente relajar*. Let's take a listen."

From the corner chair in the waiting room, Taylor watched Claire walk with a patient toward the reception desk. She was talking softly to him, while he nodded and flicked worried glances at her face.

Next to Taylor, a little girl coughed, and her mother helped her blow her nose. Near the front window, an elderly couple held hands and discussed the man's prostate problem in voices loud enough to reach the nosebleed section of Safeco Field from the pitcher's mound. Classical music played in the background, and a woman standing at the front desk, filling out paperwork, tapped her heavily ringed finger in time. The small waiting room was filled to near capacity, and Taylor wondered how long it would be until Claire was free.

He saw her touch her patient's arm and obviously say some encouraging words because he shifted his stance, clutching a piece of paper in one hand and a brown paper bag in the other.

Taylor had loved once before, badly. He intended to do it right next time . . . *this* time . . . this woman, if she'd let him. But he needed to find a way past her barriers and that might take some doing. After all, there was nothing he could say, no guarantee he could make to convince her what had happened to her father and brother would not happen to him. Hell, he didn't know what the future held, but, watching her now, he knew what he wanted it to hold.

She kept her hand on the man's arm, guiding him to the reception desk as she spoke. The click of computer keys reached him across the room as the receptionist checked the computer to schedule a follow-up.

Catching the patient's eye, Claire bent her head and explained something to him, reassuring him. She was completely focused on her patient's needs; at that moment, nobody else existed in the world for her.

Dr. Claire Hunter was good at her job; he should know. When he'd been her patient a year ago, her attention to him and his care had been a hundred and ten percent. He'd not only come to admire her, he'd fallen pretty hard for her. She was attractive, dedicated, sincere, strong. It was one alluring package.

Yet, strong and capable as she was, she'd gotten tears in her eyes at the news her grandpa's wheelbarrow had been destroyed. Imagine that. Crying over a junky old wheelbarrow.

Any woman who could cry over an ugly-assed wheelbarrow, *and* beat him at basketball, he wanted in his life.

His heart pinched as a smile crept across his lips. Yeah, *this* woman. Forever, if he could manage it.

At the reception desk, the patient nodded once more, and thrust the paper bag he held into her hands. She took it, thanking him.

As the man walked to the exit, Taylor stood. It was then she saw him.

Her expression altered as he moved around the magazine rack to come and stand facing her. The smile she'd given her patient changed into something much brighter, sweeter, much more personal. Her eyes gleamed as she looked at him with a mixture of wariness and anticipation.

She started to say something, but he cupped her face in his hands and kissed her—and he didn't stop until he heard the receptionist giggle.

He pulled away, but their lips clung. It took another quick kiss to free them.

Grabbing his arm, Claire hurried him out of the room, away from the curious faces of the patients, and down the hall into a cubbyhole office.

When she let him go, he pulled her close and kissed her again.

Squirming, she took a step back. "You've got to stop doing that!" she groused, but she had a half grin on her face when she said it.

Instead of responding to her remark, he gestured to the bag. "Urine sample?"

She laughed. "I hope not." She opened it and peeked inside. "Ooh. Mexican chocolate. Ever had it? It's delicious in coffee."

"Your patients give you food?"

She set the bag on her desk. "We occasionally get a patient who has no insurance and no money. Even though we never turn anyone away, they feel obligated to bring us something in exchange for their care. Eggs, jams, homemade bread, produce, whatever they grow or farm. In summer, it's strawberries or corn; in spring, it's cherries; apples in the fall." She blinked and averted her eyes for a moment, then said, "There's something I want to discuss with you."

"I don't like the sound of that."

"It's not what you think. It involves a patient."

"Okay. Let's hear it." He took the chair next to Claire's desk and eased his legs out in front of him, shoving his hands in his pockets.

She sat down and tossed the brown bag of chocolate onto her desk. "The patient claims to have been assaulted. Punched in the abdomen, but he's afraid to go to the police for fear of repercussions. What's your advice?"

Taylor mulled this over for a moment. "What kind of repercussions?"

"The man threatened to cut off his dick if he told anybody about it. The kid's young, and scared to death of this guy."

"Any witnesses?"

"N-no." She averted her eyes.

He cocked his head. "Was there a witness or not? What aren't you telling me?"

She licked her lips and picked up a pen from her desk. Twirling it between her fingers, she said, "Nobody saw the actual assault. However, a witness did notice later that the man's knuckles were scraped and bruised. He said he'd banged them on a door."

"When did this happen?"

"A couple of days ago."

He narrowed one eye on her. "You're still not telling me the whole story. What are you holding back, Claire?"

Tossing the pen onto the desk, she said, "It's not my story to tell and unless the patient decides to press charges, I can't break doctor-patient privilege. I simply wanted to know what his options are."

"I don't like grown men who beat up on kids," he growled. "The boy needs to contact us. We'll investigate and we'll protect him. Tell him that."

She nodded, nibbling on her lip the way she always did when she was thinking. "I'll see what I can do." Swiveling in her chair, she said, "Another thing. It's about Adam."

Oh. Him. "What's Dr. Dingleballs done now?"

She didn't snap at him as she usually did when he called Thursby names. Curious.

"Well, he came by unexpectedly a while ago, and . . . to make a long story short, our conversation ended badly."

Sitting straight up, he said, "What does *badly* mean? He didn't try to hurt you, did he?"

Claire's brown eyes widened. "Oh, no. Nothing like that. But what he said concerned me very much. He's divorced and lost custody of his two young children and they seem to be in an unhealthy situation with a reckless mother and potentially dangerous new father."

"Shit, that's horrible."

"I agree."

"I mean, that pompous dickhead actually found some woman to procreate with?"

Claire's mouth flattened. "Taylor—"

"I'm not being insensitive," he rushed to assure her. "It's just that I can't stand the guy. But the kids, that's not cool at all. Where are they?"

Taking out a pen, she picked up a scrap of paper from the desk and wrote down as much information as she knew. Handing it to Taylor, she said, "Could you just do some unofficial checking? If the children are in any kind of danger, the authorities need to be notified."

He shoved the paper in his pocket, then said, "I'll see what I can do. In the meantime, I'll be back at five to pick you up."

"What if I don't want to be picked up?"

"How's your little finger?"

She wiggled it at him. "All better."

"Good," he said. "I'm demanding a rematch. And this time, I'm going to beat your pants off for real."

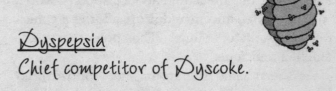

Dyspepsia
Chief competitor of Dyscoke.

Chapter 15

As the day wore on, Claire took a break to pour herself some coffee. It was nearly four in the afternoon, but if she didn't get some stimulation soon, she'd literally drop in her tracks. As she lifted the steaming mug to her mouth, she remembered the Mexican chocolate, and glared at the oily liquid in her cup. The carafe had obviously been simmering away for a while; maybe a little chocolate would turn the bitter to sweet.

Going down the hall to her office, she opened the bag and took out the red-and-yellow metal canister.

Mexican chocolate was strong; a little bit went a long way. She measured about a spoon's worth into the coffee and mixed it up, adding a generous amount of sugar. The potent mixture smelled delicious.

As she inhaled the aroma, her mind drifted back to Thad Kleinman. His X-rays had been clear; his ribs were sore, but presented no fractures. The kid was tougher than he looked. She'd written him a prescription for pain meds and referred him to a private physician for follow-up. To her disappointment, he'd decided against pressing charges.

Damn. She was riding a fine line here. Thad wasn't a minor; if he didn't want to contact the police, there was nothing she could do about it. If she said anything to Adam, he'd know the boy had spoken to her and—difficult as it was for her to believe—might actually seek some kind of revenge on Thad.

And then there was the problem of Adam's children. If he was capable of harming a waiter over spilled wine, she wondered how he'd interacted with his kids. Maybe the wretched ex-wife wasn't so wretched after all. Maybe she was protecting her kids from their own father.

What a mess. In any case, she was well rid of him and was thankful she'd never become romantically involved with the man.

Absently, she lifted the coffee mug to her lips.

"Dr. Hunter?" Sally peeked around the door-jamb. "We have a child out here with a lacerated knee. Looks pretty deep. You want to check her out before I suture?"

"Is that who's screaming?"

Sally's mouth quirked. "Quite a set of lungs on that one."

Claire set the cup on her desk. "Sure. Let's see if we can calm her down." Glancing longingly at the liquid caffeine, she silently promised to come back soon.

A few minutes later, she returned to her desk. The little girl's injury had been superficial after all, and a cherry-flavored Tootsie Pop had gone a long way in soothing her hysterics. No muscle tissue or ligaments were affected, so Claire let Sally finish up.

The mug wasn't quite so steamy as when she'd left it, but that was okay. As she went to take a taste, her desk phone rang. She shifted the cup to her right hand and answered the phone.

"This is Dr. Hunter."

"So, you are there!" Betsy rushed. Her voice held an undercurrent of relief mixed with worry. "Are you okay? Why didn't you tell me about your run-in with some road-raging lunatic?"

Claire set the cup on the desk.

"It's been hard to take a breath," she said. "I

wanted to call you, but it's just been one thing after another."

"You're all right, though."

"I'm good."

"I hear you're working closely with Taylor."

"Yes."

"How closely?" Betsy said in a low, sultry voice.

Claire chuckled. "Not *that* closely, you pervert."

"Damn." Betsy let out a long, weary sigh. "And I'm not a pervert. If anything, I'm a voyeur, except I wouldn't be voyeuring anything but simply using my imagination while you describe your encounter in explicit detail."

"There is no encounter to describe."

Betsy snorted. "It's just a matter of time. He'll wear you down. I have faith in the McKennitt charm. Hey, tell me about the investigation."

As briefly as she could, Claire explained about the truck incident and break-in, Aunt Sadie and Mort, the barn fire, and how lucky they were the only casualty had been Grandpa's dear old wheelbarrow.

"Now that I've brought you up to speed, how are you feeling, very pregnant lady?"

"I'm tired all the time," Betsy grumbled. "The baby's good, though. I'll be glad when this phase of our little production is over. Soldier looks at me like I'm a hot air balloon loose in a cactus farm and am going to explode any second. And I want my old bladder back. And I want my husband's arms to go all the way around me, like before, instead of his fingertips barely touching at my spine."

Claire picked up her coffee. The mug was cool in her hand. "I'm still planning on taking next week off to help you finish up the baby's room," she said. "Did you see? Harbisson's is having a big sale on newborn stuff."

Betsy chattered on about the baby, the supplies she still needed, the cute little pink booties her mother had bought. As Claire listened, enraptured by her friend's delight, she brought the mug to her lips. Tepid. Well, what the hell, she thought. Scalding or Siberian, caffeine was caffeine. With a little smile, she took a swallow.

Taylor closed his laptop and shoved it into its case. Finally, they were making some headway. *Some.* Not *lots*, but you took your leads where you found them.

They knew the SUV that had run Claire off the road was black. And Sadie had seen one when she was with Mortimer. As luck would have it, the tire tread Taylor picked up after the barn fire was standard on late-model Excursions. However, while Mortimer owned a Caddy and two other vehicles, none of them was an SUV.

It was enough, however, for Taylor to connect the dots and form one big squiggle. The picture itself would come later, but it would come; he was sure of it.

He set the laptop case behind the seat of his truck and glanced at his watch. Almost time to pick up Claire at the hospital, but first he had to make a quick stop at the art supply store. Leaning across the seat, he reached into the glove compartment and retrieved the photograph he'd gotten from Sadie that morning. Just looking at the damn thing made him smile. He studied it, making a mental note of the colors he needed, then slipped it into his laptop case.

Twenty-five minutes later, tossing the plastic bag from Art's Art Mart next to his laptop, he checked his watch. Almost five. Perfect.

Entering the hospital through the sliding double doors, he stopped at the reception desk and asked for Claire. The woman behind the computer screen lifted her head and blushed.

"I remember you from this morning," she said, her smile toothy and white. "I suspect she's down in her office just waiting on you." Then she snickered.

He nodded his thanks and headed down the hall.

The door was slightly ajar, so he tapped on it and pushed it open. Claire sat hunched over her desk, her back to him, her head down. One hand was extended as though she was trying to reach the phone but didn't have the strength to pick it up.

"Claire?" he said, moving into the room, alarm rushing through him like a cold tide. "Claire? Are you sick?"

Turning her head, she lifted her eyes to his, but before she could speak, she brought up the wastebasket gripped in her other hand and buried her face in it. He slid his arm around her shoulders, steadying her. She felt fragile, as though a stiff breeze could topple her.

When she'd finished, he let go of her for a moment, rushed to the open door, and yelled into the hallway. "Hey! I need a nurse in here. Now!"

Returning to Claire, he crouched beside her chair. "Try to take it easy. Got some towels coming."

"Thanks," she choked.

Her voice was weak, her balance unsteady. How in God's name had she gone from perfectly healthy six hours ago to this?

A nurse appeared in the doorway. "Is something—"

"Wet towels, please," he ordered. "And use *warm* water."

The nurse took one look at Claire, nodded, and scurried away.

Turning back to Claire, he said softly, "Is there some kind of virus going around?"

She shook her head. "Don't . . . think so."

"Can you walk okay? I'll take you home."

He was becoming more worried by the minute. She looked like hell. Her skin was pasty and her hands trembled. Her lovely brown eyes were rimmed with red and she held her stomach as though she'd been stabbed. Oh, God. She was going to retch again. This time, he held the wastebasket for her.

"Not . . . home," she managed. "Get ER doc for me, pl-please."

She looked up at him, and he saw it then for what it was. The light in her eyes, normally so bright and lively, was weak and dull, gone sleepy and glazed, almost as though it was on the verge of going out.

She was in pain. It didn't seem possible a person could be the picture of health in the morning and deathly ill in the afternoon. This couldn't be an ordinary virus.

The nurse returned, bearing a handful of wet cotton towels. She tried to move past Taylor to help Claire, but he grabbed one from her hands, slipped his arm around Claire's shoulders, and gently wiped her swollen mouth, tossing the towel on the floor when he was done. With a clean cloth, he stroked her forehead, trying to soothe away the pain.

"If I got you some water, could you keep it down?"

In his arms, she felt so fragile. His heart tightened in fear. Had she been exposed to some virulent strain of the flu? Was this some kind of food pois—

His brain stopped functioning. Words and images clicked into place. "Did you drink that Mexican chocolate?"

She nodded weakly as two more nurses rushed into the room and began tugging at him, trying to force him away from her. But he held his ground.

Whispering, she begged, "Don't . . . let anybody else . . . Toxic . . ."

"Where is it now? Claire? Hang with me, baby. *Where is the chocolate?*"

She swallowed and pointed to her desk drawer. "Ingested . . . hour ago . . . only a teaspoon . . ."

Too weak to finish her sentence, she collapsed into his arms.

"Hey," said a warm voice in the dark. *Him. Him. Yes, always him. Only him . . .*

Claire rolled her head in his direction. "Hey, yourself," she rasped.

"How you feeling?"

She blinked up at Taylor, working him into focus. Even shrouded in fuzzy fog, he was beautiful.

"Alive," she chuckled softly.

As she shifted a little to get more comfortable, she became aware he was holding her hand. The fit was so perfect, she hadn't realized they were touching.

Palm to palm, they were connected, the circuit complete. His warmth, energy, his passion for life coursed through his body and into hers, reviving her, giving her strength. His thumb circled the back of her hand in soft, lazy circles.

Leaning forward, with his free hand, he smoothed her brow. The caress was familiar, intimate, reassuring. He smiled into her eyes, and she felt her resistance dwindle like rainfall after a summer storm.

Curling her fingers around his, she gave his hand a gentle squeeze.

He bent and placed a kiss on her mouth.

When he finished, she put her fingers to her lips. "I'm sorry. I must have stinky breath."

"I don't care." He slipped a lock of her hair over her ear, then settled back into the chair. His eyes went serious.

"It was morphine, in the chocolate," he said. "Narcotine to be exact. Another couple of hours, and the antidote wouldn't have worked. You're going to be okay, Claire."

"My knight in shining armor, yet again," she whispered.

"Bad habit. I know how youse broads like to save yourselves these days."

"I won't hold it against you, Detective."

She scooted up a little and he handed her a plastic cup. Taking a few sips of water, she let the cool liquid ease down her parched throat.

"Did you get any prints off the container?"

"No such luck. He'd wiped it. There were none on it but yours."

"That's too bad."

"Not really," he grinned. "Criminals are stupid. He wiped the container, but he forgot about the paper bag. Ramon Sierra, real name Paul Fuentes, has been a very bad boy. He has a sheet a mile long, including a sealed juvie record. I've got a warrant out on him. The next time he comes out of his hidey-hole, we've got him."

She took another sip of water. "But why would he poison me? He doesn't even know me."

Taylor brought his chair closer to her bed and slipped his arm across her stomach. She liked the weight of it, the heat. She felt secure, protected, and, all things considered, it was a very good feeling to have.

"Three reasons," Taylor said. "One, he's

weird. Two, somebody put him up to it. Three, both. My guess, it's our SUV guy. And it appears our SUV guy has access to morphine, and knows what dose to administer to obtain the desired results." He rubbed his chin with his free hand. "Have you pissed off any medical professionals lately?"

Claire closed her eyes. It was not possible, made no sense at all, but she couldn't ignore reality. Denial wouldn't get anybody anywhere.

"Actually, I have," she said quietly. "Adam."

"Dr. Dickbreath?" he snorted. "Tell me why?"

She averted her eyes. "Because he asked me to marry him, and I turned him down."

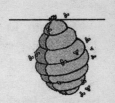

<u>Congenital</u>
Very, very friendly.

Chapter 16

Taylor stared at Claire, her remark scattering his brains like beans in a blender.

"He asked you to marry him." He squeezed her hand, just to make sure it was still there.

"Yes."

"But you turned him down."

"Yes."

"And he got pissed." He rubbed his thumb across her knuckles, enjoying the softness of her skin—and the fact he was the one holding her hand and not . . .

"Enough to want to hurt you? *Poison* you? That's pretty radical, even for Dr. Numbnuts."

She relaxed back against the pillow. Closing her eyes for a moment, she said, "I'm probably being unfair, maybe jumping to conclusions, but I've recently come to suspect he may be capable of violent behavior, when he feels provoked."

Images, words, gut instincts, experience . . . all clicked and snapped inside his skull. "Thursby's the one who assaulted that kid you were talking about, isn't he."

"I didn't say that."

She didn't have to. Her eyes told the truth even if her words were designed to protect her patient's rights and privacy.

"He still doesn't know I'm a cop, right?"

"I haven't said any—"

"Claire!" At the sound of Thursby's voice behind him, Taylor sat straight up and twisted in his chair.

In the dim light of the room, the two men locked gazes.

Thursby blinked and slid his eyes away, hurrying to the other side of Claire's bed. He fumbled for her free hand, but the IV she was hooked up to made things difficult, so he shoved his hands in his pockets.

Glaring at Taylor, he said, "Would you kindly excuse us, McKennitt?"

"No." Taylor settled back into his chair, Claire's hand still resting comfortably in his.

Obviously flustered, Thursby said, "I'd like a private word with Claire."

Taylor shrugged. "Take a number, pal. I had first d-d-d-d-d-dibs."

Adam eyed Taylor, but said nothing.

"Listen," Taylor said. "The tox report says somebody laced Claire's chocolate with narcotine. You wouldn't happen to know anything about that, would you?"

Thursby's sharp gray eyes narrowed. "No, I wouldn't." He turned his attention to Claire. "Is that what it was? Narcotine?"

She nodded.

"Dear God," he whispered. "If you hadn't gotten the antidote in time . . ." His voice trailed off and he looked with pitiful eyes at Claire. "I'm sorry. It . . . must have been painful."

Taylor watched Thursby like a hawk watches a rat. "You know a guy by the name of Ramon Sierra, aka Paul Fuentes?"

Thursby's gaze slid from Claire to Taylor. "Who?"

"He's the guy who gave Claire the poison. Used the name Ramon Sierra, but the cops lifted a fingerprint from the bag he'd used to carry it. Apparently, this Fuentes has a long criminal record."

"Is that a surprise?" Thursby laughed. "I guess anybody who'd try to poison someone would probably be the criminal type, now wouldn't he."

"So, you know him, or what?"

"Hell no, I don't know him."

"Taylor," Claire said softly. "I'd like to talk to Adam privately." Her cool fingers curled around his palm as she gave his hand a gentle squeeze. "Please?"

"I think I should stay," he mumbled.

"Just for a minute."

Reaching for the call button, he placed it in her hand. "I'll be right outside the door."

He wanted to kiss her—right in front of Thursby—but that would be so juvenile.

Bending, he placed a soft kiss on her mouth.

Hey, he could behave like an immature jerk if the situation called for it.

He felt Thursby's gaze on his back all the way to the door. Just as it closed behind him, a wild-eyed Aunt Sadie rushed off the elevator, nearly knocking him down.

"Where is she?" she choked. "Is she all right? Who did this horrible thing to her?"

A heartbeat later, Betsy stepped out of the

other elevator, Soldier right behind her. Taylor moved the whole herd into a small waiting room across the hall, and explained what had happened.

"But is she all right?" This from Betsy, who was holding her giant tummy with both hands. "Was there any permanent—"

"No, not at all," he assured her. "She received the antidote in time, and can go home tomorrow. They tell me she should feel much better within just a few hours."

"Thank God," Sadie sobbed, holding a handkerchief to her swollen eyes. Betsy slipped her arm around the old lady and gave her a gentle hug.

Taylor heard Claire's door open, so he checked the hallway. Thursby was stomping down the corridor like an unhappy ogre. Good.

"Why don't you two go on in and see Claire," he said to the women, "while I have a word with my brother."

Running in that hour before dawn always made Taylor feel like he was the only living man on the planet. Before him stretched a dark ribbon of road, his to conquer. It rose in places to challenge him, curved to entice him, flattened to let him catch his breath. The steady rhythm of his footfalls changed depending on the surface. Asphalt smacked the bottom of his feet, spiked blades of grass on soft earth absorbed the sound, making him feel like he was flying through the stratosphere. The brittle crunch of gravel, when he happened upon it, annoyed him, and he hurried to find a smoother, more eloquent voice to keep him company.

Running before dawn gave his brain a chance to unfuzz after a hard sleep, or revive when rest had eluded him. His mind worked best just after a run, his lungs having pumped out inertia, sucked in new energy for the menial or monumental tasks that lay ahead.

Running before dawn let him smell the leftover night, damp from the sea, and briny. The fragrance of wood chips in a rose garden reached him, evoking the memory of when he'd been a kid and pushed open the heavy lid of his mother's old hope chest, to breathe the mellow scent of cedar for the first time.

Running before dawn, pain and pounding fell away until only movement remained.

He licked his lips, salty from his own sweat, salty like Claire's kiss when she cried. He licked his lips again, because it brought her there with him, next to him, inside him.

Grabbing the square of towel stuffed in his waistband, he wiped his face and neck, running, and running, the sound of his breathing like a saw through ice.

He'd posted a police officer outside Claire's hospital room; she was safe and would stay that way until they sorted this mess out. It pissed him off that he couldn't approach Thursby directly. If the man *was* involved, knowing the cops were sniffing around would blow everything. The creep would go to ground and they'd lose him. With no hard evidence, they had nothing to hand the DA.

When he reached Harbor Street, Taylor made a sharp left, slowing his pace. One twenty-seven was a two-story white clapboard three doors up on his right. Dark, like all the other houses in the neighborhood, like all the other houses in Port Henry at four in the morning.

Across the street and down, somebody's dog launched into a high-pitched yap fest. Little dog, from the sound of it. Good alarm system, irritating all the same.

In front of Taylor, a streetlamp bathed the pavement with a bright circle of light. Skirting it, he approached the property. No car in the driveway. Staying in the shadows of the tall boxwood hedge lining the drive, he eased himself toward the garage. No window on the door.

Crouching, he examined the cement driveway for tire tread, but it was still too dark to make anything out. He had a penlight in his fanny pack but wouldn't use it until he was ready to leave.

The house was leased, but the interesting thing was, the lease was month-to-month at Thursby's request. Not exactly the kind of thing a man would do if he expected to bring his two kids to live with him, as Claire had mentioned. And why lease? Why not buy? The good doctor seemed to have plenty of money.

Silently, he approached the kitchen door. Working quickly, he unzipped his fanny pack, removed the powder and brush and dusted the door handle and around the frame, using tape to pick up four latent prints. Of course, no evidence he collected could be taken to court, but they might get a lead on the guy's real name—if his prints were in the database. According to the report Taylor received late last night from the Portland PD, Adam Thursby had indeed been a highly respected orthopedic surgeon, well known in his field, and well loved in the community—right up until the day he died seven years ago at the age of ninety-one.

It had been three days since Claire was poisoned. Her stomach muscles weren't sore anymore, her stamina was beginning to return, and she had eaten a full meal at dinner—always a good sign.

She glanced at the bedside clock. Ten-forty P.M. Tomorrow, she and Betsy would hit the department stores, and she'd need to be fully recovered in order to ooh and ahh over tiny pink tigers, baby blue elephants, yellow duckies, and white lace bonnets.

Curling in on herself, she fluffed her pillow and relaxed into the soft mattress, wishing she wasn't alone in her bed. Ever since awakening in the hospital with Taylor beside her, holding her hand, she'd developed a deep-rooted yearning for him.

Maybe she was getting used to his being around, or maybe, as Betsy had warned, he was simply wearing her down. Either way, he'd become important to her in the way she'd feared he would, and now she didn't know what to do about it, about him.

But if he was here right now, the way she was feeling right now, right now would be the right time for—

The knock on her bedroom door stirred her from her thoughts. "Aunt Sadie? Come in."

"Not Aunt Sadie," came the husky reply. "Not even close. Can I still come in?"

Claire's heart skittered around inside her chest and her throat tightened. He was here, at her bedroom door. Even though her common sense was quick to insist that nothing really would happen between them, her hormones—open-ended and ready for anything—jumped into a happy dance of astonishing proportions.

She held her breath while the doorknob turned and the door squeaked open. He had a sheepish grin on his face, and his head was slightly bowed as though he was a kid about to make up some excuse for being caught where he shouldn't be.

"Aunt Sadie let me in," he said, closing the door behind him. "In fact, when she saw me, she practically grabbed my collar and yanked me inside." He cocked his head. "She didn't say it in so many words, but I think she likes me." He grinned, and by the light of the moon shimmering through the open window, Claire had to admit Aunt Sadie knew a good thing when she saw it.

He wore jeans and a black shirt under a short leather jacket. His lids were a little sleepy and he looked like he could use a shave.

Somehow, all the air in the room vanished, and Claire had trouble breathing. Her heart *thrum-thumped* rapidly against her ribs.

She felt her body begin to respond, and it was all she could do not to slide down in the bed, slip off her nightgown, and invite him to put his hands all over her bare skin.

"Why are you here?" she choked. "Have you made any headway on the case?"

Moving to the side of the bed, he took off his jacket and placed it on the back of her dressing table chair. Then he sat and began casually taking off his shoes. Her eyes followed his every move, but she was afraid to ask him what he was doing—afraid he wanted to spend the night with her, even more afraid he didn't.

"Got some prints we're checking out," he said, slipping off his shoulder holster and setting it on her dresser. "I can't tell you much right now. I'm hoping that tomorrow, we'll have some answers." Emptying his pockets, he set his wallet, comb, loose change, and handcuffs next to his weapon.

Why the sight of those items on her dresser made her insides quiver, she couldn't say.

"To answer your first question," he said, "I'm here to protect you." Yanking his shirt free of his waistband, never taking his eyes from hers, he began unbuttoning it.

"There's a guest bedroom across the hall." Amazing. She managed to say the words without mumbling or stuttering.

He removed his shirt and her mouth went dry. It turned to the Sahara when he unbuckled his belt.

"I'm not staying in the guest room," he murmured, sliding down the zipper of his jeans. In five long seconds, he was naked, the tanned perfection of his body making her hormones not only jump, but laugh and pound on the door, demanding to come out and play.

"We don't have to do anything," he said, walking toward the bed. "Not if you don't want to, and as cajoling guy-speak as that sounds, I mean it. I just want to hold you, Claire." He stood next to the bed, waiting. "I need to. Can you understand that?"

Maybe it was the look in his eyes, maybe the set of his jaw, or soft curve of his lower lip. Maybe it was the note of yearning in his voice— the same yearning she felt, if she was being honest with herself—that finally shattered her resolve.

Watching his eyes, she pushed the covers away and rose to her knees, reaching for the hem of her nightgown. Slowly, she inched it up her body, and off. In the moonlight, she saw his mouth twitch, among other things.

"You're right," she murmured. "We don't have to do anything. But I think—"

He had her in his arms, his mouth on hers, before she could finish the sentence. She eased onto the mattress as he settled between her thighs. He ran his hands over her breasts, and she kicked the covers down and off the bed, leaving only their limbs to tangle.

Taylor's kisses were deep and hot, just as she remembered. His tongue slid against her own, his hands moved around to grasp her bare bottom, pulling her against his erection.

By the time the first kiss was over, she was panting. So was he.

He trailed his wet tongue across her nipple, and his name formed on her lips. His rough hand slipped between her legs to rub and tease her, and even the most remote thoughts in her brain evaporated into a veil of pleasure.

Nuzzling her neck, he cupped her breasts, then lowered his head for another taste. He licked and suckled, teasing her nipples into taut peaks.

Claire felt like she was floating on a cloud of sensation. She nearly gasped at his every touch; her skin warmed in the wake of his gliding fingers.

Nudging her thighs farther apart, he moved so the tip of his erection pressed against her, taunting her, setting whorls of desire up through every part of her body.

Beneath her palms, his skin was damp and his whole body seemed to tremble. Sensing his deep need for release, not to mention her own, against his open mouth, she whispered, "Don't wait on my account."

Waving his arm over the edge of the bed, he shoved his hand into his jeans pocket, and pulled out the packet. Tearing it open, he sheathed himself, and with one smooth thrust, he was inside her, leaving her sighing with pleasure.

"Claire . . ." he murmured against her neck, softly repeating her name as he thrust into her until his breath was spent, and all she could hear was the rhythmic rasp of his shallow breathing.

He kept his movements slow, torturous, making her silently beg for him to get on with it. But he held back, knowing just where to touch her, how hard, how soft, when to kiss her, when to pull back, bringing her to a near frenzy of need. Curling her legs around his, she brought him closer, tighter until . . .

When her orgasm hit, she writhed and bucked under him, sighing his name, feeling the release in every muscle, every bone. Her head fell back and she let herself go, let herself feel, let herself fall.

Two more thrusts, and another, and Taylor came, rocking the bed as his orgasm overtook him.

They lay there together, arms and legs entangled, pounding heart to pounding heart, and smiled into each other's eyes. Leaning forward, he kissed her on the mouth, and his eyes went serious. "Thank you."

She wanted to say it, too, but her throat tightened, closing around the words until they died away. What in the hell was the matter with her? She wasn't going to cry, was she?

Taylor wound his arms around her, rolling until she was on top of him. Against her breastbone, she could feel the rapid beating of his heart.

"Hey, you're heavy," he chuckled, tucking a stray lock of her hair behind her ear.

"Am not," she said, sliding off him to cuddle against his side. She raised her hand and ran a fingertip along his bottom lip. "You kiss good. And everything."

He quirked a grin. "Yeah?"

"You must have practiced on thousands of women to perfect your technique."

Averting his eyes, he grumbled, "Not so many as you might think."

Right. With looks like his, he'd probably had too many girlfriends to count. He'd played sports in high school and college. No doubt, he'd had cheerleaders and pom-pom girls and every female in student government hot for him.

Claire looked more closely. Was he blushing? He *was*. She felt her heart give a little tug.

"Okay, like what, a thousand?" she chided.

He grunted.

"More?"

He scowled.

"Okay, less than a thousand," she purred. "Five hundred?"

"Five hundred?" He snorted. "I needed to eat and sleep, too, you know."

"Well, then, two hundred?"

He shook his head, avoiding her eyes.

"One hundred?"

Nothing.

"Fifty?"

He closed his eyes and turned his head away.

Her own smile faded as she looked long and hard at him. She tried to remember things he'd said about his ex-wife, things Betsy and Soldier had mentioned about her, but nothing was making sense.

"Twenty?" she said on a half laugh.

He slipped his arms from around her and sat up. Raising his knees, he crossed his arms over them and leaned forward, resting his chin in his forearm. "Keep going," he said quietly.

Claire rose slowly, yanking the quilt from the floor and covering herself with it.

"Fewer than twenty?" she smiled. "Wow, you must be very select—"

The truth smacked her in the face, halting her words, her thoughts. Her mind tried to wrap itself around reality, but it was a tight and uncomfortable fit.

Watching him carefully, she whispered, "One."

He shrugged. With a dry laugh, he said, "In the last year, I've doubled the score. How many men can say that?"

Claire's heart crimped into a tiny ball, and her

mind raced. But before she could apologize for intruding so thoughtlessly into his personal life, he spoke.

"I met Paula when we were both fifteen. She was my first. We got married right out of high school." His low voice held no inflection whatsoever. "I was faithful. She wasn't. When I met you, the ink wasn't even dry on the divorce papers yet."

Claire swallowed the bitter taste in her mouth. "And the night of your brother's wedding," she whispered, her voice choked with tears. "That was . . . I was only the second . . ."

Reaching for him, she put her fingertips on his bare shoulder, then scooted nearer until her body curved around his back.

The stubble on his jaw made a rasping sound as he scratched it with his thumb. "Paula slept around. She told me it was because I wasn't . . . enough . . . to satisfy her. After she and I separated, my brother told me I should cut loose, have a few flings, get her out of my system. But then I met you."

On his shoulder, her hand began to tremble. "Taylor. Since we . . . have you . . . have there been . . ."

He turned his head and looked straight at her. "No."

Tears slicked her face now, and she wiped them away.

"Me, too," she said, unable to keep the tears from her voice. "Since the wedding, there hasn't been anyone. Whenever I got close, I somehow couldn't . . . you were . . . I—I couldn't forget . . ."

She stared at her fingers, gone all blurry though her tears. "I'm so *sorry* . . . that morning, for leaving you like that. What you must have thought . . . oh, God. I'm so sorry . . ."

He turned and pulled her to him. She wrapped her arms around his neck as tightly as she could, burying her face against his chest, and let out a long sob.

"Oh, Taylor," she cried softly, her tears salty on her lips. "That night . . . I . . . my dearest friend married your brother. The look in their eyes as they spoke their vows. I've never seen two people more in love. I wanted that, wanted a piece of that somehow."

Taylor nodded and placed a soft kiss in her hair, but said nothing.

"The music," she went on. "The sweet romance of it all. The champagne toasts and happiness that permeated the place. Then I was in your arms and we were dancing and I felt like I'd found heaven on earth. I wanted to be with you in every possible way. I wanted to make love with you so I could take and keep a part of you, of that night with me forever."

Still, Taylor said nothing.

Dabbing her eyes with the quilt, she said, "I know it was probably silly and foolish and all one big deceitful fantasy, but it's what I wanted. And I was rewarded. That night with you was more than I could have ever hoped for. You were everything I'd ever dreamed of." She closed her eyes, afraid to look at him. "Then the night was over and reality set in and the music stopped playing and the romance had turned to truth and the truth was, I had to leave. Leave it all behind. Leave you behind. I didn't want to. But I didn't know how to tell you. I'm sorry. I'm sorry for everything."

"Hey," he soothed. "I understand now. It's okay."

She pulled away and looked into his eyes. "No, it's not. I was afraid of you, and I ran. You were, you *are* an awesome lover. What you do to me. How you make me feel. And to think you thought that I thought . . ."

"Think nothing of it." He chuckled. "I must have inherited the monogamous gene from one of my parents. I just haven't ever wanted flings. If I hadn't met you when I did, I probably would have caved. In fact, I probably would have caved as often as I could. A man has needs, after all." He slid her a sly grin.

As she placed a kiss on the corner of his mouth, his cell phone bleeped to life, and he cursed.

"Sorry," he said to her, reaching for his pants. "McKennitt." His spine straightened and his eyes narrowed as he listened intently to whatever the caller had to say. "I can be there in fifteen."

"What?" she asked as he ended the call.

Placing a soft kiss on her mouth, he said. "Gotta go to work. Get dressed. You're coming with me."

Coroner
Jogging partner.

Chapter 17

Taylor pulled his truck to a halt amid a PHPD patrol car, an aid unit, and the coroner's van. On the opposite side of the narrow street, a small crowd of curious neighbors huddled and whispered like children in a library.

Yellow tape surrounded the perimeter of the property, identifying the house as the place where death lived. He knew that, even after the tape was removed, the survivors and neighbors would never view the home in the same way again.

Switching off the ignition, he turned to Claire,

"Stay in the truck unless I send for you. Winslow said the husband's pretty shaken up. I might need you to take a look at him."

Claire nodded.

Leaning forward, he kissed her. "This may take a while."

"Go do what you have to do," she said softly. "I'll be fine."

Taylor met Officer Sam Winslow at the open front door of the post–World War II clapboard house. Marigolds had been planted around the perimeter, their yellow faces shiny and bright against the backdrop of death.

"What have we got?" As he spoke, he reached into his jacket pocket for his notepad.

Winslow frowned. "Vic's name is Mindy Ketterer. The husband, one Joseph Ketterer, found her about two hours ago. Caucasian female, age forty-two. Appears to have slipped in the tub, hit her head on the tile. Water was still running when the husband got home. Bathroom floor's flooded, living room carpet's soaked. Nobody else was home at the time. Very little blood."

Mindy Ketterer. Taylor knew the name, knew the woman was an employee of the mortuary, and was Mortie's personal secretary. Alarm bells went off inside his head and the back of his neck felt itchy.

Their whistle-blower had been an anonymous

female, and now Mortimer's secretary had had a fatal accident.

More bells, a few whistles, and a quiet *oh, shit* sounded inside his head.

Taylor lifted his eyes to meet Winslow's. "She slipped? I'm homicide. Why'd you call me in?"

Winslow's mouth quirked into an edgy smile and one eye narrowed. "Yeah, well," he said with a shrug. "Seemed like a straightforward accident at first, but I don't know. I've just got a feeling about this one. Wanted a pro to take a look at the scene before we wrap things up."

"Where's the husband?"

"The kitchen's already been photographed and dusted, so we put him in there for now. He's in pretty bad shape."

"What's your gut tell you. Did he do it?"

Winslow rubbed his nose. "My gut tells me no, but that could be just because I missed dinner."

Taylor made some notes. "The coroner have any ideas on time of death?"

With a nod, Winslow said, "Maybe four hours. She got another call, but said to tell you the body lying in the water made pinpointing time of death a little iffier. Said you'll get her report tomorrow."

"Thanks, Sam," Taylor said before making his way down the hall. Two aides worked just outside the bathroom door, carefully strapping

Mindy Ketterer's mortal remains to the stretcher.

Taylor nodded to them, then unzipped the body bag. Closing it again, he turned and peered into the small bathroom where a woman's life had come to an abrupt end.

Commode with a frou-frou pink cover on it, tub with shower, small window, open. Overhead light on. White tile floor saturated with water. Blue fingerprint powder smeared the tub and cabinets like bruises on pale flesh.

A pink floral shower curtain had been ripped from its rings as though somebody had made a grab for it. It lay like a vinyl shroud across the wet tile floor. A smear of blood on the porcelain sink indicated where Mrs. Ketterer might have hit her head. Another smear stained the oval rug in front of the commode where her body had come to rest.

Taylor viewed the scene with detachment. Not a lot of blood. Death must have been almost immediate.

He spent the next fifteen minutes looking around. Things seemed to be consistent with an accidental death, but damn if something just wasn't right. Maybe talking to the husband would help.

As he passed Winslow on the way back, he said, "Dr. Hunter is out in my truck, Sam. Would you escort her to the kitchen in a few minutes? Just make sure she doesn't touch anything."

Taylor found Joe Ketterer sitting slouched at the kitchen table holding a half-empty glass of water.

"Mr. Ketterer?"

The deceased's husband appeared to be a man of middle years, balding, whose beverage of choice was most likely beer, judging from the roundness of his belly. He wore a blue-and-black plaid shirt with the sleeves rolled up to the elbows, over a white undershirt. At the mention of his name, he raised his head but only stared vacantly into Taylor's eyes.

"Mr. Ketterer," Taylor repeated in a low voice. "I'm Detective McKennitt. Can we talk for a couple of minutes?"

Joe nodded. His tired eyes seemed to beg Taylor to be brief, beg for this all to end, for it all to be a huge mistake.

Taking the chair across the square oak table from the man, he said, "Things been okay between you and Mindy lately, Joe?"

Joe took a drink of water from the glass. "Okay?" he asked slowly, as though he were trying to recall what the term meant. "Sure."

"Did she seem nervous or upset about anything?"

"Not really."

"Can you think of anyone who'd want to hurt her?"

Joe's head reared up. "Hurt Min? No way. She is . . . she w-was a sweet woman. You ever know a sweet woman, Detective?"

Taylor nodded.

Joe took another drink, then set the glass down as though it were made of crystal so delicate, it might shatter if he wasn't careful. Running his finger around the rim, he said, "She did seem a little preoccupied lately, but she didn't say nothing. I just figured maybe it was her job, or, well, the other thing. She always gets kind of skittish just before she gets her . . . uh, her period, see. When we was first married, I didn't understand how all that stuff worked. But Mindy and me, we been married a long time now. Long time."

He looked away from Taylor to stare into the glass. "You get used to a woman's ups and downs, and it's okay, see, 'cause you know she's getting used to all your crap, too. You learn to cut each other a little slack. You know how it is."

"Yeah," Taylor said quietly. "I know how it is."

Joe picked up the glass, then set it down again, keeping his thick fingers wrapped around it. Without warning, a sob escaped his throat and he blinked hard several times. Looking into Taylor's eyes, he said, "Mindy, she's a fine wife. Caring. Real smart. We got a couple of kids. This is gonna hit 'em hard. Man, yeah. This, this is gonna . . . Min and me, we been together a long time. I tell you that already?"

"Yes, sir."

Joe nodded, then swiped his knuckles along his jaw. "Women like Mindy, they don't just die like this, do they, Detective? I mean, I kiss her good-bye this morning, and she makes some smart-ass remark about how I left my socks and underwear on the bedroom floor and didn't I know where the laundry basket was after all these years, and I go off to work thinking, yeah, yeah, I'll pick 'em up when I get home, if it'll make her happy."

Another sob worked its way to the surface and he pinched his eyes closed. "Min and me, we been together a long time. Once I seen her, you know, back in the day, she was the only one, you know? You married, Detective?"

"I was."

Joe seemed to not hear him. Nodding absently, he said, "I go out for a beer after work with some of the guys, and I get home, and there's water on everything, and I'm mad because I think the main's broke or something, and this is gonna cost me a shitload. Min's car is in the driveway, so I'm calling for her, pissed as hell. Then I go into the bathroom . . ."

He looked up at Taylor, his brown eyes rimmed with red, his mouth an open wound on his face. "I don't want to remember her like that. You know? I don't want to remember her like *that!*" His bottom lip quivered as another deep sob escaped.

"I'm sorry, Mr. Ketterer," Taylor said. "I have to ask you . . . had Mindy said anything about her employer, John Mortimer? Was she having any kind of trouble with him? Did she ever complain about him?"

"N-no," Joe said. "I didn't like the guy, and I thought Min working for an undertaker was kind of creepy, but it's a living, ya know? She liked him well enough, I guess."

"In the last month or so, did she say anything to you, anything at all about things Mortimer might be doing that could be considered improper? Did she ever mention contacting the police?"

Joe lifted his head, confusion plain to see in his weary eyes. "Like I said, she was nervous, a little more stressed out than usual, but if she thought Mortimer was doing somethin' under the table, she didn't say nothin' to me about it. What's that got to do with Min falling in the tub and getting herself dead?"

* * *

From the kitchen doorway, Claire silently watched Taylor talk to the victim's grieving husband, the irony of her position not lost on her.

She stood in the threshold, a nonplace. A few inches of space through which people passed, but seldom lingered, like the stillness between breaths, the silence between heartbeats. Never a destination, simply the passage to whatever waited on the other side.

Or the point of retreat.

She paused there, neither in nor out, emotionally teetering in that safe space between her two worlds. Behind her lay a carefully planned, thoughtfully arranged life. Ahead of her, a man, and everything loving him could bring. Maybe great sorrow . . . maybe great joy.

She could take a step toward that man, toward all he offered with his blue eyes and wry grin, his humor, boyish charm—and the crushing pain she'd feel if she lost him. The choice was hers whether to cross that threshold, go with him, see for herself what could be.

Or she could step back.

She closed her eyes and saw her brother in his wheelchair, her father's headstone, her mother's grief-stricken face. Barriers all, to Claire's happiness.

God, how selfish was that? And disloyal. And

disrespectful. If her mother were here, would she encourage Claire to follow her heart, or would she admonish her daughter for being so foolish as to fall in love with a cop?

Yet, even with the barriers between them, Taylor was the one Claire's mind turned to when she thought of a man capable of filling to the brim the remaining days and years of her life. It was his face she saw when she let herself drift into thoughts of partnership and family and fulfillment.

God knew she'd tried to suppress those thoughts, even as months rolled by without any contact with him. Yet, all it had taken was for him to walk into the room, call her name, and she was hooked all over again.

Claire watched as Taylor spoke in low tones to poor Joe Ketterer, so unexpectedly bereft of his wife, his own life's partner. And in watching Taylor struggle to help this poor man find some measure of comfort, she realized that, for the last twenty years, she'd been a complete coward. She'd feared a moment like this so much, she'd closed her eyes to any chance of real happiness. How did that old saying go? A coward dies a thousand times, a brave man only once?

She'd already died a thousand times— whenever she thought of her parents, whenever she dwelt on Zach, whenever she read in the newspapers of a police officer's death. They were invariably young, leaving a wife and small children. And she died another death because she knew exactly how much it hurt.

Taylor. *I'm sorry for your loss*, she heard him say, and the pain in his voice and the shadows in his eyes grabbed her heart in a fierce and powerful grip. And she let it.

Yes, she'd *been* a coward; maybe now it was time to be brave.

She must have made some kind of sound, for Taylor turned his head and looked straight at her. Their eyes met and held. Taking a breath, she waited a heartbeat and stepped through the threshold, into a brand new world.

"Officer Winslow said you wanted to see me."

Taylor nodded. "Joe," he said. "This is Dr. Hunter. I thought maybe she could prescribe something for you to help you get some rest tonight."

Joe lifted his gaze and stared at her.

"Would you like me to do that, Joe?" she said.

His nod was slow. Another hard sob escaped his throat and he looked at Taylor, then back at Claire. Convulsions overtook him as tears washed his face. He brought up a trembling hand to wipe them away.

"That might be good," he choked. "Min and

me, we was together a long time. I tell you that already?"

Sadie put Hitch back in his cage and secured the door.

". . . Attica! . . . Attica! . . ."

"Shut up, Hitch," she admonished. "You be a good boy now. You have plenty of food and water, and fresh air wafting in through the window."

". . . show me the money! . . ."

"I have some errands to run," she said, slipping her purse through the crook of her arm. "Claire will be home as soon as she and her handsome young detective are through on that case I told you about last night."

". . . I'll be back . . . hasta la vista, baby . . ."

"Yes, yes," she cooed. "You're a clever boy. Now shut up."

A few minutes later, Sadie locked the kitchen door behind her, and headed for the garage. Her keys jangling in her hand, she stopped when she heard a car turn into the driveway. A black Cadil— Mortie!

Oh, dear. Now what? Detective McKennitt wanted her to get information from Mortie, but over the phone. And now here he was, ambling down her driveway. Should she ask him to say? Ask him questions? Send him away?

As the car rolled to a stop, Sadie turned the situation over in her mind. This *was* the role of a lifetime, after all, and since Mortie didn't have the balls to hurt a turnip, she'd undoubtedly be perfectly safe, *and* be doing her civic duty at the same time.

So, when Mortie stepped out of the car, smiled, and said, "I'm real sorry about what happened, Sadie. How about coming for a drive in the country with me and we can talk about things?" there was nothing for it but to say yes.

By the time Taylor got Claire back to the farm, it was midday. They were both somber, both tired, but she could tell he was still wound up. So was she.

He parked behind Aunt Sadie's truck and turned off the ignition. Quiet surrounded them. Through her aunt's open bedroom window, Claire could hear Hitch softly warning Sadie she was going to need a bigger boat.

Turning to Taylor, she said, "I need to go for a walk. Care to join me?"

Without another word, she got out of the truck and began walking toward the pond. A moment later, Taylor fell into step beside her.

The air was filled with the heady bouquet of summer. The fragrance of roses and clover blossoms mixed with the boggy scent of the pond, as well as a touch of salt from the sea only a few miles away. Somewhere in the tall grass, crickets played their spindly tunes, while frogs, nestled unseen in the cool mud, sounded like a hundred basement doors creaking open and closed.

They stopped walking when they reached the edge of the pond where a slight breeze rippled the water's surface, splintering the sunlight into dashes and winks.

"You want to talk?" he said.

"Talk is good." She stared at the water. "About what?"

"About how much you like me."

Biting back a laugh, she said, "What on earth makes you think I like you, Detective?" Inside her chest, her heart picked up speed.

"C'mon. I know you like me." Out of the corner of her eye, she saw him grin sheepishly. "Is it because I'm so damn good-looking?"

"No."

"So much for my ego. Then is it because I'm so smart?"

"If you mean smart aleck, then yes, you're smart."

He pursed his lips and squinted at her. "I'm clever, if that counts for anything. I like that in me. And I'm honest and trustworthy."

"You sound like a German shepherd."

"Woof. Which reminds me. I love children and animals. And I like being the good guy."

Without turning to him, she said, "I've been thinking and I . . ."

Though he said nothing, Taylor moved closer to her. Cupping her shoulders, he turned her toward him, enveloping her in his arms.

He held her head to his shoulder while she slipped her arms around his waist. Letting her lids drift closed, she simply stood there with him, safe in his embrace while he rocked back and forth as though they were moving to the rhythm of a slow, slow dance.

Taylor, tall and stalwart and ever vigilant, her self-appointed champion.

She was a strong woman, had made tough choices and seen them through. She'd lived life on her own terms and gotten where she wanted to go. As fulfilling and satisfying as her career was, however, there was still the occasional empty space.

But now, standing like this with Taylor's arms around her, their bodies touching, his heat and energy swirling through her, those niggling little voids she'd been ignoring for years began to fill. The part of her soul that had gone for so long untended, maybe even unacknowledged, began to respond.

She raised her face to him, closing her eyes as he lowered his head and kissed her.

Soft, it was, and gentle, a mere touch of his lips on hers. He tasted of sweet and salt and Taylor. His arms tightened around her, and she moved into him, opening for him. His thumb grazed her cheek. He slid his tongue inside her mouth as his kiss became ardent, urgent, sending trills of pleasure up her spine and down . . . way down.

The breeze ruffled her hair, and he gently slid a wayward lock from her brow, leaving a wake of sensation across her skin. His hand trailed down her neck, and down, to cup her breast, and she moved closer.

Touch me, she silently begged.

But he didn't. He let his thumb circle her nipple, refusing it, tormenting her until her pulse went wild, her lungs begged for more air.

She molded her hand around his, trying to get his fingers to do her bidding. He refused.

Frustrated with desire, she broke the kiss and nearly stomped her foot.

"Hey, b-baby," he quietly chuckled. "You must be a broom, 'cause you just swept me off my feet."

She snorted a laugh and opened her mouth to give him a smart-ass remark, when he took her again, thrusting his tongue deep, sliding it along hers, stealing the breath from her body.

His hands moved quickly, popping the buttons of her blouse, shoving the fabric away. The garment slipped from her shoulders to fall behind her in the tall grass. He had her bra undone and off in less than a breath, then his rough hands were on her, cupping both breasts, lifting them, squeezing them. Her nipples ached for his touch, his tongue, his mouth, but still, he refused.

"Taylor," she begged. "Please . . ."

"C'mere . . ." He lowered her into the grass, cool, and sweet-smelling. The soft blades bent and bowed over them, enclosing them in their own little world. She let her lids drift shut. Sensation washed over her as he took one nipple in his mouth.

A flick of his tongue and she cried out from the pleasure. Between her legs, the throbbing ache felt delicious, and she silently pleaded for him to slide his hand inside her pants, touch her there, send her over the edge into delirious oblivion. She parted her legs and rolled her hips into his.

He kissed her once more, his mouth teasing her lips, sliding down the column of her throat, returning to her mouth. His kisses were wonderful, intoxicating. He was a master at the craft. Dear God, his kisses alone could bring her to orgasm.

In the silence of the meadow, he bent to her breast once more, tugging on the nipple, scraping it with his teeth, sending shards of desire through her body, sharp as glass, warm as honey.

Sliding her zipper, he eased her jeans and panties down her hips, and off. She was naked while he was fully clothed. She felt like a wanton wood nymph making love in a secluded glade, aroused beyond coherent thought, able only to feel, to experience, to respond.

She was so aroused, if he so much as breathed on her, she'd come.

Desperate to feel his skin, she tore at the buttons of his shirt, then pulled him down on top of her, reveling in the warmth of his hard muscles, his flesh on her, driving her insane with flat-out lust.

He moved down her body, and down, and down. Her brain ceased to function. All she could think about was where he was heading, what he'd do when he got there, what it would feel like.

And then, he was there.

His tongue licked her once, and her back arched. Every muscle in her body tightened and she dug her hands into the matted grass at her sides.

He licked her again, sending ripples of pleasure through her, and she sobbed his name. Through her delirium, she thought she heard him laugh softly.

She lifted her head to see, just as he pushed her legs apart and licked her once more. Her head dropped back and she felt the orgasm build. Afraid to move for fear the pleasure would end, she stiffened as he used his tongue against her, and she came, choking for air, crying his name.

Slowly, her body relaxed against the warm grass. She felt the sting of tears in her eyes as her heart thundered against her ribs. Her chest rose and fell in an effort to simply breathe.

He shifted, reached in his pocket, tore open the packet, and sheathed himself. Gently parting her thighs, he entered her in one long glide.

She clamped around him as he filled her, moaning his name. Desire began to build again, and within moments, she was on the brink once more, desperate for the release he'd give her. Desperate, now, to feel him go wild in her arms.

She curled her legs around his, bringing them tightly together, squeezing him, increasing the friction.

He made a low, groaning sound, slammed into her, then stopped. Panting, he bent over her, motionless. Another thrust. And another. He gasped for air and pounded into her one last time as his orgasm overtook him, making his breathing choppy, his words mere gasps of pleasure.

He collapsed on top of her, his mouth against her neck. His lungs were like bellows, fighting for breath.

Claire wrapped her arms around him and held him so very close. With one hand, she ran her fingers through his damp, silky hair, caressing him, soothing him.

They lay in the grass with the warm summer breeze blowing across their skin, lost in each other's arms. She wondered what he was thinking, but didn't want to break the magic to ask.

Taylor. Hers. There was no denying it. Being with him, lying wrapped in his arms, feeling his chest expand and contract with each breath, listening to the sound of his murmured words . . . her senses were attuned to him and had been since the moment they'd met.

"You're aware, aren't you," he said softly, "that you've just taken another step toward the Dark Side."

"I'm aware," she whispered.

"You're okay with it?"

She bit her lip, then snuggled closer. "I'm okay with it."

Raising his head, he looked down into her eyes, but said nothing.

<u>Illegal</u>
Large, sick bird.

Chapter 18

As the miles between her and Port Henry grew, so did Sadie's feelings of apprehension. She'd only agreed to go with Mortie so she could pump him for information, as the saying went, but in the whole time they'd been driving, he hadn't said two words to her! He hadn't even glanced her way, just kept muttering to himself, adjusting the rearview mirror, looking over his shoulder, like Bogey used to do when he was on the lam.

Wiggling in her seat, trying to get more comfortable, she watched Mort's fingers curl around the steering wheel in a death grip. He kept his bright rodent eyes on the country road, barely even taking the time to blink. And even though the interior of the car was cool, his face was all puffy and red, and sweat beaded on his forehead.

Irritated at his reticence, she cleared her throat. "What was it you wanted to say to me, Mortie? If you're going to apologize, it had better be good."

Flicking her a glance, he returned his attention to the road. "We can talk when we get there," he snapped.

"Where is *there*?"

His mouth turned down. "The place we was before. Where I took you that time I forgot my cell phone." He arched a brow. "You remember the place I'm talking about, Sadie?"

Inside her chest, her heart tripped over itself. *That* place. The place Detective McKennitt wanted her to find. That what-this-whole-thing-was-about place. Hot dog!

"Not really," she said breezily, not wishing to appear anxious. "I think I was asleep most of the time. Couldn't find it again if my life depended on it."

"Criminy, that's what I *told* him, goddammit."

Her brows lowered. "Told who? What are you talking about?"

They rounded a lazy curve in the road and the

scenery began to look vaguely familiar. Though they were surrounded by tall trees, to her right stood a thick stand of Douglas firs so dense, broad daylight didn't even penetrate. Mortie slowed the car. Was it her imagination, or was there a tall fence running parallel to the road, just behind those trees?

"Never you mind," Mortie snarled. He huffed out a short breath. "We're almost there. I'll tell you everything then." Reaching up, he swiped his damp forehead, then rubbed his palm on his pants.

"Are you ill, Mort?" Sadie said. Why on earth would the man be sweating bullets?

Flicking a glance in his rearview mirror, he muttered, "This is as good a place as any."

Mort pulled the car to the side of the road and into a small clearing under a canopy of fir branches. The car was surrounded by trees, their long limbs creating a living roof over their heads as she and Mort stepped out of the Cadillac.

The scent of evergreens mixed with damp needles and wild rhododendron was fresh and invigorating. Except for the drone of bees and the occasional chirp of a bird, the world was quiet.

"Are we going to have a picnic?" she said.

Mort was sweating like the pig he was and Sadie wondered if he was in the early throes of a heart attack. "This ain't no picnic, Sadie, and that's for damn sure."

He came around to her side of the car, and then she saw exactly what the problem was. A gun. In his hand. Aimed at her heart.

Oh, my.

"I need to take a shower," Claire whispered to Taylor as they climbed the stairs to her room. "Care to join me, *quietly*? Don't want to disturb Aunt Sadie."

At Claire's bedroom door, he kissed her. He felt like he was returning her home after the prom. He liked the feeling; he liked it a lot.

"I need to call in for the status of the lab tests," he said softly. "I'll go down to the kitchen."

Damn, he wished they had more time before the real world had to intrude. Pulling her into his arms, he kissed her hard, letting her know they had unfinished business. When he finally released her, she smiled up into his eyes, then quietly closed her bedroom door.

As he pushed the kitchen door open, he thumbed the autodial. A moment later, "McKennitt."

"Anything come in?"

"Hey, yeah, little brother," Soldier said. "I was just reading it over now."

Taylor heard papers being flipped and shuffled, and then, "Okay. Tire tread analysis. It seems the impressions you picked up after the barn fire are a match with BF Goodrich radials, the kind that come standard on SUVs."

The phone in his left hand, Taylor opened the fridge with his right. *Milk.* He reached for the carton. "Not a surprise. What else you got?"

"Mindy Ketterer was a homicide."

"Not exactly a surprise, either," Taylor said, hunting through the cupboards for a glass.

"Yeah," Soldier continued. "According to the autopsy, she had a skull fracture, but the violence of the trauma wasn't consistent with a fall. There were indentations on the back of her neck, like from fingers. Somebody grabbed her and slammed her head into the sink. No defensive wounds, no struggle. She died instantly."

Reaching into a cupboard, Taylor pulled out a clean glass and poured himself some milk. "So, somebody follows her home, does the deed, leaves the water running to obliterate trace evidence. By the time the husband gets home, his living room looks like the delta of the Mississippi River." He took a gulp of milk.

"Motive?"

Taylor set the glass down. "It's gotta be damage control. I'd bet even money she saw Mortimer's silent partner. Maybe even knew who he was."

"Winslow went by the mortuary this morning

to bring in Mort for questioning," Soldier said, "but nobody was there. Place is locked up. I put out an APB on him."

"Thanks." Dropping into one of the kitchen chairs, he said, "Anything on those prints?"

Soldier snorted. "Oh, yeah. Are you sitting down?"

"I just did, but I can do it again if it's that good."

"It is. We ran the prints and they popped up one Kevin A. LeRoy, age forty-two, last known address, Portland, Oregon. Arrested three times for wife battery. Served thirty days on one charge; the others were dropped. The now ex-wife has full custody of two minor children. LeRoy's allowed monthly visits in the presence of an officer."

"Sounds like a prize. Does he care enough to show up?"

"Never missed a session," Soldier said. "Apparently, he adores his kids and talks of nothing but getting custody."

Taylor leaned back in the chair and thrummed his fingers on the table. "Got a photo ID of this guy?"

"Hang on," Soldier said. "First, there'll be a little quiz. Twenty points if you can tell me what kind of vehicle he owns."

Taylor straightened. "SUV?"

"We have a winner," Soldier said. "He drives

an Excursion. Price tag of about fifty grand. Eleven feet across, nineteen feet long. Seats nine adults, five hundred bags of groceries, or ten thousand puppies. Forty-four-gallon gas tank."

"Christ, that sucker would shove a 747 off the runway, let alone an old pickup truck."

"Indeed. But wait," Soldier said, "there's more. For fifty extra points, you can answer our bonus round question."

"What a coincidence," Taylor drawled. "Fifty points is exactly what I need to get me that new toaster oven."

"I thought so," Soldier said. "On a hunch, I ran the DNA from the blond hair you picked up in Sadie's kitchen . . ."

"And it's a match."

"Could we have ourselves a silent partner?"

"And maybe Mindy Ketterer's killer," Taylor finished for him.

"Got your laptop handy?" Soldier said. "I'll e-mail you LeRoy's picture. Handsome bastard, I'll give him that. Blond hair, gray eyes. Don't care much for the sneer, though . . ."

Sadie stared at the gun in Mort's trembling fingers. The poor man's hands were so sweaty, she was surprised he could hold on to the gun at all!

She took a step back, just to see if he was paying attention. He was.

"Don't go nowhere, Sadie," he choked as he wiped sweat from his eyes. "I mean it. I h-have to do this, you see? Don't want to, but it's come down to you or me, and it ain't gonna be me."

Nodding, she kept her eyes on the gun. "Your crooked partner wants me dead, is that it, Mortie?"

He licked his lips and swallowed. "Yeah. Now, just stand there, real still. I just want to get this over quick, and don't want to mess it up." When he finally looked at her, his eyes had a sad sort of pleading quality. "Because if I mess up, you might suffer, and I'm just not that big a bastard, Sadie."

Taking another step back, she said, "You're not going to kill me, Mort. You can't." She wished she was sure about that, but she'd bluffed her way through auditions, maybe she could bluff her way out of death.

She took another step back. True, she was no spring chicken, but neither was he. If she could make it to the woods, she might have a chance, if he didn't shoot her in the back before she got that far.

Mort licked his lips again, and pulled the hammer back on the gun. "I told you to hold still!"

Taking another step back, she said, "And let you shoot me? I'm old, but I'm not stupid, Mortie. Besides, the police know all about you and your illegal disarticulations. Killing me won't do you a speck of good."

Over the barrel of the gun, his eyes widened. "Cops? The cops know? But how . . ."

His voice quivered. Putting his palm to his forehead, he let his gaze drop, and with it, his arm. Ah. Just the opening she was looking for.

Sadie turned on her heel and made a dash for the trees. Perhaps *dash* wasn't the right word, not with her hip being stiff and achy as it was, but hopefully fast enough to outrun a badly aimed bullet.

Just as she reached the first trees, she heard Mort yell after her. "Sadie? Where . . . Sadie! I warned you! Gadzooks, woman!"

But Sadie kept her eyes on the darkest part of the thicket. With her head down and her legs pumping, her purse strap firm in the crook of her arm, she trudged over the rough ground like a bargain hunter in search of the discount table at Bloomingdale's. Over snapping twigs and sharp rocks, through scratchy bramble and low branches that grasped at her sweater, she didn't so much as glance over her shoulder. Not when she heard him shouting curses. Not when she heard him come crashing through the bushes. Not even when she heard the gun explode . . .

* * *

Claire towel-dried her hair and quickly dressed. God, she was absolutely starving. Great sex would do that to a person, she thought, grinning to herself as she slipped into her sandals.

She was a little surprised Aunt Sadie wasn't up and about yet. The clock on the bedside table read ten-seventeen. Hmm. As long as Claire had lived with her aunt, Sadie had never been one to lounge in bed of a morning.

". . . no wire hangers! . . . no wire hangers! . . ."

"Damn. How am I gonna hang up my jacket?"

Claire turned to see Taylor standing in her bedroom doorway, a charming grin on his oh-so-handsome face.

"Yeah," Claire laughed, "he's really on a roll this morning."

Taylor cocked his head. "You'd think all that racket would wake up your aunt."

Claire nodded. "Yeah. You'd . . . think." In the back of her mind, tiny wheels began to slowly turn. "Her truck was in the garage when we got back, right?"

"Yes," he said, leaning his hip against the doorjamb. "Winslow has an officer doing a drive-by every thirty to forty minutes. He hasn't reported anything unusual."

" 'Kay," she said absently. "And the door was locked."

He straightened. "Does she normally sleep this late?"

Claire shook her head.

Backing out of her doorway, Taylor headed down the short hallway to Sadie's room. Behind the closed door, Hitch was screaming his birdy guts out.

". . . Detective McKennitt . . . that'll do pig . . . that'll do . . ."

Taylor snorted. "Little bastard's got quite a repertoire."

"Doesn't he though." Claire knocked on the door. "Aunt Sadie? Aunt Sadie, are you awake?"

With a quick look at Taylor, she turned the handle and slowly opened the door, sending Hitch to flapping and squawking in his cage.

The little room was neat as a pin, as usual. The bed was made, and the window stood open, letting in a cool morning breeze.

Hurrying to Sadie's bathroom, she knocked on the door, then opened it. Empty. A damp bath towel hung from the hook by the tub.

Taylor came up behind her. Turning, she placed her palms on his chest. "She was here this morning. There's still a little water around the drain in the bathtub."

"Maybe she's out with the bees."

Claire let her gaze flit around the room until it

came to rest on the chair in front of Sadie's dressing table, the empty chair.

"Her purse," Claire rushed, cold blood suddenly coursing into her heart, making her stomach cramp, her skin prickle. "She always sets her purse on that little chair."

"Stay here," Taylor ordered. "I'll check the house and property."

As he ran from the room and down the stairs, Claire felt panic thicken her senses. Sadie was here, somewhere. She must be. Nothing could happen to Aunt Sadie, *nothing*.

Pacing the room, Claire went over and over possible scenarios, but nothing she could come up with fit the situation. Sadie wouldn't take her purse to go check on the bees, or sweep the barn, or take a stroll down by the pond.

In his cage, Hitch paced back and forth along his perch.

". . . I see dead people . . . dead people . . . uh-oh . . ."

Sadie kept her head down, and her feet moving. Her knees felt like Jell-O—not like it was when you let it set overnight, but Jell-O after about an hour.

Another blast zipped past her, missing her by a mile. Handguns were notoriously poor weapons when it came to hitting the mark at a distance, especially in the hands of a Nervous Nelly like Mort. She'd learned that the time she did that guest appearance on *Dragnet*, by God.

Reaching the shelter of the thicket, she ducked down as far as her stiff back would let her, and veered off to the right, toward the road.

Another gunshot sang out through the trees, sounding much, much closer this time. In fact, it sounded like it came from a different direction altogether! Why, the old fart was faster on his feet than she'd imagined! She'd better get a move on if she expected to get out of this little predicament alive.

Scurrying through the undergrowth, she realized minutes had passed in silence. Instead of Mort's curses and gunfire, she heard the revving of an engine. A moment later, the squeal of tires filled the air as the Caddy left the glade and hit the pavement. Through the rough tree trunks that nearly obscured her view, Sadie could barely make out the black car tearing off up the road like the proverbial bat out of hell.

So. He'd gone and left her out here in the middle of nowhere, had he? Probably expected her to die. Well, she wouldn't!

Straightening her spine, she scoffed and turned, and ran smack into a solid wall of muscle and bone. She gasped for air as strong hands took hold of her arms.

Her first thought was that Mortie hadn't taken off. So who was in the car . . .

Raising her chin, she looked into her captor's face, and gasped again. Why, it wasn't Mortie a'tall.

"Hey, Sadie," he said, smiling down into her eyes. "You okay?"

"Fl-Flynn?" she muttered, on what little breath she had in her lungs. "Flynn Corrigan? What on God's green earth are you doing out here?"

Oh, my, she thought. *This could be very good, or very bad.*

Releasing her arms, he said, "You're quite a woman, Sadie Lancaster."

"I know. Now, what *are* you doing here?"

He shrugged, gently took her arm, and began escorting her back the way she'd come. "Followed you," he said. "I've sort of been watching your farm. When I saw you leave with Mortimer this morning, I trailed along behind. Good thing, too, considering."

"You followed us?" She narrowed one eye on him. "How come Mort didn't see you? He looked in the rearview mirror every two seconds."

Flynn smiled again, and those ice blue eyes glittered. "I'm real good at what I do."

And just what might that be, exactly? He'd been

watching her farm? That could either be very good, or very bad.

As they walked, she noticed that big fence again, off to her right, buried deep in the thicket. Now that she'd had a chance to think about it, she realized where it must lead.

Taking in a fortifying breath, she figured she might as well get this show on the road. Flynn was either going to help her, or not. She was all run out, so the jig was up, no matter how you looked at it. "Do you have a cell phone?"

"Yes, but the reception down in the valley is pretty iffy." He tilted his head. "Who do you want to call?"

Giving him the once-over, she decided to tell him the truth, everything, at least as much as she knew of everything. "I hope you like surprises, Flynn, because this one's a doozy."

As she explained about Mortie, the disarticulation, Detective McKennitt, and the place with the gate Mortie had taken her to that time, Flynn remained quiet. When she finished, she said, "So I need to use your cell phone to call Detective McKennitt to let him know I found the gate."

Flynn stopped walking and turned her to face him. "You say you found the gate?"

She gestured toward the trees. "See back in there? You can just make out a chain-link fence.

If you follow it a little more north, I'm betting you'll find that gate."

Flynn peered into the thicket, pursed his lips, then blew out a long breath. "I'll be damned." Nodding slowly, he reached under his jacket. But instead of pulling out a cell phone, he pulled out a revolver.

"Well, Sadie. I hope you like surprises, too, because now it's my turn."

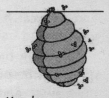

Ransom
What you did after you walked some.

Chapter 19

Kevin LeRoy's ass was numb. He'd been sitting in the damn bushes for an hour, slapping at bugs, trying to keep his legs from going to sleep while he watched the farmhouse. But so far, that handyman's truck hadn't budged, and there was no way he was going to approach Claire with that prick anywhere on the property.

LeRoy had found a damn good spot near the blackberry vines at the back of the house from which he could observe, yet remain unobserved. He could see the kitchen door and the barnyard, and even catch conversation, when the wind was with him.

Smacking his forearm, he cursed every mosquito on the planet. Though he'd had to park a mile away and hike to the farm, he was glad he'd been so cautious. Some PHPD cruiser kept driving by every half hour or so, checking the place out. Something was going on, and he really wanted to know what.

". . . and keep the doors locked." A man's voice, familiar. LeRoy peered through the branches. McKennitt, emerging from the kitchen door. And Claire. He cocked his head to listen.

"Don't go outside for any reason," McKennitt warned. "And don't open the door to anyone . . . especially . . ."

What was that? Especially *who*? Shit, he missed it.

". . . We'll find her. I promise."

Hmm. Perhaps that was information he could use to his advantage.

Then McKennitt put his arms around Claire and kissed her. He felt his fingers curl tightly into his palms. He knew it, he just knew it. Handyman, his numb ass.

As McKennitt got in his truck and tore off, Claire closed the kitchen door.

When the truck was out of sight, LeRoy stood, brushing dirt and leaves from his clothes. His right leg was tingly, but a little exercise should clear that up.

Moving silently across the small side yard, he edged up close to the house. The day was heating up, the upstairs windows were open. He could climb up there, but he was wearing the wrong shoes, and besides, that cop car might come along when he was halfway up or down, and that would be awkward to explain.

He thought he heard a noise, like somebody talking, then he remembered the old lady's parrot. Must be Hutch or Dutch or whatever in the hell the bird's name was, chattering mindlessly away.

The closer he got to the open window, the louder the bird got. Too bad he couldn't get in and kill the little son of a bitch. That'd shake everybody up. Not only would he be getting back at Claire for spurning him, it would escalate her fear factor.

"... men are bastards ..."

Yeah, tell me about it, beak brain.

"... you talkin' to me? ..."

Parrot au vin, he thought. Slowly roasted over an open fire. He could have the little fart plucked and barbecued before—

"... Detective McKennitt ... men are bastards ... Detective McKennitt ..."

LeRoy froze, then slowly backed behind a large rhododendron. There must be some kind of mistake, or maybe it was a joke. That bird could not *possibly* have said . . .

But Claire had told him the little shithead was smart, repeating nearly everything it ever heard. Still . . .

". . . you talkin' to me? . . . McKennitt . . . Detective . . . shut up, Hitch! . . ."

Well, now. If that didn't just change everything.

She'd not only spurned him, she'd betrayed him. Worse, she'd betrayed his kids. And after he'd told her about Brenda, after he'd practically gotten down on his knees and begged Claire to help him win back custody of his kids.

Rubbing his temples, he fought to keep his anger under control. Damn. How could she? How *could* she!

Did the cops know about the harvesting? Was that why they'd enlisted her help? If they thought they could use her to try and trap him, they were every bit as stupid as they looked.

All the way back to his car, he thought of Claire and what he'd do to her when he got her alone. Without her help, he'd lose his children. After all his hard work, after all his sacrifices, he'd lose his kids because the stupid bitch had betrayed him!

She needed to be punished for that, needed to be shown how painful that kind of loss could be. Her duplicity would cost her; the price would be

high. But first, she needed to be taught a lesson.
A good, hard lesson.

As he slid behind the wheel of the car, he
pulled out the cell phone he'd copped from
some guy's pocket a while back. Adjusting the
rearview mirror, he looked into his own eyes for
a moment, feeling like the sucker he was.

Connecting with the Port Henry PD, he said,
"I'd like to speak with Detective McKennitt."

"What does this concern, sir?"

"I have information on the Ketterer murder."

"I see. It would be best if you could come in—"

"No," he rushed. "No, I just want to talk to
him. I want to remain anonymous."

"All right. I can take the information, if you
like, and pass it on to one of them."

"One of them? You have two Detective
McKennitts?"

"Yes, sir. One's with the Seattle PD, and the
other works out of Port Henry."

No shit. "Are they related or something? Father and son? Brothers?"

There was a momentary pause, then, "Did you
wish to leave some information about the Ketterer case, sir?"

He ended the call. *Two.* Two McKennitts, and
one of them was Claire's boyfriend. Well, if nothing else, it confirmed the parrot's idiotic chatter.

Think, think, think.

Yes, okay, yes. If he couldn't get into her house, maybe he could coax her to come outside. Of course he could. It might take a bit of doing, but he was smart, and more than that, he was clever.

Grinning, he cranked the ignition and put the SUV in gear. A phone book. He needed a phone book.

How much did the cops know? he wondered. Ah, hell, it didn't matter. He'd just change his identity again and start over somewhere else. But Crystal and Josh were another matter. Damn Claire for doing this to him!

Well, the game wasn't over yet. She *would* help him get his kids back, whether she wanted to or not.

Claire stood in the silence of her bedroom, gazing out the window at the stars twinkling high above in the indigo sky. A wisp of cloud veiled the moon, heralding the arrival of fog in the morning.

"Please be all right," she whispered to the darkness. "Aunt Sadie. Please, please be all right."

She glanced at her watch. Half past ten. Taylor had been gone all day and evening. He'd called her several times, but so far, no new information.

Her phone rang. "Yes, hello, Taylor? Any news?"

"Not yet," he said, his voice weary, yet somehow reassuring. "Try not to worry, okay? We're on it, and won't rest until we have her home again."

It was suddenly too much. She caved. Hot tears scalded her cheeks, and she hurried to wipe them away. "I understand," she whispered. "Do you have any leads at all?"

"Mortimer's still missing, too," he said. "We think they're together. Maybe he came by to talk to her, they went for a drive, and the car broke down. That's probably all it is."

Wiping her tears on her sleeve, she said, "Sure. That's probably all it is."

"Oh, and we have a positive ID on Thursby. His real name's Kevin LeRoy. We think he's Mortimer's partner."

"I see." Adam. A criminal. Bizarre, but not totally unexpected, given his actions of late.

"I meant to tell you all this earlier," Taylor continued, "but we've been busy following up leads all day. I'm sorry."

"It's okay," she said. "I understand. It's hard to believe, about Adam, I mean, but when I think about it, it makes the most sense."

She walked back to the window and stared out

into the nothingness. "He ran me off the road, stole my stuff, tried to burn down the barn, and poisoned me." Shaking her head, she said, "*Why*? I didn't know a thing about his business with Mort."

Taylor blew out a long sigh. "That wasn't it. Based on the reports I'm getting from Portland, it's been his MO when he wants something, especially from a woman. He thought by secretly intimidating you, you'd turn to him for strength. Even marry him."

"But why *me*?" Her throat hurt from choking back more tears. She needed to be strong, needed to keep it together. It wouldn't do her aunt any good for her to fall apart.

"You'll have a chance to ask him when I catch the son of a bitch," Taylor said. "For your own safety, I'd like to have Winslow bring you down to the station."

"No," she said. "No, I'm staying here in case Aunt Sadie comes back. The house is locked. I'm safe, and as you say, you've got the cruiser coming by every half hour or so. I'll be fine."

"Claire?"

She sniffed. "Yeah?"

"I won't let you down," he said softly. "I swear it."

Nodding to the phone, she ended the call, and

wiped the tears from her eyes. Just as she sat on the bed, her phone chimed again.

"Yes, Taylor?" she rushed. "Was there something else?"

"Sorry, honey. It's not your boyfriend."

Adam.

For a moment, she didn't know what to say. *I know all about you, you son of a bitch!* probably wouldn't get her far. Was he aware she knew who he was, what he'd done?

Swallowing, she took a moment to settle her nerves.

"Adam," she said slowly. "Aunt Sadie is missing. Do you know anything about it?"

There was silence for a moment. "Why would I know anything about your aunt?"

"Well, you wouldn't, but it's a fairly small town. I thought maybe you might have seen her."

There was silence for a moment, then, "Maybe I have."

Her stomach tightened and she placed her palm at her waist. "What do you mean?"

"I want to see you." It was a statement of fact, not a request.

"I'm afraid that's impossible right now. Like I said, Aunt Sadie—"

"Claire," he growled. "I want to see you, and I will. I am a little miffed at you, though. Why didn't you tell me your handyman friend was a detective?"

"H-how did you—"

"Let's just say a little bird told me."

Okay, find out what he's up to, and call Taylor.

"All right, Adam. I'll meet you. Where are you?"

"Nice try," he said. "Now, here's what you're going to do. The cruiser that's been circling the wagons all day isn't due back for another twenty minutes. You're going to walk out the back door, up the driveway, and onto the main road. When you get there, start walking toward town. I'll pick you up."

"No. That's no good. Aunt Sadie might come back, and I need to be—"

"Aunt Sadie isn't *coming* back, Claire," he bit out. "But you *will* meet me, and you will do it now, and here's why."

Claire heard movement, a rustling sound, then Adam's voice again. "Say hello to your friend."

She listened as a heartbreakingly familiar voice panted, *"Don't do it*, Claire . . . Stay *away* . . . Call Soldier. He'll know—"

The woman's words were cut off by what sounded like a slap.

"Betsy!" she screamed, clutching the phone in a hand suddenly gone sweaty. "No! Betsy! Are you all right? Betsy!"

Cold chills ran down her spine and her brain

ceased to function. Her eyes filled with angry tears. She felt her jaw tighten, her fingers curl into tight fists.

"She's fine," Adam drawled. "For the time being. You know, for a small town, there sure are a lot of cops named McKennitt, and as luck would have it, one of them has a very pregnant wife."

"No!" she sobbed. "You can't! Let her go! I'll do what you want. I'll do *whatever* you want. Please—"

"Yes," he snapped. "You *will* do whatever I want."

Pausing for a moment, he said evenly, "If I don't see your fine little ass up on that road in the next three minutes, your friend dies. And you know what else? It'll be very slow and very painful."

"Adam," she begged in as calm a voice as she could muster. "Adam. Don't do this. Please Adam don't . . ."

But the line had already gone quiet. She stared down at her watch, then at her dressing table. She had two minutes left.

Smuggler
Self–righteous sneak thief.

Chapter 20

Taking off at a dead run, Claire was down the stairs and into the kitchen in five seconds. Her fingers shook so hard, she had trouble throwing the lock on the back door. Finally, it clicked and she flung it open, holding her cell phone in front of her so she could see the display, but before she could hit the speed dial for Taylor's number, the phone chimed.

"Taylor?" she panted as she raced across the barnyard.

"It occurs to me," Adam said, "that you are one of those rare women who can walk and talk at the same time, so I am going to occupy your cell phone until I pick you up. That way, you can't alert anybody."

Damn! " 'Kay," she choked as she tore up the driveway. It wasn't a steep incline, but she'd never tried running up loose gravel in sandals before.

She checked her watch. Fifteen minutes and the cruiser would come by. Could she stall Adam that long?

But he knew about the drive-bys. He'd timed his plan to avoid them. She was on her own.

Taylor. If you're psychic at all, hear me, hear me, hear me! I need help. Please, God, hear me!

By the time she reached the end of the drive, she was out of breath. The cell phone to her ear, she turned right and began walking toward town. How long until Adam got there?

As though he read her thoughts, he said, "I'll pull up next to you. Get in without making a fuss, and I might let your friend breathe another five minutes."

She heard the car behind her now, but no headlights flared. He must have turned them off, making him nearly invisible in the night. When he reached her, he slowed to a crawl, and she glanced warily to her left.

It wasn't the Mercedes. It was a black Excursion, and even in the dark, she could see it had a dented front bumper.

Too many thoughts to sort out collided in her skull as she reached for the door and opened it.

Adam sat behind the wheel, his expression unreadable in the shadows.

"Fancy running into you," he chided. "Get in."

"Where's Betsy?" she huffed, still trying to catch her breath.

With a tilt of his head, he said, "In the back. She was tired, so she's taking a little rest."

Claire climbed into the passenger seat. "You didn't hurt her. If you hurt her, I'll—"

"*What* will you? Close the goddamn door," he snarled. Darkness and light played over his handsome features, suddenly gone cruel. The moment the door slammed closed, he flipped on the headlights and accelerated, jerking Claire back in the seat.

"What will you *do*?" he bit out. "All the good cards are in my hand."

Claire twisted as much as she could and looked over at the bench seat behind her to where Betsy lay, her hands and feet bound. Her eyes were closed.

"What did you give her?"

"She's got quite a mouth on her," Adam said dryly. "I'm sure her husband will thank me for shutting her up for a while."

"She's pregnant!" Claire snapped. "What did you give her, you son of a bitch?"

"Really, Claire," he said solemnly. "Play nice. I don't have to keep her alive, you know."

Choking down her anger, she said, "Why Betsy?"

He lifted his shoulder in a slight shrug. "You'd mentioned her a couple of times. It was obvious to me you have deep feelings for her. She's *important* to you, which makes her very convenient for my purposes."

"You can't truss her up like that. Untie her—"

"Shut up!" Adam yelled. Pressing a button on his side of the car, as though he were speaking to a child, he said, "Childproof locks, Dr. Claire. Ain't modern technology great? Now, shut the fuck up until I tell you to speak, or all the rules go away, and so does your best friend."

"What!" His cell phone to his ear, Taylor was out the station door and halfway to his truck before Winslow finished speaking, Soldier hard on his heels.

"I'm at the farm," Winslow said, alarm clear to hear in his voice. "She's gone. Kitchen door's wide open. She left a message on the dresser mirror. It's in lipstick or something."

"What does it say?" Taylor shouted as he slammed the key into the ignition.

"Kinda hard to read, but it looks like it says *Adam* and then *Betsy*."

Taylor shot a look at his brother next to him, just fastening his seat belt. *Holy shit.* "Uh, copy. Anything else?"

"I've done a perimeter check of the property," Winslow said. "Her car's here. She either walked away, or somebody picked her up."

How long had she been gone? How much of a head start did LeRoy have?

"Jackson," Taylor said. "Call home."

Soldier looked his way, then frowned when he gazed into Taylor's eyes. "What? Why?"

Reaching across the seat, Taylor gripped his brother's forearm. "I'm sorry," he said. When Soldier's brow creased in confusion, Taylor delivered the blow. "I'm . . . It's LeRoy. I think he . . . has Betsy."

As long as he lived, no matter what wretchedness his work would force him to witness, nothing could ever hold the power to wound him, break his heart like the look he saw in his brother's eyes the moment Soldier realized the woman he loved . . . was gone.

Until, that is, Taylor gazed into the rearview mirror, and into his own empty eyes.

As the miles fell away, Claire tried to concentrate, form some kind of plan that would get her and Betsy out of this mess.

Did Adam plan on killing them? And what

about Aunt Sadie? Why wasn't she in the car? Had Adam already k— No. *No*. It wasn't possible. She would not, could *not* go there.

A chill made its way down her spine, cooling her blood, and despite the warmth of the night, she shivered.

She realized she couldn't assume anything at this point. Even if she could somehow overpower Adam, unless she rendered him unconscious and took control of the car, her chances of getting the unconscious Betsy away safely were zero.

She'd wait, look for her chance, then go for it. He had to make a mistake. She was strong and smart. There was a way out of this. She'd find it.

And if he hurt Betsy or the baby in any way, she'd have the bastard's liver for breakfast.

Thanks to the lighted display on the dashboard, Claire watched the clock, monitoring how long they'd been on the road. Forty minutes and counting. Adam had kept up a steady speed of about forty-five miles per hour. Not fast enough to snare the attention of the cops, but certainly fast enough to get out of town and into the countryside where there were fewer houses and cars.

She did the calculation in her head. Forty-five miles per hour in forty minutes. That meant they'd traveled about thirty miles. Even though it was dark, they'd headed out of town on an unfamiliar road in a southwesterly direction. If he kept going, they'd run into the Olympic National Forest. Where in the hell was he taking them?

Then she remembered what Aunt Sadie had said about the place out in the country.

Her eyes on what she could see of the road ahead, she said softly, "The police know all about your activities, Adam. Kidnapping Betsy and me won't do you any good."

"Sure it will," he said. "I have a big fat ton of money now, and more coming in all the time. And you're going to marry me. Then we're going to head on down to Portland, and get my kids back."

"Adam. Didn't you hear me? The police know about the harvesting. They—"

"I don't care." He chuckled.

She stared at him. "Your arrogance is eclipsed only by your stupidity."

He shrugged. "Sticks and stone, Claire. Sticks and stones."

"Okay," she said. "I'll marry you. I'll do it right now. Drop Betsy off at the nearest—"

He burst out laughing as though she'd just told him a hilarious joke. "No way. *First* we get married, *then* I release your friend."

Shaking her head, she whispered, "Adam, you can't possibly think marrying me will get your kids back. I'm sorry about your situation, but this isn't going to solve anything."

He kept his eyes on the road, but lowered his head like a ram about to butt a wall. "This will work," he growled. "As soon as I met you, I knew you were the one who could help me make it work. You're smart and beautiful, and a doctor. And now that I have the money to fight Brenda—"

"But Adam," she pressed. "The fact that I'm a doctor means nothing to the courts. That's just silly. Why, you're a respected surgeon who—"

"I'm not!" he choked, then slammed the wheel with his fist. "I'm *not*. I was a washout. I never made it through med school. They kicked me out, Claire. Me! I had the talent, the smarts, but they kicked me out. Said I had anger management issues. They confused an artistic temperament with anger. Can you believe it!"

If it hadn't been so tragic, Claire would have laughed. Yes, she could believe it, all right. His volatility and lack of self-control seemed to manifest at the merest provocation. But anger was one thing. He was also deluded if he thought marrying her would get his kids back.

"I'm sorry, Adam," she muttered, stalling, trying to think of some way out of this. "I had no idea about med school."

He nodded a few times, his lower lip jutting out like that of a kid who'd been sent to his room.

Watching him, she realized that Adam was a

boy in a man's body. An unruly child who wanted his way and couldn't have it. And now he was hurt, angry, and desperate, and he was going to make everyone pay for his misery.

"Brenda married me when things were good," he said. "I was going to be chief of surgery someday, and she knew it. But when they cut me loose, she found all kinds of excuses to leave me." Under his breath, he said, "She took my kids. Crystal and Josh. They idolize me, you know." He shot her a quick glance. "*They* think I'm wonderful. They want to come and live with me. Why, the last time I talked to Crystal, she *begged* me to come and get her."

Claire nodded slowly, and let the conversation drop.

The night was heavy, oppressive. The dark settled over Claire, making her feel as though she were entombed as she forced her brain to work harder to come up with a viable plan of escape. But everything she thought of involved too much risk to Betsy.

Claire had no idea where they were. The trees were so tall, the stands so thick, moonlight couldn't penetrate. Only the headlamps and dashboard lights provided relief from the predatory darkness.

"Where are we?" she ventured.

He waited so long to answer, she gave a little jump when he finally spoke.

"Where all the magic happens," he said. "Or used to. I'm going to have to abandon this particular operation now. But there are other people, other places. You and the kids will be well provided for, so don't worry. You won't be sorry you married me, Claire." He smiled over at her. "I promise."

Claire's stomach tightened into a hard knot.

He slowed, as though looking for something off to the side of the road. Behind a thick stand of trees, a small ball of light eased the darkness.

"Hi, honey, I'm home!" He chuckled as he turned off the main road and onto a narrow drive. In front of them stood a barrier of iron bars. Reaching above his head, he pressed the electronic opener, and the gate began to slide away.

Off to her right, she thought she caught a glint of something, a reflection. Eyes in the night? A deer? A coyote? Deep into the woods as they were, it could be anything.

As the car passed through the entry, she glanced in the side view mirror. Shadows, movement, another glint of light, then stillness. The iron gate slammed closed.

Wherever this place was, she and Betsy were trapped inside.

* * *

Taylor watched his brother go slowly insane.

Betsy's mother, Loretta Tremaine, her red hair teased and sprayed into what appeared to be an imitation of a candle flame, paced Soldier's kitchen, hugging the geriatric Piddle to her bosom. The chihuahua's head bobbed up and down with each step she took.

"Find my daughter!" she screamed. "Castrate that man! No, wait. I'll do it! If he harms one hair on my Elizabeth's head—"

"Loretta," Soldier growled. "You need to calm down and tell us exactly what you saw." Taking his mother-in-law by the elbow, he escorted her to the nearest chair, where she sat and crossed her legs. Licking her glossed lips, she nodded and took in a deep breath.

"As Pids and I were driving up the street, I saw a tall, exquisitely handsome man helping Elizabeth into the backseat of a very large automobile."

"What color?"

"He was white."

"The car, Loretta."

"Oh. Black. It was enormous, one of those, what do you call them, subterranean vehicles."

"All-terrain sports utility vehicle?"

"Yes, that's it. An SUV thing. But by the time I drove up, he was driving away. I honked and waved, but she appeared not to notice me. Imagine that."

Soldier sighed. "A difficult feat. What did you do then?"

"Well," she said, as if the answer were obvious. "That was when I noticed the kitchen door was wide open. I went to close it, and saw her purse sitting on the table. The room was as you see it now, a complete disaster, as though there had been a, well, a struggle. That's when I knew something was wrong."

"Because of the struggle?" Taylor asked.

"No, because a woman would never go *anywhere* without her handbag. I mean, honestly." She rolled her eyes and shrugged.

"What direction did they take?" Soldier said.

She gestured with her free hand while the chihuahua snoozed in the crook of her other arm. "That way. Away from town."

The brothers exchanged glances. Taylor had issued an all-points for the SUV, but they could be anywhere by now.

He tamped down the anxiety in his gut. Claire, at that bastard's mercy. Betsy . . . well, a man only had to look in Soldier's eyes to see the anguish there.

LeRoy had made a big mistake kidnapping Claire and Betsy—bigger than he could possibly imagine. Even if he did manage to get clean away, the McKennitt brothers would hunt him down like the dog he was. They would never give up until they found the son of a bitch. *Never*.

And if either Claire or Betsy was hurt. . . .

Taylor shook his head. It wasn't going to happen. LeRoy would be a fool to hurt either one of the women, and he had to know the consequences of what he was doing. But being arrogant and cocky could make him reckless . . . and very dangerous.

In the background, Loretta was still chattering away.

". . . beautiful women, such as myself, but since I am not nearly as dumb as I look, I have it, if you want it."

He shook his head, trying to clear his mind of the debris left by the woman's constant babbling. "Want what, Mrs. Tremaine?"

She scowled at him. "Why, the license number of the SUV."

"*You got it?*" Taylor and Soldier blurted out the words at the same time.

Her glance shifted between the two men. "I am rather smart," she stated. "I saw it as he drove away, made a mental note, then wrote it down." From her dress pocket, she drew a slip of paper. "Here you are. Now do your duty, detectives. Find my daughter and my grandbaby!"

Taylor took the paper from her and looked at it, showed it to Soldier.

BABMGNT

Taylor smirked. "Babe magnet. Yeah, right."

"No wonder we couldn't track him," Soldier said. "That's not the license number on the SUV on file."

"He switched them. Damn. We've got an APB out on the wrong plates."

Taylor's stomach soured. Every cop in the state was looking for the wrong frigging SUV. *Goddammit*.

As his brother's cell phone rang, Taylor closed his eyes for a moment, and saw Claire as she'd been when he'd held her in his arms, and made love to her . . .

It wasn't *over*, he swore to himself. He'd get her back. They had years and years, decades ahead of them. No. It wasn't over.

"On our way," Soldier said, just finishing up the call. Slapping the phone closed, he turned to Taylor. "Saddle up, little brother," he growled. "We just got our break."

Chapter 21

Claire tried to make out objects through the windshield as the SUV journeyed down the narrow dirt road. Outside, the darkness was so complete, they might just as well have been tunneling through a cave. Dense forest effectively shut out the moon and starlight, limiting her view to only those things the twin beams of Adam's headlights touched. Rough brown trunks stood near the road as if stationed there to forestall intruders. Boughs heavy with thick needles dipped low to the ground. Gigantic ferns arched into the air like fountains of green and gray feathers.

The car bumped around a gradual curve in the road. Off to the right, nearly obliterated by the forest, stood a single-story farmhouse and low-ceilinged barn. Judging from their architecture and condition, Claire figured them to be well over a century old, and objects of neglect for more than half that time.

A low-wattage bulb from a dangling porch light was all that kept total darkness at bay. So well hidden was this place, you could pass right by it in the dark and never know it existed.

Parked next to the ancient barn were three very modern cars. She recognized Adam's Mercedes, but she'd never seen the other two before.

Adam brought the SUV to a stop in front of the house. Although no lights shone from inside, the front door opened immediately and two men stepped out onto the porch. Even though they both wore white lab coats, they looked like a couple of thugs. One of them, she recognized.

The bigger of the men came around to her door and opened it, while the other, somewhat less intimidating of the two, opened the back where Betsy lay unconscious.

Claire stared at him. He lowered his eyes for a moment.

"How's the heart problem, Mr. *Fuentes*?"

In response, he simply shrugged.

"I'd have thought she'd have come around by

now," Adam said casually, looking into the rearview mirror at Betsy. "Sure hope I didn't overmedicate her." He flicked a smile at Claire.

"You'd better pray you didn't," she said softly, glaring into his eyes.

He reached out and ran his thumb along her cheek. She recoiled as though she'd been struck by a snake.

"Don't make threats you can't keep," he said. "If you'd been nicer to me, I wouldn't have had to involve her."

As he got out of the car and slammed the door, he said to the bigger man, "You know what to do, Baker."

A moment later, Claire felt thick fingers curl around her arm. She tried to jerk free, but the man Adam had called Baker was strong, and he yanked her from her seat to stand close beside him. Way too close.

She doubled her fist and took a swing at him and he shoved her against the car, whooshing all the air from her lungs. His broad hand splayed against her chest, he warned, "Don't give me any trouble. It'll go real hard on you if you do." His breath smelled like rotten food and she nearly gagged.

Ignoring her nausea, she begged softly, so only he could hear, "Let my friend go. She's going to have a baby. Please . . ."

By the meager light from the porch lamp, she couldn't see his face clearly, but he was big, broad, and had hair cropped so short, it was impossible to tell what color it was. His brows were dark, but his eyes were an eerie light blue, too small, too bright. Just looking at him terrified her.

"C'mon," he said, grabbing her arm again and nearly dragging her across the yard to the barn. She wanted to fight him, but he was enormous. She felt like a rag doll clutched in a giant's fist.

Digging in her heels, she pulled back against him. "No," she choked. "I'm not going anywhere without Betsy."

"Not a problem," Baker said. "Fuentes has got her. Now shut up and come quietly."

She didn't want to give up, give in, but with Betsy still unconscious, she had no choice.

It was so dark, she could barely see a thing. If Baker and Fuentes weren't in white lab coats, they'd be virtual ghosts. How did these guys find their way around in such low light? They must have every inch of the place memorized.

When they reached the barn, Baker opened the old door and shoved her inside. Her nostrils were immediately assailed by the unappetizing blend of formaldehyde, decomposition, and body fluids. He slammed his hand against the wall, and suddenly, the place was ablaze with light. She blinked several times, trying to adjust to the glare, then she took a hard look around.

From the outside, the place appeared to be a broken-down old barn, but inside, it was a thoroughly modern morgue, from the glistening white tile floor to the stainless steel table to the cooler that defined the far wall. Tools of the trade were neatly arrayed alongside jars of formaldehyde, and a digital thermometer claimed the air temperature was a near-icy thirty-eight degrees. Not low enough to freeze, but cold enough to obstruct bacterial growth.

Behind her, Adam said, "Impressive, isn't it."

She turned to face him. "You make me sick."

He laughed. It was a hearty, yet humorless sound, and it prickled her skin to hear it.

Fuentes, carrying Betsy's limp body, moved past them. "Where do you want this one?"

"Put her on the couch in my office," Adam ordered. "You want a tour, Claire, before you join your friend?"

"Not particularly," she said as Fuentes moved off down a long corridor. She watched him go, making sure he was careful with Betsy. Turning her attention to Adam, she said, "Did you kill Mindy Ketterer?"

Behind her, she could feel the heat from Baker's big body. She'd tell him to back off, but she knew if she did, he'd only move closer.

Adam shrugged. "Couldn't be helped. She wasn't very bright, but it seems she could add two and two. That made her a liability."

"What have you done with Aunt Sadie?"

His brows arched, then he looked annoyed. "How the hell should I know where the old bat is."

"You don't have her? But you said—"

"I was a bad boy." He grinned. "I wanted you to believe I had her to make my job a little easier."

If Adam didn't have a clue as to where Aunt Sadie was, if he hadn't kidnapped or hurt her, then where was she?

Worry gnawed at her insides. God, this situation was getting worse by the minute.

The good news—if there was any good news under the circumstances—was that Claire's only immediate problem was Betsy.

"Baker," Adam said. "Escort Dr. Hunter to my office, then come back out to the house." With that, Adam spun on his heel and headed for the door.

"What are you going to do with us?" Claire said to his retreating back.

"Nothing, for the moment," Adam replied, without turning. When he reached the door, he stopped and slowly swiveled in her direction. "In the morning, you and I will be married. It's all arranged."

She shook her head. "We don't have a license."

He smiled in a way that made her stomach clench. "Yes we do. *Money*, Claire. Money talks, and it also gets things done. We're getting married tomorrow, license and all. Sleep well."

A minute or so later, with Baker close behind her, she stopped in front of what must be Adam's office. Caught between the closed door and her hulking escort, Claire could do nothing but wait until he opened it and let her in. That was when she felt his fingers digging into her bottom.

His breath stirred the hair on the back of her neck, making her want to retch. Lowering his head, he nuzzled her ear and whispered, "You and me. What do you say?" He squeezed her buttocks. "Right up against this door."

"Another time."

He laughed, and stepped back a little. With one hand, he opened the door; with the other, he shoved her into the room.

Though there was no light burning inside the office, she could see Betsy's form on the sofa next to a tall bookcase. Ignoring the humiliation of being groped by such a disgusting Neanderthal, Claire rushed to the couch, went down on her knees, and began checking Betsy's vitals.

Behind her, the door slammed shut, enveloping the two women in total darkness. She heard a metallic *chink* as the lock engaged.

Lowering her head onto Betsy's warm shoulder, she whispered, "I'm sorry. I'm so sorry for getting you into this."

"Damn," Betsy drawled, her voice rough and sleepy. "I thought that creep would never leave. What do you say we blow this Popsicle stand?"

Claire sat back on her heels, joy filling every corner of her heart. "You're all right?" she choked. "How long have you been awake?"

She felt Betsy's fingers seeking her own. Grabbing hold, the two women held hands and clung to each other in the terrible dark.

"I began coming around about an hour ago," Betsy answered groggily. "I pretended to be out just in case I got an opportunity to do something. Unfortunately, nothing ever presented itself."

"How do you feel? Any after-effects from the drug?"

"A bit of a headache," she confessed. "I sure could use some water."

"Stay here." Claire stood and looked around the small office. Over the last few minutes, her eyes had somewhat adjusted to the darkness. Under the door, a thin strip of light gave just enough illumination for her to make out a lamp on Adam's desk. She made her way over to it, and switched it on. Behind her, Betsy sat up.

"There's a pitcher by the phone," Betsy said. "Water, do you think?"

Claire looked inside, sniffed the contents, then

took a sip. Handing the container to Betsy, she said, "There's not much, but it should help hydrate you."

As Betsy took the pitcher and chugged its contents, Claire began going over every square inch of the office, starting with the phone. Like Adam was going to hold them hostage in a room with a functioning telephone. She picked up the receiver. Nothng.

Betsy wiped her mouth. "Do you think anybody followed us?"

"No. I kept checking the side view mirror. We were alone the whole trip."

Rubbing her tummy, Betsy said, "I feel like such an idiot."

"Why?" Claire moved to sit on the sofa beside her friend. "This is *my* fault. I had no idea Adam was so . . . desperate."

"That's not the word I'd use," Betsy said dryly. "I feel stupid because he got the drop on me, and I never saw it coming." A long, weary sigh escaped her lungs. "I should have realized something was up when he parked in the driveway right next to the kitchen door. He knocked like it was the most natural thing in the world. I opened the door, and the next thing I know, I'm struggling with this guy, and he shoves a gun against my side."

"He has a gun?"

"Oh, yeah," she said. "But then, it's not like I haven't been kidnapped at gunpoint before, so I stayed cool. Until he shot me, that is."

"With a hypodermic, not a .38."

Betsy sent Claire a worried look. "He wouldn't have given me anything that could hurt the baby." Fear shone brightly in her eyes as she slid her hands over her swollen tummy.

"Oh, God, no," Claire rushed. "No, I'm sure he didn't. He wants me to cooperate, and he knows I'd kill him with my bare hands if he did anything to hurt you or the baby."

"Would you have?" Betsy rasped, still clutching her belly, holding her child as close to her as she could. "Killed him?"

Claire felt her heart grow cold as fury infused her blood like a deadly virus. Looking into her dearest friend's eyes, she hissed, "Yes." She patted Betsy's hand, hoping like hell what she was about to say was the truth. "Your vitals are fine, and you've come around quickly. That's a good sign. When we get to the hospital, we'll do a thorough check, but I'm sure everything's okay. Is the baby moving?"

Betsy nodded, a slow smile replacing the fear on her pretty face. "Moving and kicking," she said. "Same old, same old." Her smile faded. "Why is he doing this? What does he want?"

As Claire stood and went to the door to check

the lock, she quickly related the highlights of the story. When she was finished, Betsy made a face.

"And he really thinks he'll get his kids back after all this?"

"I get the impression he left reality in the dust a long time ago."

Claire walked the perimeter of the room. Plain walls, nearly empty bookshelves, a desk, a chair, the sofa. No windows, and only a single wooden door. She pressed her body against it. The wood gave a little, and the lock rattled. Hope sprang to life in her heart.

Behind her, Betsy groaned.

"You okay?"

She nodded. "Gotta pee. Bad."

Looking around, Claire said, "I don't see a restroom key. You may have to use that pitcher."

Taking the container in hand, Betsy said softly, "I guess I'm grateful this isn't a soda bottle. I just don't think my aim is that good."

Claire turned away while Betsy proceeded to relieve herself. Jostling the lock again, she said, "You know, this door isn't all that secure. I'm sure this office wasn't meant to be a prison cell, so I'll bet with a little work, I can bust the lock."

Straightening her clothing, Betsy sat back on the sofa. "What if they hear?"

Claire shrugged and eyed the door again. "We'd be no worse off than we are now. They all went back to the house. Maybe it's far enough away so they won't hear."

Dropping to her knees, Claire lay on her back and put both feet against the door. "The femur is stronger than concrete. Coupled with the quads, they exert more force than ten men."

"Really?"

"No. But I'm trying to psych myself up here. Keep your fingers crossed."

Holding her breath, she pulled back, then punched the door with both feet. She felt the vibrations shudder up her legs and into her lower back. With a sharp crack, the wood splintered and her left foot went right through.

Pain shot up her leg, and she choked down a cry. She kicked the door again, and more wood splintered. Sitting up, she began pulling the loosened shards from the bottom of the frame, then she reached through the hole and felt for the doorknob. Nothing. The door wouldn't budge, so she yanked more wood out until the opening was big enough to crawl through.

"It didn't make very much noise," Betsy whispered, coming to Claire's side. "I'll bet they didn't hear."

"I'm not waiting around to find out," she

growled. "Listen, your tummy won't make it through this hole so I'm going through and getting something I can knock the lock off with."

As she started through the opening, Betsy said, "You're bleeding!"

"I know," she panted as she eased herself through the gaping hole in the door. "Big splinter. Hurts like hell. I'll be fine. Wait here."

As soon as she was on the other side, she made her way down the lighted corridor to the makeshift morgue. The lights there were out, and she didn't dare turn them on. She remembered seeing some instruments on a table when they'd first entered the room, so she made her way across the cold tile, feeling her way as she went. When her hand found the shape of a hammer, she curled her fingers around it.

Running her palm along the table, she also picked up a couple of knives, and a towel.

Quickly retracing her steps, she arrived back at Adam's broken office door a few moments later.

Wrapping the towel around the door handle, she prayed it would muffle her strokes. One, two, three whacks, and the door handle fell loose, easing the lock enough to pry it open with one of the knives. A minute later, and the door swung open.

Betsy sat across the room on the sofa, holding

her stomach. Rushing to her side, Claire took her hand and pressed one of the knives into her palm. "Don't be afraid to use it," she whispered. "C'mon. We have to find a way out of here, get back to that gate, and pray we can get it open before they discover we're gone."

Betsy swallowed, then stood, clutching the knife in her hand. " 'Kay," she said breathlessly.

As they scurried across the room as fast as Betsy could go, Claire panted, "Don't worry. I'll get you out of here. Somehow, someway, the men will track us down. They'll find us, I promise."

"Which men?" Betsy breathed.

Claire looked into Betsy's worried hazel eyes, and smiled. "Ours."

Deep inside her heart, she hoped she was telling the truth. Taylor and Soldier had no way of knowing where Adam had taken them. It fell to Claire to get her friend to safety, but her leg hurt like hell where the wood had sliced her calf. She knew she was losing blood, and hoped it wasn't going to impair her strength.

They shuffled through the darkened morgue toward the only door into—or out of—the place. Since the lights were off, it might not be obvious when she cracked it open. They could move off unseen into the woods and work their way back to the gate. When they got there, well, she'd deal with that problem if they got that far.

Easing the door open, Claire peered into the shadows. Squares of light across the yard told her they'd gone inside the farmhouse. Nobody seemed to be roaming about the place. Between the doorway where she'd paused, and the dark forest, stood about twenty yards of open space, but if they crouched low and hurried, they could make it.

"I don't see anyone," Claire whispered. "You ready?"

Betsy nodded and grabbed Claire's hand. Bending as low as possible, the two women moved out the door and across the open expanse of dirt. Claire kept one eye on the farmhouse as they shuffled along, silently praying their captors would stay inside for a long, long time.

As soon as they were well into the undergrowth, Claire pulled them to a halt behind the trunk of an enormous fir. Betsy was breathing hard, but said nothing.

Across the yard, the front door opened, spilling light onto the porch, illuminating Baker, who glanced over at the barn. He yelled something back into the house, then ran across the yard and through the partially open door, Fuentes and Adam close on his heels.

"Damn," Claire choked. "We've got to get farther into the woods. They'll have flashlights and—"

Next to her, Betsy seemed to bite down on a gasp.

"It's okay," Claire assured her. "You'll be fine."

Betsy shook her head, her fingers curled tightly around Claire's. "I'll do my best," she panted. "But while you were . . . knocking off the lock . . . something happened."

"What are you—"

"Leave me," she rasped. "I'll only slow you down. Leave me and go for help."

"I'm not going *anywhere* without you."

"Claire," Betsy sobbed quietly. "You may have to. God, I'm sorry. My water broke. I'm in labor."

<u>Benign</u>
What you be after you be eight.

Chapter 22

"It's okay, Betsy," Claire whispered. "Take deep breaths. Focus. Let the contraction pass."

Betsy sucked in air and blew it out, then panted like a dog. When she'd calmed a little, she said, "I'm . . . s-sorry. Took me . . . by surprise. I'm not due for three weeks. Contractions are more . . . painful than I ex . . . pected."

"I know."

"No you don't!" Betsy snapped. "Oh, God. I'm sorry." She wrapped her trembling fingers around Claire's arm and looked up into her eyes. "I'm scared. What if the injection made the baby come early? What if something is wrong?" The words were no louder than a breath. "I'm supposed to be in a hospital, where they can take care of my baby. This shouldn't be happening!"

"It'll be okay, I promise," Claire said, patting Betsy's trembling hand. "First things first. Do you think you can walk? We need to get out of here and get you to that hospital."

Betsy nodded enthusiastically. "Yes . . . move I can. God . . . I sound like . . . Yoda."

Searching the dark woods for lights or movement, Claire helped Betsy to her feet. "You're doing great," she whispered. "We'll make it. You'll see."

As the two women shuffled through the dense undergrowth, Claire's leg began to throb in earnest. She hadn't had time to look at it, let alone apply any kind of pressure bandage. She hoped to hell she wouldn't bleed to death—not until she got Betsy to safety, anyway.

"Claire? Oh, Claire!"

At the sound of Adam's voice, both Claire and Betsy dropped to their knees, ducking as low as possible.

A beam of light bounced off the tree trunks and bushes, illuminating sharp needles, jagged rocks, dry, curled leaves.

"I know you can't have gotten far," he shouted. "Clever girl to kick down the door. I underestimated you. I won't do that again. Why don't you come on out and we can make your friend more comfortable."

Claire's heart thudded inside her chest and she fought down panic. Next to her, Betsy covered her own mouth. *Please, not another contraction*, Claire thought. *Not so soon.*

Her fingers dancing over the ground, she found what she was looking for. Picking up the rock, she hurled it as far as it would go. In the distance, it slapped against a tree trunk, then fell into some bushes, making a rustling sound.

Footsteps. Adam, running toward the noise.

Wow. It had worked. Just like in the movies. Aunt Sadie would be so proud.

"I'm not going to hurt either one of you," Adam shouted from farther away. "You know what I want, Claire. You can't get past the gate, so you might as well come out."

Betsy's breathing changed, and Claire knew another contraction was upon her.

"Steady, Betsy. Steady."

Betsy buried her face in Claire's shoulder to muffle her ragged breathing. When the contraction had passed, she choked, "I can't have this baby out here. I want Soldier . . . want to be with him. Help me, Claire . . . please. What can we do?"

She heard Adam yell something, then a beam

of light passed over their heads and disappeared. The sound of men running, shouting . . . going away from them. Claire took advantage.

"Let's see how far we can get before the next contraction."

Together, they stood and began shuffling through the undergrowth. Time ceased to have meaning. In the dark, they ran, staggered, limped, but kept moving.

What if I can't get the gate open? What if Adam's just waiting there for us to show up? What if . . .

They stopped for a moment to catch their breath. In front of them, the undergrowth rustled.

Easing Betsy to the ground, Claire dropped to her knees and gripped her knife tightly in her fist.

A beam of light caught her eye, and she pulled back the knife, ready to thrust it.

"Claire?"

She halted. That voice was familiar . . . wonderfully familiar.

"Claire?"

"Aunt Sadie?" she mouthed. "Aunt *Sadie*?"

Before her astonished eyes, Sadie burst through the bushes, Flynn Corrigan right behind her. In one hand, he held a flashlight, in the other, a gun.

As Sadie reached Claire, she wrapped her arms around her in a tight hug.

"There isn't much time," Sadie whispered.

"Flynn stuck a log in the gate to keep it from closing when you drove in. We followed as quickly as we could."

"So that's what that was," Claire said. "I thought it was a bear or something."

On the ground, Betsy moaned.

"Aunt Sadie, Betsy's in labor."

"Of course she is," her aunt said calmly. "In a drama, the worst thing that can happen always does, and that's about the worst thing I can think of right now."

Claire cocked her head and listened for Adam. In the distance she heard him shouting. He and his thugs were thankfully going the wrong way—for now.

"Auntie," Claire said, "what are you *doing* here?"

Sadie patted her on the cheek. "Long story. Flynn here is FBI. He's been trying to find this place for weeks."

"But how did you—"

Betsy moaned again and covered her mouth to stifle a cry. Flynn stepped forward and bent over her.

"Can you walk, ma'am?" he said, keeping his voice low.

"Her water broke," Claire said quickly, as they helped Betsy to her feet. "The contractions are only a few minutes apart. I haven't been able to time them. We have to get her to a hospital—"

Gunfire ended what she was about to say. Behind them, a tree trunk splintered into sharp blades of wood, and Flynn yelped, covering his face with his hands.

"Damn," he choked. "Damn." He blinked and wiped his eyes, smearing blood on his face. "Shit, I can barely see."

"They're coming," Claire rasped. She licked her dry lips, but with no moisture in her mouth, it was useless. "Get Betsy out of here. Get her to a hospital. I'll lead Adam away. Promise me." When both Flynn and Aunt Sadie started to protest, Claire snapped, "Promise!"

Claire turned and cupped Betsy's hot cheek in her hand. Bending, she kissed her on the temple. "Love you, duckie."

Betsy tried to say something, but another contraction was upon her and she could only cry out softly.

Standing, Claire tried to find the beam of Adam's light again. It was closer, moving in.

She thrust the knife into her left hand, picked up a stick with her right. As fast as she dared, she began running through the undergrowth, creating as much noise as she could, banging the trees and bushes with the stick, making it sound like a dozen people were rampaging through the forest.

Immediately, the beam of light shifted and began to track her progress. Then another beam joined the first, then a third. Adam shouted something to Baker, who yelled at Fuentes. Good. They were following her. Flynn and Aunt Sadie would get Betsy out of there. Good.

There was barely enough light to see, but she was able to make out tree trunks and larger bushes. Her leg hurt like hell, but she was running to save her best friend's life. And the baby's. And Aunt Sadie's, and even Flynn's. One for four. It was worth it. She wouldn't go down without a fight, but it was definitely worth it.

She began panting, running for all she was worth to put as much distance as she could between her and the people she loved. Branches tore at her clothing, pain shot up her leg, but she kept running.

Was it her imagination, or was it growing lighter? Morning. Daylight. She'd be able to see much better . . . and be seen much better.

A beam of light illuminated the bough above her head and another shot rang out. She ducked and crawled into a hollowed-out log, pulling moss and fern leaves over the rotted opening.

There had to be bugs and slimy things in

there, but nothing nearly as slimy as what waited for her outside.

Footsteps. Breathing. Nearby. Above her. She slowly scrunched back into the log and prayed she was invisible.

"Where the hell did they go?" Adam. Furious.

"Look," Baker said, "Why don't we just clear out? What good's it gonna do you to catch them? We could be gone by now. Wait around much longer, and the cops are gonna show up."

"Yeah," Fuentes said. "I'm outta here. You're nuts, man. I'm taking my share and getting the hell out before—"

The gun blast nearly made Claire scream. Clamping her hand over her mouth, she choked down any sound.

Fuente's body hit the ground about two feet in front of her. From her hiding place, she saw his face. His eyes were open, he was looking straight at her, but didn't see her. A small stream of blood trickled from his temple.

Claire thought her heart would burst. It pounded so hard, surely her two pursuers could hear it.

"Police!" a man yelled. "Drop your weapon!"

Claire's heart jumped, and tears of relief and gratitude blurred her vision. *Taylor*.

"They can't see us, Dr. LeRoy," Baker whispered above her. "And they think you're alone. Get him to come closer."

Baker was going to ambush Taylor. *No. No, no, no!*

"Over here!" Adam shouted. He stuffed his gun behind him, tucking it under his belt at the small of his back, then raised his hands. "Right here!"

Baker edged his way back behind a tree, and waited. From where she lay, Claire could see his face. He was enjoying this. He would kill Taylor, and he would enjoy it.

If she shouted a warning, she'd give her position away. They'd either kill her or take her hostage and use her against Taylor. If she kept quiet, Baker would kill him.

"It's a *trap*!" she screamed. "There are two armed men!"

Hands were on her, dragging her from the rotted-out hollow.

"You stupid bitch," Baker growled as he drew his hand back to strike her.

She kicked him in the groin and he yelped, releasing her. Her knee came up, hard, catching him under his chin. His jaw snapped shut and she was sure she heard some teeth break. Baker's eyes closed and he went down like a bag of wet cement.

"Claire?" Taylor shouted. "Claire!"

In the gray dawn light, she could see Taylor making his way toward her through the dense undergrowth, his weapon drawn, held in front of him with both hands. There were other cops, too, but he was the only one she could see clearly, the only one who mattered to her heart.

Before she could move toward him, she felt strong fingers curl around her arm.

"Don't even think about it," Adam warned. He yanked her in front of him, using her as a shield. The barrel of his gun jammed into her ribs.

As Taylor moved closer, Claire could see his face. He was scowling, his blue eyes focused like twin laser beams on the man who held her hostage.

Adam shouted, "Stay back. I'll kill her! I will!"

Claire still gripped the knife from the morgue tightly in her left hand. Taking a deep breath, she blindly plunged it behind her, aiming for Adam's thigh.

But he caught her wrist, crushing her bones, forcing the knife out of her hand. As she struggled, Adam quickly raised his arm and fired at something, then placed the gun against her temple.

Her ears rang from the blast, her nostrils felt singed. She gasped and tried to turn her head away. Tears slicked her cheeks as she locked eyes with Taylor. He stumbled forward and mouthed something to her.

I'm sorry . . .

"No!" she screamed. "No!"

Helpless, she watched as Taylor clutched his stomach, dropped to his knees, then crumpled to the ground.

"Taylor!" Her cry echoed through the forest like the keening wail of a wounded animal. She tried to push herself away from Adam, but he held on and began dragging her farther into the forest.

"No!" she choked, squirming, kicking, flinging her fists against his legs.

Adam jammed the gun against her jaw. "You're going to get me out of this mess," he growled. "Shut up or I'll put a bullet in you right *now.*"

She could hear him panting, sucking in huge breaths. He was out of options, cops were everywhere, just waiting for her to move far enough away so they could get a clear shot.

Her racing mind went to Taylor. Was he bleeding to death while she was being carted off by his killer? He needed medical attention, a doctor, *her.* If he thought he was going to get away from her by dying, well, he had another think coming!

She let her knees buckle and her body go limp. Falling abruptly, she jerked Adam off balance.

Crouching with her, he brought the gun around to point at her forehead. "Get. Up."

She glared into his eyes. In the distance, she heard men shouting. A siren blasted through the quiet. Overhead, the beating of helicopter blades was nearly deafening.

Her mind raced. How to stop him . . . how to stop him . . . how to get back to Taylor . . .

"Get up," Adam spat, "or I'll put a bullet through your brain."

"You need me," she choked. Her mouth was so dry, speech was nearly impossible. "Without a hostage, they'll gun you down the minute you pull the trigger."

"Maybe," he snarled. "But you'll be dead, won't you, and so will your boyfriend."

Out of the corner of her eye, she saw Officer Winslow crouched in a clearing. To his right stood another uniformed officer. On the left, a third. All had weapons trained on Adam.

Where was Taylor? Was he still lying there? Was anyone taking care of him?

Fifty years or five . . . that's what Betsy had said. Claire wanted the next fifty years of Taylor's life, and dammit, she'd have it.

Winslow yelled, "Release her, LeRoy. You've already killed a police officer. Don't add—"

A sob escaped Claire's throat. It wasn't true. It was a ploy. Please, let it be a ploy.

Another sob lodged in her throat. Tears blurred her vision as she stood and faced Adam.

"Let her go, LeRoy!" Winslow shouted. "Don't be a fool! Kill her and we'll be all over you!"

Sweat trickled down her back and her clothes felt damp. Her legs wobbled, her fingers shook.

Adam yelled something. He was nervous, unsure what to do, surrounded, trapped. She was his only ticket out of there, and the cops weren't letting it happen. They were at a standoff. Something had to give.

It was all up to her.

"Adam," she whispered. The world went silent as he glared into her eyes. Sweat dripped down his face. His eyes were red, bloodshot. His hand trembled as he trained his gun on her face.

Looking deeply into his eyes, she smiled.

He blinked, then furrowed his brow. His eyes darted about, watching her, watching the cops, watching the woods around him. He was alone and if not for her, he'd be dead.

"Adam?" she whispered again. "Listen to me."

"Shut up!" he squealed. "You ruined everything for me. Why shouldn't I ruin everything for you, huh? My kids, Claire. That's all I wanted."

He was crying now, tears slicking his face.

"Ruined . . . everything . . ." he sobbed. Reaching for her, he grabbed her shirt collar with his free hand. "Head for my car," he choked, "and don't give me any trouble."

He began to move, but she stayed put.

"I said come on!"

The collar of her shirt was crumpled into his fist. She would have to wait. Provoke him. If she was just patient, she'd have him.

He yanked at her collar again, bringing her to her feet. Still, she dug in and wouldn't move. Thrusting the gun in her face, he growled, "I don't know what you think you're doing, but it won't work. Now, move your ass!"

Again he yanked, and again she stood her ground. In a moment of fury, he released her and pulled his hand back to slap her. The movement threw him slightly off balance. The barrel of the gun tilted away from her face.

As soon as it did, she cupped her hands and slammed them over both his ears as hard as she could, forcing air pressure into his ear canals.

He screamed and staggered back, reeling from the pain inside his skull.

She dropped to the ground and curled into a ball to protect her chest and head.

A blur of movement rushed past her as something big tackled Adam, bringing him down with a yelp and a grunt.

She lifted her head to see Taylor wrestling with him, trying to pry the gun from his grip. The two men rolled through the grass and ferns, crashing into the trunk of a nearby tree. A fist came up and she heard a solid smack as knuckles connected with flesh.

Taylor rose up, Adam's shirt in his clenched fingers. In a lightning-quick movement, Taylor's fist connected with Adam's gut, then his elbow caught Adam on the side of the head. He grunted and went limp. A second later, three police officers stood over the two men, their weapons trained on Adam's head.

"Drop the gun!" Taylor ordered. "Now!"

Adam froze under Taylor's knee, planted firmly against his chest. Adam snorted, then let his head drop and lowered his hand.

Taylor slammed Adam's arm into the dirt, pried the gun from his fingers, and pushed himself to his feet. Winslow flipped the prisoner onto his stomach, yanking his arms behind his back, and cuffed him.

Pulling him roughly to his feet, Winslow shoved him toward Baker, lying flat on his stomach, his hands cuffed behind his back.

Only then did the other officers stand from their crouched positions.

Claire sat up and watched as Taylor bagged Adam's weapon and handed it to Winslow. As he did, he raised his head and looked straight into her eyes, and smiled.

He holstered his weapon and began walking toward her. His shirt was torn, his face dirty and streaked with blood. He was rumpled and sweaty and a glory to behold.

Crouching beside her, he started to say something, but before he could get the words out, his face paled, his lashes fluttered for an instant, and he fell forward into her arms.

"Taylor," she breathed. "What . . ."

Blood. Blood saturated his jeans. Adam's bullet had found its mark after all and Taylor was bleeding to death, right there in her arms.

He awoke to pain. His skull throbbed and his leg was on fire. He tried to open his eyes, but his lids wouldn't cooperate.

In the darkness, he heard the sound of someone calling his name . . . a woman. His very own. He loved her. He wanted to tell her so, but he began to fade again, and in a moment, his world ebbed back into darkness.

When he came to again, the room was silent. A dull light penetrated his closed lids, and he fluttered them open, then pinched them shut. Somebody was shining a bright light into his pupils. Though his throat was parched, he growled, "Get that goddamn light out of my eyes."

With a little click, the beam went dark.

"Welcome back, my love." The voice was decidedly feminine, and he recognized it. And how. "Why don't you open your eyes again?" she urged. "I promise not to bite."

He opened one eye to see her smiling at him. If he was lucky—and he knew he was—he hoped to see that smile every time he opened his eyes for the rest of his life.

"You a nurse?" he chided. They had come full circle, he the injured patient, she the attending physician. Would she remember?

"Ah, not nearly as good," she said, just as she had the day they'd met. "I'm a doctor. *Your* doctor. Can you tell me your name?"

He cleared his throat and suppressed a grin. "Tell me yours first."

She laughed a little, but it sounded husky, as though she'd been crying. "Ooo-hoo. Aren't you the stubborn one?"

"Do I have another concussion?"

She ran her fingers through his hair. Mmm. Felt good. "Not this time, Detective," she said. "Just a big, fat bullet to the thigh. Did a bit of damage, lost a lot of blood, but your brother gave you some of his. You'll be up and around in no time."

He squirmed a little, trying to get more comfortable. Damn, his leg hurt. "So I'm going to live after all, huh."

"It's looking that way." She lowered her voice. "What are you thinking?"

His lips quirked into a sly grin. "I'm thinking you're the cutest doctor I've ever had. What are you thinking?"

She caressed the ridge of his ear. "I'm thinking we've had this conversation before."

Raising his hand, he touched his fingertips to her cheek. Softly, he said, "Tell me, Doc. Do all your patients fall in love with you?"

She moved a little closer and placed her palm tenderly on his jaw. "Only one that I can recall."

"Smart guy. Must be a man among men."

"Oh, he's okay. Passably good-looking. Fairly smart. Considers himself some kind of Don Juan. Stutters when he gets excited. Very annoying." Her brown eyes smiled down at him.

"You love him."

"Yes."

"But he's a cop, right?"

"Yes."

"How'd you come to grips with that?"

She lifted one shoulder in a small shrug. "One day, he got hurt. Nearly bled to death. For about ten minutes, I thought I'd lost him." Looking deeply into his eyes, she murmured, "They were the longest ten minutes of my life. The most painful. And I regretted we hadn't had more time together, that I had been keeping us apart."

She tilted her head and he realized she had tears in her eyes. "I came to the conclusion that I'd rather take my chances than spend one more minute away from him. When you love someone the way I love him, it's all or nothing." Looking deeply into his eyes, she whispered, "I choose all."

He stuck out his lower lip as though he was considering her words. "Has he asked you to marry him?"

In a little singsong way, she said, "No, but he will. Any second now."

"You're very sure of yourself."

"Not really. But I am very sure of him."

"Sounds to me like he adores you."

"Ya *think*?"

He slipped his hand around her neck to pull her down for his kiss. Against her soft lips, he murmured, "I *know*."

Endocrine
To weep no more.

Epilogue

It was a double wheelchair ceremony.

Claire's brother, Zach, arrived a couple of days before the wedding with his girlfriend, Mary Rose, a lovely woman Claire liked immediately. For the nuptials, Mary Rose had decorated Zach's chair with flowers and ribbons, while Claire had done the same for Taylor's, even though he'd be leaving his behind eventually. Each day, his leg got stronger, and soon, he'd graduate to a crutch or a cane. The prognosis was good; all he needed was physical therapy and time.

After the wedding, the celebration had gone on all night, but the best man and matron of honor had to leave early to get home in time to feed four-week-old Molly Claire McKennitt, the gurgling delight of everyone's life.

Betsy had held on long enough for her and Soldier to be airlifted to the hospital, where Molly had entered the world screaming her lungs out, to be immediately placed in her dumbstruck father's arms. It was love at first sight, and by all accounts, it was mutual.

The bullet that had torn up Taylor's leg might have kept him from walking around for a bit, but it hadn't even slowed him down in the bedroom, as evidenced by Claire's wedding dress, which now lay draped over a chair in their honeymoon suite. A small fire crackled in the fireplace, taking the chill off the early autumn evening.

Naked, Claire nestled in her new husband's arms, and ran her finger over his bare chest until he wrapped his fingers around her wrist.

"Stop it." He chuckled. "That tickles."

She sighed and snuggled closer. "No it doesn't. You just want me to quit playing around and get on with it."

"Goal-oriented bastard that I am." He sighed. "Just like all men. Damn our rotten hides."

"Speaking of which." Claire chuckled. "Did I tell you Aunt Sadie and Flynn are getting married? They're going to wait until after Mort and Adam's trials so they can make their honeymoon into a fishing trip to Canada."

"Yeah." Taylor sighed. "Poor old Mort didn't get very far. They nabbed him just this side of the Canadian border with everything he could stuff in his Cadillac." Then he scowled. "Sadie's marrying Flynn, huh. A Fed in the family? I feel sick."

She smacked him. "A *retired* Fed. And you like Flynn. If it hadn't been for him, Betsy would never have gotten out of there alive. And the baby . . . God, I shudder to think."

He nodded, then bent and placed a kiss on her nose. "Yeah, poor washout Kevin LeRoy. Didn't get his M.D., didn't get the girl, and didn't even score big in the previously owned bones department."

"But now he's in the joint."

Taylor arched a brow. "That was pathetic."

Claire chuckled. "Hey, I've always been very *humerus*."

He let his head fall back as he laughed and she admired, and not for the first time, his strong neck, smooth muscles, sexy . . . well, everything.

Snuggling closer, she let herself enjoy the feel of his body next to hers, the warmth of his skin. She placed a kiss on his chest and sighed with more contentment than she'd ever dreamed possible.

"Oh," he said. "I almost forgot. I have a wedding present for you."

Reaching over the edge of the bed, he brought up a rectangular object wrapped in silver paper with curly white ribbons. He handed it to Claire as she sat up.

"It's almost too pretty to unwrap," she said. "Thank you."

Taylor stretched out and put his hands behind his head. "You haven't even seen it yet."

"But it's a painting, isn't it?"

He nodded. "Open it."

Slipping the ribbon off one edge, she picked off the tape and slowly unwrapped the gift. As she turned it over, her breath caught in her throat and she knew without a doubt she was going to cry for a long, long time.

When she didn't say anything, Taylor scooted up next to her. "Sadie found the photograph for me. I used that. She said you were about five. Do you remember—"

"I remember," she whispered, her throat too tight to speak. "God, I remember."

The day had been sunny and Grandpa had tossed her in the wheelbarrow and rolled her out to the fields, laughing and squealing. They'd ended up at the pond where they'd thrown dry bread to the ducks. Grandma had been alive then, and she'd snapped a photograph of them just before they'd headed up the path. Taylor had captured that moment in oils. Grandpa's eyes gleamed with life and laughter, his smile huge and warm, while Claire, in a blue denim jumper, was laughing, her long hair in pigtails, her small hands gripping the side of the wheelbarrow, hanging on for dear life.

"Thank you," she choked again. "It's . . . perfect."

He smoothed his palm along her arm. "I saw the look on your face when you lost Grandpa's wheelbarrow. The thing was ugly and weighed a ton, but I could see what it meant to you. I knew right then, I was going to find some way to replace it for you, if only on canvas."

Bending her head, she kissed him, and it was the sweetest kiss she had ever known. When she raised her head, he said, "Are you sure you're okay with all this? I can take a desk job, if you want."

She shook her head and looked deeply into his glittering blue eyes, eyes that would never, ever cease to fascinate and attract her.

"No," she said. "I'm okay. When you got shot, when you fell, my heart . . . changed. As you came through the trees, came after me, your weapon drawn, your eyes steady, focused, I knew at that moment you were doing exactly what you were born to do. I don't have the *right* to ask you to change. How arrogant and selfish of me it would be to demand such a thing."

He kissed her again and grinned. "I only offered because I knew you'd say that."

She laughed and set the painting carefully on the nightstand, then slipped her arms around his neck. In a light, breathy voice, she said, "I know."

Blinking down at her, his mouth quirked into a sexy, flirty grin, and she knew she was in for it.

"Hey, b-b-b-baby," he murmured as he settled between her thighs. "You want to see something swell?"

Coming in May from Avon Romance

Duke of Scandal by Adele Ashworth

An Avon Romantic Treasure

Lady Olivia is a wife in name only, returning to London determined to confront her dastardly husband. But the man who stands before her is her husband's twin, the Duke of Durham, and now Olivia must make a scandalous choice.

Vamps and the City by Kerrelyn Sparks

An Avon Contemporary Romance

Can the undead really find love on Reality TV? Producer Darcy Newhart thinks so. But this sexy lady vampire is distracted by a hot, handsome contestant named Austin . . . who just happens to be mortal, and a slayer! What next?

What to Wear to a Seduction by Sari Robins

An Avon Romance

Lady Edwina is putting on clothes . . . only to take them off again! But she's determined to seduce notorious rogue Prescott Devane, the one man who can help her find a black-mailer . . . and also steal her heart.

Winds of the Storm by Beverly Jenkins

An Avon Romance

Archer owes his life to Zahra Lafayette. Now, in the days after the Civil War, he needs the help of this beautiful former spy again. Posing as an infamous madam, Zahra is willing to help in his cause, but she's unwilling to grant him her love.

Visit www.AuthorTracker.com for exclusive information on your favorite HarperCollins authors.

REL 0406

Available wherever books are sold or please call 1-800-331-3761 to order.

Don't miss any of the sensual, sexy, delectable
novels in the world of
New York Times bestselling author

STEPHANIE LAURENS

On A Wicked Dawn

0-06-000205-0/$7.50 US/$9.99 Can

When Lucien Ashford proposes marriage to Amelia Cynster,
she's torn between astounded relief and indignant affront.

The Promise In A Kiss

0-06-103175-5/$7.50 US/$9.99 Can

When Helena discovers a handsome man in a moonlit
convent courtyard, she decides to keep his presence a secret.

The Perfect Lover

0-06-05072-9/$6.99 US/$9.99 Can

Simon Frederick Cynster sets out to find a mate who will
be a perfect lady by day . . . and a wanton lover by night.

The Ideal Bride

0-06-050574-5/$7.50 US/$9.99 Can

Michael Anstruther-Wetherby's future in Parliament
appears assured, except he lacks a wife.

The Truth About Love

0-06-050576-1/$7.50 US/$9.99 Can

Gerrard Debbington chafes at wasting his painting talents on
a simpering miss, only to discover that Jacqueline Tregonning
stirs him as no other.

Visit www.AuthorTracker.com for exclusive
information on your favorite HarperCollins authors.

LAUC 1105

Available wherever books are sold or please call 1-800-331-3761 to order.

Avon Romances

the best in
exceptional authors and unforgettable novels!

DARING THE DUKE
by Anne Mallory
0-06-076223-3/ $5.99 US/ $7.99 Can

COURTING CLAUDIA
by Robyn DeHart
0-06-078215-3/ $5.99 US/ $7.99 Can

STILL IN MY HEART
by Kathryn Smith
0-06-074074-4/ $5.99 US/ $7.99 Can

**A MATCH MADE
IN SCANDAL**
by Melody Thomas
0-06-074231-3/ $5.99 US/ $7.99 Can

SCANDALOUS
by Jenna Petersen
0-06-079859-9/ $5.99 US/ $7.99 Can

RULES OF PASSION
by Sara Bennett
0-06-079648-0/ $5.99 US/ $7.99 Can

KEEPING KATE
by Sarah Gabriel
0-06-073610-0/ $5.99 US/ $7.99 Can

GYPSY LOVER
by Edith Layton
0-06-075784-1/ $5.99 US/ $7.99 Can

SCANDALOUS MIRANDA
by Susan Sizemore
0-06-008290-9/ $5.99 US/ $7.99 Can

A KISS BEFORE DAWN
by Kimberly Logan
0-06-079246-9/ $5.99 US/ $7.99 Can

THE BRIDE HUNT
by Margo Maguire
0-06-083714-4/ $5.99 US/ $7.99 Can

A FORBIDDEN LOVE
by Alexandra Benedict
0-06-084793-X/ $5.99 US/ $7.99 Can

Visit www.AuthorTracker.com for exclusive
information on your favorite HarperCollins authors.

ROM 1105

Available wherever books are sold or please call 1-800-331-3761 to order.

DISCOVER CONTEMPORARY ROMANCES at their
SIZZLING HOT BEST FROM AVON BOOKS

Running on Empty   by Lynn Montana
0-06-074255-0/$5.99 US/$7.99 Can

The Hunter   by Gennita Low
0-06-059123-4/$5.99 US/$7.99 Can

How To Marry A   by Kerrelyn Sparks
Millionaire Vampire
0-06-075196-7/$5.99 US/$7.99 Can

Wanted: One Sexy Night   by Judi McCoy
0-06-077420-7/$5.99 US/$7.99 Can

Flashback   by Cait London
0-06-079087-3/$5.99 US/$7.99 Can

The Boy Next Door   by Meg Cabot
0-06-084554-6/$5.99 US/$7.99 Can

Switched, Bothered   by Suzanne Macpherson
and Bewildered
0-06-077494-0/$5.99 US/$7.99 Can

Sleeping With the Agent   by Gennita Low
0-06-059124-2/$5.99 US/$7.99 Can

Guys & Dogs   by Elaine Fox
0-06-074060-4/$5.99 US/$7.99 Can

Running For Cover   by Lynn Montana
0-06-074257-7/$5.99 US/$7.99 Can

CRO 1205

Visit www.AuthorTracker.com for exclusive
information on your favorite HarperCollins authors.

Available wherever books are sold
or please call 1-800-331-3761 to order.

Avon Romantic Treasures

Unforgettable, enthralling love stories, sparkling with passion and adventure from Romance's bestselling authors

TILL NEXT WE MEET   *by Karen Ranney*
0-06-075737-X/$5.99 US/$7.99 Can

MARRY THE MAN TODAY   *by Linda Needham*
0-06-051414-0/$5.99 US/$7.99 Can

THE MARRIAGE BED   *by Laura Lee Gubrke*
0-06-077473-8/$5.99 US/$7.99 Can

LOVE ACCORDING TO LILY   *by Julianne MacLean*
0-06-059729-1/$5.99 US/$7.99 Can

TAMING THE BARBARIAN   *by Lois Greiman*
0-06-078394-X/$5.99 US/$7.99 Can

A MATTER OF TEMPTATION   *by Lorraine Heath*
0-06-074976-8/$5.99 US/$7.99 Can

THIS RAKE OF MINE   *by Elizabeth Boyle*
0-06-078399-0/$5.99 US/$7.99 Can

THE LORD NEXT DOOR   *by Gayle Callen*
0-06-078411-3/$5.99 US/$7.99 Can

AN UNLIKELY GOVERNESS   *by Karen Ranney*
0-06-075743-4/$5.99 US/$7.99 Can

SCANDAL OF THE BLACK ROSE   *by Debra Mullins*
0-06-079923-4/$6.99 US/$9.99 Can

Visit www.AuthorTracker.com for exclusive
information on your favorite HarperCollins authors.

RT 1105

Available wherever books are sold or please call 1-800-331-3761 to order.

AVON TRADE... because every great bag
deserves a great book!

DATE DUE

JUL 1 2 2006	
AUG 0 8 2006	
DEC 2 8 2006	
JUL 2 4 2007	
MAY 0 1 2010	
JUN 2 5 2008	
JUL 1 6 2008	
AUG 1 5 2009	
OCT 1 3 2009	
NOV 0 3 2009	
NOV 2 4 2009	
Jul 21/10	
AUG 3 1 2011	
FEB 2 2 2013	
DEC 1 9 2013	

GAYLORD   PRINTED IN U.S.A.

information on your favorite HarperCollins authors.

Available wherever books are sold, or call 1-800-331-3761 to order.

ATP 0406